RUN Ragged

KARI AGUILA

This is a work of fiction. Names, characters, places, and incidents either are the product of the author's imagination or are used fictitiously, and any resemblance to actual persons living or dead, businesses, companies, events, or locales is entirely coincidental. Medicinal and edible plant descriptions are for fictional purposes only. Never eat anything unless you know what it is.

Cover design by Jessie W. Chandler

ISBN: 0991165049

ISBN-13: 978-0-9911650-4-9

For Captain Judy Gregoire, sailor, teacher, mentor, scientist, adventurer, cross-country driving partner, and friend.

To Alex: Thank you for always supporting and guiding me with your honesty, courage, and strength. You are my home.

To Michael Fassbender: No, I will not marry you. Please stop asking.

RUN Ragged

Prologue

Joseph watched Rhia tug up one long sleeve, exposing her small brown hand. She grasped the handle of a grocery basket at the top of the stack, and as the basket bounced to her side, her sleeve fell down again, concealing the only skin that showed below her face. He pressed his own large hand into her back and guided her inside.

They moved along the outer edge of the store, avoiding the dusty shelves and the ragged-looking men that prowled and pawed at the boxes and bins along the inner aisles. At the small selection of fruits and vegetables, Joseph let her go, the warmth of her shoulder lingering on his palm. He picked up an apple, examined it, and discarded it for the bruises and blotches on its skin. He selected another and, turning it over in his dark hands, decided it would have to do. He dropped it into the basket, and caught her eye. Quickly, so none of the other men would see, he wiggled his eyebrows. Rhia had to look away to stifle her smile. He returned his hand to her back and led her on.

Together, they made their way through the store, gathering food and supplies they would need for the week. The basket full and Joseph's mental list all crossed off, they went to check out.

"Morning, Joseph," the man behind the counter greeted them. His thin skin was the color of sand under the fluorescent light.

Joseph saw the man's pale-brown eyes dart quickly over Rhia, from her floor-length skirt to her long sleeves and high neckline. "Morning, Higbee," Joseph said. "Just a few things this week." He nodded to Rhia, and she began unloading their items onto the conveyor belt.

"I see you brought your daughter in again."

"Rhia's only eight. It's not right to leave her alone on the boat."

"I suppose." The grocer watched Rhia tug her sleeves up, several inches above her wrists, and fasten the small snaps that held up the fabric. He wrinkled his nose as if he'd smelled something foul, but scanned the items and slid them down the line.

"Good thing you got your milk rations. I've only got one more case in the back, and my supplier told me he's not expecting more any time soon. Everything's going to the front lines."

"Have they started drafting cows now, too?"

The grocer chuckled. "No, not yet. Still just eighteen- to thirty-five-year-olds, but even that might change."

"Did you hear some news?"

"They're talking about taking sixteen to forty-five." He glanced over the top of his wire-rimmed glasses briefly before looking back at the groceries.

Joseph watched his daughter pack the items carefully in a fabric sack. He knew she was listening.

"General Brighton says things are looking good, though," the grocer added. "He's saying the Oil Nexus can't last another six months against us. Says he expects a million barrels of crude to be liberated by Christmas."

"Even with Canada occupied? How's he gonna get it to us?"

He shrugged. "Maybe that's why they need more troops. Hold the lines. Push 'em back."

"Easy for you to say. They're not talking about drafting over seventy."

The grocer smiled, his tan skin wrinkling around his eyes and mouth. "Not yet. Not yet. Anyway, no more milk for a while. We all need to tighten our belts a bit to help out the troops."

Joseph shifted his weight for a moment, debating his answer. "Well, anything for the troops, I guess."

"Yep." The grocer finished ringing up the items and looked at his screen. "That'll be $104.95, Joe—$74.35 blue rations for the food, $30.60 red rations for the nonperishables."

"Okay." Joseph pressed his thumb to the screen and waited for the beep. Nothing happened. He pulled back and tried again. Still nothing.

"What the hell's wrong with this thing now," the old grocer grumbled as he tapped at the screen. After several seconds of frustration, he shrugged. "System's down again."

"That's been happening a lot lately."

"Can't you do anything about it? The city should have some protections in place. Backups or something."

"They keep hitting the grid. Hard to protect against something that changes shape every week."

The grocer rummaged in a small drawer below the counter and pulled out a handheld device. "Sign this one. I'll charge it to you when it comes back up."

Joseph pressed his thumb onto the screen, then turned to go, his hand firmly guiding Rhia to the door.

"Cover up that girl's hands, now," the grocer called after them. "You don't want to tempt anybody."

~

Rhia carried the sack of groceries as they walked down First Avenue. The town was quiet, robbed of a generation of young men who had gone to fight for the oil that both created and destroyed everything. Left behind were the middle-aged and older men who manned the tech and service jobs that helped the country limp along, the few rich and powerful men who would never be asked to sacrifice, and millions of women. Women could have worked, maybe could have helped to avoid this war if they hadn't been banned from active duty, banned from positions of power, and eventually, a dozen years before, banned from even the most menial jobs.

The rich men said it was for the best. The economy had been in shambles and their power was waning, so they had bribed and manipulated and frightened voters until they were able to pass the ten Family Focus Acts, one by one. These acts purported to restore the moral compass of society and benefit children, but their true goal was the slow and steady removal of women from public office, from universities, and from businesses until they were safe at home and no longer in danger of taking jobs from men desperate for work. The resulting rapid degradation of everyone's rights meant that now all women and most men, including those who had once supported and encouraged their daughters, sisters, and wives, no longer had a voice.

Rhia watched the feet of the men who passed them on the sidewalk and heard her father say hello. The few girls or women they passed were as modestly dressed and well tended as Rhia, out of doors only with their older husbands or fathers at their sides. Like them, Rhia had been taught not to tempt men with her body. She politely kept her eyes to the ground and deferred to the men around her, but she imagined the girls' faces, imagined looking into their eyes and smiling. She secretly believed, secretly hoped, the girls were imagining her, too.

When they reached the corner of Houghton Street, Rhia looked across the quiet intersection at an abandoned building. The boarded-up windows and cracked façade had been like that since before she was born, and now blended in with the crumbling shops and apartments all around the small town of Miranda. And yet, something about that one building always made her stare.

Above three of the long-shuttered doors were faded signs that someone had attempted to paint over years ago. In their haste, or in their dissent, they had done a poor job of it, and Rhia could make out the names of the shops that had once occupied those spaces—The Happy Nails Salon, The Frock Shop, Gilda's Books. Rhia's lips moved as she mouthed the names.

Then her father pressed her forward, and they crossed the street and made their way toward the harbor.

~

The water made small slapping sounds against the dock as the boat rocked gently in the evening breeze. Inside, Joseph sliced the apple he had gotten from the store and stirred rice into a small pot of boiling water. He turned to take plates out of the cupboard and saw Rhia hunched over the books and papers that littered the fold-down table in the corner.

"You're gonna go blind, girlie. Turn on the lamp. Better yet, open the curtains and let some light in."

"Someone might walk by." Free from the long clothes that weighed down her skinny limbs, Rhia stretched her arms over her head.

"Nobody's out there now. Nobody will see you. Besides, you're a little kid. They can't expect you to stay bundled up all the time."

Rhia pursed her full lips and looked up at him. "Dad, I'm not that little anymore. And even if they didn't care about my clothes, they'd certainly fine you for letting me read this stuff." Her frizzy hair stuck out from her head in every direction, dark brown with streaks of copper that haloed her face.

Joseph shook his head. "The culture tsar doesn't live on *my* boat. I'm your father, and you can read whatever I say." He turned back to the stove. "You need to know how everything works around here. For safety. It's not like in town, where there're men to do the skilled work while the women cook and clean. It's just you and me out here. You need know how to do things. Make things."

"Jennifer Benet says girls only need to know how to make babies."

"And that's exactly why I don't let you go to the Girls' School." Joseph banged the lid on the pot of rice and sighed.

"Look, we'll get diesel up here sooner or later, and then we'll be able to head out again. When we're on the water, I need you to know everything I know."

Rhia pulled one of the tattered paperbacks from under a stack of maps. "How does *The Life and Struggles of Fred Korematsu* help me run the boat? He's just some Japanese man from over a hundred years ago."

"That's history. It's important. We're in a war, and he lived through a war." Joseph stirred refried beans into a pan, then turned off the propane.

"Mr. Higbee said the war will be over in six months." When her father didn't answer, she added, "Do you think he's right?"

Joseph hesitated. Would it do any good to lie to her? All the good news and propaganda being thrown around couldn't hide the acrid smell of sulfur and death that crept down from the Canadian border on a strong wind. "I don't know. They've been at it two years now, and it doesn't seem to be getting any better. Boys go away and they don't come back."

"Do you think you'll have to go?"

Joseph could feel Rhia's dark eyes boring into the back of his head. "Hard to say. I'm a communication engineer for the city now. That seems like a job they'd want me to keep doing, but it could be something they need in the military, too." He crossed the small cabin and set two plates down on top of the books and papers on the table.

"What would happen to me?"

That question had kept him up more nights than he could count, and he still hadn't come up with a good answer. The boys drafted to fight left behind mothers, sisters, and wives that other men did their best to care for. If there were children, extended families did their best to take them in. But he had no one, and he knew he needed to figure out a backup plan for Rhia soon or she'd be swept into the Girls' School system, where she'd lose everything he'd taught her.

"You'll be okay, girlie." Joseph smiled at his daughter and tried to hide the heaviness in his heart. "Don't worry. You just keep reading and learning everything you can. I'll take care of you."

~ One ~

Heat rippled above the deck, bending the light into waves and distorting the docks and cranes that jutted out from the distant shore. Rhia squinted through the glare and gently tugged on the wheel, guiding the *Elizabeth Maru*, her thirty-two-foot gillnetter, toward the regional trade. She wiped a drip of sweat from her temple with the shoulder of her faded T-shirt and leaned forward in the patched leather captain's chair. The old springs groaned. Her left knee bounced up and down, a subconscious tell of the nervousness that accompanied each of her biweekly trips to Piper Point. She was close now.

As Rhia surveyed the busy port through the windshield, she reached down to the clear plastic cover of the oil gauge and flicked it twice out of habit. She registered the reading even as her brain took in the sounds of a smoothly running boat—the gentle hum of the propeller blades behind her, the constant and easy spin of the anemometer, and the comforting firmness of the throttle in her right hand. From where she sat inside the cabin, Rhia could reach all the important controls on the console—the steering wheel and throttle; the switch for the floodlights; the VHF radio; the GPS and compass in its binnacle; the depth sounder. She rested her left hand near the switches that toggled power between the unrolled solar cells covering the cabin top, the wind turbines, and the hydrogenerator.

Reaching the no-wake zone at the mouth of the harbor, she pulled down hard on the old lever and cut the engine to idle. The heavy-laden boat slogged awkwardly below her.

"Play nice, Betty. Almost done."

More than a dozen boats were already being unloaded at the massive dock. Men scrambled over the decks hauling piles of lumber, sacks of grain, barrels of food, and bolts of cloth off the boats under the supervision of women in bright-red coveralls. Rhia had to navigate her boat carefully into position, turning the wheel hard to port. Looking up, she waved to the auburn-haired woman waiting for her.

The woman heaved two dark-gray fenders over the side of the dock. Each one, made from old rubber tires tied together with leather thongs, bounced hard before settling into place.

With a slight shudder, the *Elizabeth Maru* reversed slowly into place, and the woman standing above nimbly stretched her long legs over the water to board the vessel. She carried two coils of line that were tied to large rings mounted on the dock, and she efficiently secured the lines around the cleats at the stern and bow as Rhia powered down with a flick of the switches. Her boat now attached to the noisy, throbbing machine that was the trade, Rhia stepped out into the harsh glare of noon on Midsummer Day.

"Peace to you, Ginny," Rhia said to the woman, who was already climbing back onto the dock.

"Peace to you. Come on up."

Rhia deftly made her way along her deck, pausing to secure a loose bungee cord around a crab cage to the metal railing behind it before following Ginny up to the dock. Men scrambled all around her as the women in charge called out orders.

"How's your week going?" Rhia asked as she quickly hugged Ginny.

"Busy. Fifty shipping containers came in by Safe Rail on Tuesday, so we had to move all the cranes to off-load them."

"Full or empty?"

"Empty. Headed to the Re-education center." Ginny made notes on her clipboard as she talked, marking the date and time, scanning Rhia's boat and jotting down the types of goods she saw. "They turn them into fully functional houses there—basic plumbing, electric, interior work."

"Re-ed. Jesus. A rusty old boxcar isn't my idea of house."

"Well, apartment then. Better than nothing." Ginny glanced at Rhia. "From what I've heard about the Center, men there are grateful to have anything at all." Pointing her pen toward the barrels, sacks, and boxes on Rhia's boat, she asked, "From New Hope, Campbell, and Miranda, right?"

"Yep." Rhia hesitated, then dropped her eyes to the soft leather sandals tied around her feet. "I heard a man from Jenkins got sent there last week."

"Where?"

"The Center."

"Well, half the men working here have been through it. It

seems like they're sending people for even the littlest things these days."

"Do they ever talk about it?"

Ginny's voice dropped to a whisper. "You hear rumors, horror stories, but these guys won't say much about their time inside. If they say anything, it's always positive. You know, 'Re-ed helped me realize my full potential as a man' or 'The Center taught me how to use my skills for good instead of evil.'"

"Sounds just like the billboards plastered all over the towns."

"Exactly. Seems like the Re-ed centers are getting their message across."

"Well, that's what propaganda is for, right?" When Ginny smirked, Rhia added, "They never say anything about the rumors?"

"No. But they don't say much at all."

"Do you think any of it could be true?"

"'Course not. And even if I did, I wouldn't say anything, right? What woman would want to threaten the peace we worked so hard for? I'm a model citizen fully on board with the New Way Forward." Ginny said it in a singsong voice, as if parroting other people's words. She lifted one eyebrow and added, "Just like you."

She leaned closer and looked intently into Rhia's eyes, as if searching for something there. After a moment she said, "Miranda hasn't sent anybody to Re-ed yet?"

"Of course not," Rhia said, offended. "Our men aren't raiders."

"You don't have to be a raider or a recruiter to get sent to Re-ed. You just have to complain a little too loudly. Doesn't anyone complain about the new rules where you come from?"

"I'm not saying that. It's just . . . I mean, sure, women and men in Miranda are just like everywhere else—some rules they agree with, and some they don't. But we've got a good group of leaders. It's not perfect, but the women are doing their best. Most of them." Rhia shifted her weight from one foot to the other. "Some of us . . . Look, it's certainly better now than when we were kids, during the war. Or even during the Family Focus Acts before that."

"Of course," Ginny touched Rhia's arm. "But, haven't you noticed there've been a lot more reports about raiders lately? Men trying to take back some power? And it isn't just wild groups of men anymore. Women are joining."

"Gin, I don't know." Rhia shook her head. She'd worked with Ginny every other week since she started running goods for the towns around Miranda, and she felt they were friends, but it was dangerous to talk this way. "Besides," she said, "these days nobody really knows what to believe. It's all just rumors."

"But it's our responsibility to stay informed, isn't it? You're twenty-five years old. Isn't it your job to question what's going on?"

"My job is to trade for my towns up the coast. I'm just a runner. I don't have any power to change what the government's doing."

Ginny hesitated. "Don't you ever wonder if we went too far?"

"Gin . . ." Rhia tugged a ratty blue baseball cap from her hip pocket and twisted it in her hands.

"Look, Rhia, I meet a lot of women in this job, from all up and down the coast. All I'm saying is, sometimes I hear about people who are getting frustrated with all the New Way rules. Including Re-education. Some people think these trades take too much food and fabric and goods from the towns. And some people think the whole promise of the New Way has been broken."

Ginny took a step back from Rhia and looked down at her clipboard as a supervisor in a bright-red coverall passed by. Once the supervisor was out of earshot, she stepped close again. "Sometimes I hear people talking about trying to change things. You know what I'm talking about? You don't have to . . ." Her voice trailed off and she was silent again.

Rhia breathed in deeply and tugged her baseball cap down onto her thick, tight curls to shade her eyes. "Better be careful, Gin. For a second, you almost sounded like a recruiter." She shook her head. "Look, after the Last War, everything was a mess. People, the ones who survived, didn't even have food or shelter. I don't know."

She thought of the cities, leveled by enemies and allies alike. The infrastructure destroyed by drones flown from the Middle East. The fires that burned everything in their path. She looked around at the men lugging heavy loads around her. "When women took control, they did what they had to do to help us all survive, right? Yes, the women went too far in the beginning, but you have to admit we've come a long way since then. Even in just the last five years. No, I don't think it's perfect, but at least now men are allowed out of the house, allowed to have jobs again."

"Yeah, but which jobs? They do our grunt work. Do you think that's fair? Do you think that's the equality we were promised?"

"We're all just doing our best."

Ginny smiled apologetically. "Of course. Hey, like you said, things are going okay for you, so why rock the boat? It's great that your town's happy. Consider yourself lucky."

"I'm not—" Rhia began.

Four deep gongs rang out from speakers above them, and both women turned to look toward shore. The long dock was flanked by colorful banners that reminded workers of the basic tenets of the New Way—Support Women! Grow More, Use Less! Pay It Forward! Share More, Use Less! The banners flapped in the gentle breeze, creating a corridor that directed all eyes toward the main storage facility at the end of the dock. A massive, curved screen glowed blue above the building, on which, as they watched, the image of a woman appeared.

"Good afternoon, citizens. Peace to you, and welcome to your Daily Update." President Asakawa, elected by a majority of women, was the third female president since the Last War ended fifteen years ago. She had campaigned on the promise of completing the solar grid and connecting the major cities, which still struggled to feed their residents. In her three years in office, she had reinvigorated the technology industry through massive government loans to corporations. Any business that followed the tenets of the New Way Forward—utilize green energy; supply jobs for both worker men and managerial women; participate in community-building exercises; promote peace—could apply.

There had been great progress in the last few years. People had gone from living by candlelight and scrounging for food to bartering for building supplies and medicines at the regional trades. Isolated neighborhoods and towns were able to communicate again via the new radio system, and the solar-powered Safe Rail trains were transporting people across the country for the first time since the Last War ended. Sure, no one knew where the money for the loans actually came from, and there was growing concern about the lack of transparency in the administration's decisions, but the president did her best to calm all fears during the daily broadcasts. People seemed willing to ignore the questions in exchange for the security the government was providing.

As the screen came into focus, President Asakawa loomed large over them all, beautifully dressed in a silvery long-sleeve tunic. Tiny pearl buttons snaked up her chest to just below her chin. She spoke slowly, with a voice like silk; her eyes were bright with intelligence.

"With the completion of the Miami depot this week, Super Lanes now web out from New Chicago to twelve stations in all corners of the country. Durable goods, medicines, supplies, and energy equipment are being delivered daily to communities via the Safe Rail. And I am pleased to announce that four new depots will be built over the next two years through government contracts awarded to the Helios Corporation."

The president smiled, and her long dark hair swung as she tilted her head slightly to the right. "Rollable solar cells and wind turbines being built in the Detroit Energy Belt will be distributed throughout the summer. Your efficient use of the energy we are able to produce has allowed us to avoid political ties with those countries that have rejected the New Way. We have freed ourselves from the shackles of petroleum dependence. I am thrilled to announce that as of this September, we will achieve complete energy independence. Citizens, all your work and sacrifices have led to this major accomplishment. Your devotion to the idea of Use Less is proving to be a glorious success. Continue on this path, and our country will surely return to its former grandeur. And remember, if your community requires additional resources, contact your regional advisor."

Rhia glanced at the people around her. As required, everyone had stopped work and faced the screen. A man to her left had paused still shouldering the heavy burlap sack he carried, his back hunched under the weight of it. Out of the corner of her eye, she could see the heave of his chest as he tried to catch his breath. His eyes remained fixed on the ground in front of him.

"On another note, I am pleased to report that recent rumors of large groups of raiders attempting to disrupt our cooperative work toward a better future are unfounded. True, some misguided men have reverted to the violence and aggression of the past, but I can assure you, we will deal with these men swiftly and justly. To that end, your Congress has responded to the voters' wishes and has approved funding for an eighth Re-education center, to be built in Arizona."

Beside Rhia, Ginny snorted quietly.

"Lastly, we remind you all to continue the excellent work your fellow citizens have been doing to rebuild our society since the destruction and devastation of the Last War. Cows, horses, goats, and pigs provided by your government are currently helping to produce food in over eighty percent of American neighborhoods, and the Pay It Forward program has been a source of aid to countless families. If your animals were blessed with offspring this year, please remember to pass along thirty percent of your bounty to citizens within your neighborhood or region. Only together can we overcome difficulty. Only together can we thrive. Continue to Use Less, to become more."

With those often-repeated closing words, the president nodded slowly, and her image faded. The four tones were repeated, and people began moving again.

"She makes it all sound so great," Ginny whispered.

"We'd better get this boat unloaded." A part of Rhia wanted to talk, wanted to vent about all the small lies and distractions the president had once again delivered in her daily pep talk. Instead, she walked away from Ginny and did not look back. She joined the back of a queue at a table where a supervisor sat, and waited a couple minutes for her turn. Reaching the front of the line, she saw the supervisor's loose red tunic clinging to her body in the heat. Rhia cleared her throat and tugged on the brim of her hat. When the supervisor looked up from her logbook, Rhia was surprised to see a thick, jagged, pink and white scar that cut across the right side of the woman's light-brown face.

"Name?"

"Rhia Malone. Runner for Campbell, Miranda, and New Hope."

"What have you got for us today, Rhia Malone?"

"One fifty-five-gallon barrel of flour, one fifty-five-gallon barrel of goat's milk, ten twenty-pound sacks of dried peas, fifty pounds of fresh fish on ice, six bolts of raw wool cloth . . ."

Rhia continued to list the goods that had been loaded onto her boat by the townspeople that week. Embarrassed by her own curiosity, Rhia watched the supervisor's face as her pencil scratched across the cream-colored paper on the table. The side with the scar didn't move as it should, and her cheek hung just a little too loosely off her skull, the skin grotesquely damaged by the deep gash, which had healed poorly. Rhia could make out a dozen or so puckered points on each side of the scar, where thick stitches must have been sewn into this woman's face.

The undamaged side seemed normal, with small and subtle movements of skin and muscles as the woman squinted in the glare or licked her lips. The supervisor looked up, and a terse smile played at her mouth. Rhia noticed she had a sweet dimple in her one perfect cheek and suddenly saw that this woman had once been young and beautiful.

"That it?"

"Yes, that's all I have today."

The supervisor glanced at a clipboard to her right, where a long chart displayed the current trade values. "That will get you sixty-three credits."

"Sixty-three?" Rhia's shoulders dropped. "No, you must be reading it wrong. That much . . . the supplies I brought should get us at least seventy."

"Sorry. It's sixty-three. Everybody's got peas and fish this month."

"But those were things on the requested list. That was what my towns thought they had to give you."

The smile vanished from the supervisor's face, and all traces of youth and beauty vanished. "Rhia Malone, you watch your tone. No one *has* to give us anything. Your region has set up this trade to help distribute supplies, but if your towns don't want to send anything, that's their business."

Rhia shook her head but didn't say more. She put her hands on her hips for a moment, then held out her right hand, palm up. The supervisor nodded and pulled two plastic cards from a peg on her table. One had a large 6 on it, the other a small 3. She pressed the cards into Rhia's palm and looked past Rhia's shoulder to the runner waiting behind.

"Next."

After carefully selecting the supplies she would load from the large bins at the shore end of the dock, Rhia walked back to her boat with the list in her hand. She grabbed the shiny silver rail that wrapped around the deck of the *Elizabeth Maru* and easily leapt on board. Ginny was on the stern deck, crouched on her haunches and pointing down into the gaping hole of the hold as she directed the man bent over inside.

"Use your hands to get the last of the ice if the shovel's too tight."

"Jesus, are you even taking my ice?"

Ginny stood. "Yep, new rules. They say the ice goes with the fish now."

"Are you kidding me? So I have to use my credits to buy new ice for the fruit I'm getting today? Ginny, that's ridiculous. I didn't even get enough to buy everything my towns need in the first place, and the women there are already scrambling to supply everything the region's telling them they have to contribute."

"Hey, lady, don't yell at me. I don't make the rules." Ginny lifted both hands. "How many creds did you get?"

Rhia exhaled loudly. "Sixty-three."

"Ugh. Yeah, everybody's been frustrated about getting less the last couple weeks. Don't say I said this, but some of us thought somebody must have been skimming off the top. But with the president's update today, it's probably because stuff is being redirected south for the new Re-ed center in Arizona."

"Well, come on. My ice isn't going to make it to Arizona."

"I know. I'm sorry." Ginny took a step closer and reached out to touch Rhia's forearm lightly with her fingertips. Her voice dropped to a whisper. "Look, I'll see what I can do this week, but just try to remember to figure in for ice next time, okay?"

Rhia smiled. "Thanks, Gin."

Ginny looked into Rhia's eyes. There was a moment's hesitation. As if deciding something, she moved closer still and let her hand slide several inches up to the soft skin at the back of Rhia's arm.

"We should really hang out sometime. Some weekend

you're free . . ."

The conspiratorial tone in the younger woman's voice and the closeness of her body both excited and worried Rhia. She smiled, shook her head, and took a step back. "Too much work to do, my friend. A runner's job is never done."

~

That evening, the *Elizabeth Maru*, holds half-full of bartered supplies, lay anchored off the coast thirty miles north of the trade. From the deck, Rhia could just see the steady waves breaking along the distant shore. Those that made it to the beach created a long white line of foam in the fading light. Other waves wrapped in curves of glittering spray around Thread the Needle, the towering sea stack that stood fifty yards offshore, partially submerged in high tide. Its black point jutted skyward, and its wide base was punctuated by an oval-shaped hole through which the water flowed in tumultuous swirls.

Several hours ago, clouds had begun to gather in the southern sky. Watching the subtle signs in the weather and the obvious changes in her instruments, Rhia had noticed a steady increase in wind speed as the barometer fell. She busied herself with preparations for a storm—crab pots, extra gear, and small nets were stowed below to reduce windage, and the dry goods from the trade were stowed safely in the two large black fifty-five-gallon barrels tied to the deck rail on the port side. She had put out her main anchor before steering into the wind and dropping a second anchor, and the line between the anchors was at a right angle to the direction of the strengthening wind. They both had a deep bite, most of the line was out, and the chafing gear was set.

As was her habit, Rhia had checked the anemometer, barometer, and radar repeatedly since leaving the trade on her homeward run, and she wasn't too worried. She'd ridden out many summer storms, which in these waters rarely packed the same punch as a winter gale. After her last check of the conditions, she removed the antennas and took down the anemometer cups so they wouldn't be damaged if the wind kicked up during the night. Anything loose was lashed down or removed, she had checked all the hatches, and the bilge pump was working properly.

"Pressure's dropping, Betty. We might be in for a rough night." Rhia stood on the stern deck in the narrow space between the back of the cabin and the electric winch she used to haul up her sun-bleached gill nets. When fishing, the curtain-like nets would be fed out at the stern perpendicular to the direction the fish were traveling as they migrated along the coast. Colorful buoys lined the top of the net, creating a float line, and lead weights lined the bottom of the net to make it sink into the sea. When fish became gilled in the net, Rhia would haul in the line with the winch, rolling it over the rubber-coated shaft fitted between the two triangles of metal she had attached to the stern as a guide.

Rhia had designed and installed the system three years ago when she had fixed up this boat, adding some parts and removing others to best suit her needs. The rust-spotted side disks of the winch glowed golden in the deepening pink of the sunset as she tied a line around the thick coil of net wrapped around the drum. Heaving her weight sideways, she snugged down the net, pulling hard on the end and tucking it under the line so it wouldn't flap in the wind.

The big black barrels, watertight plastic drums she had salvaged from an old industrial site, contained as many spices, building supplies, medicines, and paper as could be purchased with the goods her towns had sacrificed. As Rhia moved to better secure them, the pit of her stomach felt tight. How could she explain the shortage when she arrived home in two days? Angry, she shoved one of the barrels roughly, and felt it sway.

"That's not right." Rhia stepped back to look at the barrel. A two-inch-thick yellow fabric strap was wrapped horizontally around its middle. She leaned around the right side of the barrel. The zinc-plated hook on one end of the strap was still attached to the deck rail. Swinging her torso to the left, she checked the other end of the strap—still wound through the heavy metal ratchet bolted to a plate on the next rail. Wrapping her arms around the barrel, she widened her stance, tugged, saw the ratchet move and heard the scrape of metal on metal. One of the bolts was loose.

With her wrench size properly adjusted, Rhia tightened the bolt, then shoved the barrels against the rail. "Well, it's better." She looked around and noticed the rise and fall of the bow as stronger waves rolled beneath her. "Wind's picking up. Don't worry, Betty. I'm not going anywhere." She set her hand on the cool metal of the deck rail. "I feel sorry for people who don't have a boat like you to talk to, girl. We have so many great conversations. Can you imagine if anyone overheard us? They'd realize I'm really an idiot, and I get all my great ideas from you."

She smiled to herself in the last of the sunset, then sighed. "I don't know, maybe you're right. Sometimes I wonder if it might be nice to take someone on . . ." The end of the sentence slipped away into the stiffening wind, and she turned to rub a thin layer of waterproofing beeswax around the tightened bolt.

Satisfied that the exterior of the boat was secure, Rhia made her way into the cabin and put away the few pillows and books that lay on the small L-shaped couch behind the captain's chair. After stowing anything that could fall or fly into the cupboards and cabinets designed to hold them, and double-checking that everything was in its proper place, she finally stepped to her small galley, pulled a bowl from the mini-fridge, and tugged one of her two forks off the magnetic strip mounted on the wall above the sink.

Rhia flopped down cross-legged on the firm cushion of the couch. She opened the blue rubber lid of the bowl and began to eat the cold salmon, carrot, and rice stew, barely noticing the increased sway of the boat below her.

With the boat secure and dinner over, Rhia brushed her teeth at the tiny kitchen sink and went below to her berth. Without turning on the single overhead light, she pulled off her clothes and stuffed them into a small mesh hammock hanging from the low ceiling. She tugged back the faded blue-jean quilt tucked around the narrow lower bunk built into the side of the small room, and lay down naked on the cool sheet. Heaving a final sigh, she let herself be rocked to sleep.

~

Through the fog of a deep dream, Rhia began to hear a bass rumble of thunder in the distance. She took a deep breath and slowly opened her eyes. The bow of the *Elizabeth Maru* made a rhythmic thump as it rose and fell against the water, riding the growing waves. A flash of light through the small rectangular windows above her bunk cut through the darkness, momentarily illuminating the room. She quietly counted the seconds before the next growl of thunder.

"One-one thousand, two-one thousand, three-one thousand, four-one thousand, five-one thousand . . . About a mile away, Betty." Rhia arched her back and stretched her bare arms over her head, curling her hands into fists. She took another deep breath and pulled herself out of the bunk. "All right, I'm up."

Thunder rolled as Rhia pulled her rain gear from a built-in cabinet across from her berth and climbed up to the main cabin. For a moment, she stood naked in the night, her clothes held loosely in her hand as she surveyed the sea around her. The temperature had continued to drop as she slept, and wind whistled through the deck rails outside. She slipped on the cool, stiff, waterproof clothes, cinching up the waist of the too-big pants with a length of rope, and moved to her captain's chair. The hinges squeaked as she lifted the seat of the chair and looked at the fat orange PFD in the compartment below, her mind filled with memories.

~

Against all odds, Joseph had returned to Miranda, nearly a year after the Hesperides Truce ended the Last War and set in motion the matriarchy that promised peace and harmony. Gaunt and filthy, he had walked back into town and for days searched every collapsed house and burned-out building until he found his daughter, half-naked and paranoid, hiding under an overturned skiff near the harbor. Slowly, he coaxed her out into the light and carried her in his arms down to the water's edge. Rhia was eleven years old.

Their boat in shambles, they worked side by side replacing and repairing parts that they scavenged from other vessels. They scrounged for scraps of food and avoided the neighborhood women, who were already beginning to question Joseph's parenting. Together, in the jerry-rigged tub they would call home, they began the difficult journey back from the brink of despair.

He was an experienced sailor and a talented tinkerer, and he soon added a mast and sail to the old fishing boat. When it was seaworthy, a small wooden rowboat was tethered to the stern to follow behind as a dinghy. Then they left the harbor and lived separate from town, rowing to land only when necessary. They were content. They felt safe.

As Rhia entered her teenage years, Joseph pieced together a divider in the berth to carve out a small private space for her, and seeing the changes in her body and mind, began to wonder when she would grow tired of their life of isolation.

In the fifth year after the truce, the women in the towns on land began the weekly markets to barter for food and goods, and Joseph sent Rhia in his stead. He knew they would fear and mistrust him, though he had never hurt a woman in his life and had rallied for the women during the oppressive campaigns of years past. During the markets, he hid belowdeck. If they believed she was alone, he thought, they would help her, befriend her, and let her in to the new society they had formed. He had been willing to hide if it meant his daughter could have a better future.

~

Rhia's father had lived his whole life at sea. He had seen storms of legend and fought off waves much bigger than the ones they faced that night six years ago. Together, Joseph and Rhia had readied their boat for the vicious winter gale approaching, and as the rain started to fall, he crossed the deck to where she stood. His dark, weather-rough hands turned her shoulders to face him, and his brow furrowed as he began to tighten the straps of her PFD.

"It's tight enough, Dad."

"Just checking."

"Stop! You're squishing my breasts."

"Hey, girlie, those breasts aren't gonna keep you afloat if you fall in the drink. You think you're indestructible, but you're not. Make sure you're snugged up." The gruffness of his voice was canceled out by a quick wink as he looked up at her young face.

Rhia smirked. "You, too, old man. Make sure you're snugged up."

Three hours later, they huddled together in the berth, holding the wooden rail that ran the length of the wall as the boat slammed down into the trough of another wave. Rhia could see the pallor of her father's face in the constant flash of lightning. His chin was tucked low to his chest, his eyes focused on the floor several feet in front of him. Suddenly, they felt a snap as the anchor line parted, and the boat began to yaw hard to the side. He jumped to his feet and flew up the steps to the main cabin.

"I'll deploy the sea anchor! You make sure you . . ."

The constant roar of air and water pounding at the boat drowned out his shouted directions. By the time Rhia reached the main cabin, salt water was spilling over the starboard rail and sloshing across the deck. It would take her father only a few minutes to pull the series drogue bag from its locker, attach the bridle legs to the corners of the transom at the stern, and drop the weight chain overboard. A hundred five-inch yellow cones would feed into the sea, catching the power of the wind and the waves and swinging the boat into position stern to storm.

Struggling to remain standing as the boat twisted below her, Rhia dug out a bail bucket and checked the switch for the bilge pump. Once the series drogue was deployed, all they would have to do was hunker down and wait out the storm. She began to think about the annoyance of pulling in all the line for the drogue when the wind abated tomorrow. Joseph always made her recover it and stow it back in its bag, and it took hours.

"Ah, there we go," she said to herself as the boat swung around and caught. The fierce storm continued to pound, but the boat was now able to accelerate as a crest approached and ride the wave as it broke. Her legs wide to absorb the motion, she waited for her father to return to the cabin. Thick sheets of rain ran down the windows as she watched the sky, the flashes of light, and the spray of water all around her. But as the minutes passed, the sound of the raging storm seemed to disappear. Standing alone in the dark cabin, she became aware of the sound of her breathing and the growing emptiness in her chest. Her father did not return.

Had he been knocked overboard? Had he fallen? Had he called out to her for help and she didn't hear? Rhia clung to the deck during the rest of the storm, shouting Joseph's name and shining the strong floodlight across the ferocious waves. And though she spent the following weeks with her eyes on the sea, seeking any sign of his body, she knew she would never see him again.

~

Shaking the memory from her mind, Rhia pulled the faded orange life vest from its compartment below her captain's chair. She tugged the thick foam over her head and wrapped the cloth strap around her waist before clicking the ends of the clasps together in front of her belly and her chest. With her right hand, she yanked on the straps.

"Snugged up," she whispered.

Looking through the windows to the deck, she could see a light rain beginning to fall and, through the darkness, four-foot waves breaking in lines of foam in the sea around her. But her anchors kept the bow pointed into the coming storm.

"All right, Betty. I'm here now, girl," Rhia crooned softly as she sat in the dark and rested her hand on the steering wheel. "You're doing fine." Frequent flashes of lightning over the sea illuminated the tempest beginning to brew around her, and as she swiveled her chair to survey the view, she saw also a tiny orange glow on the distant shore.

Rhia squinted. If she looked at it directly, it almost disappeared, but if she looked slightly to the right of it, she knew it was there. "Campfire?" She racked her brain, mentally scanning the maps of the area around Thread the Needle, and couldn't think of a town close by. People didn't just camp for fun anymore. Why bother, when you lived so meagerly day to day?

Rhia leaned out of her captain's chair and reached over to the mini-fridge. Rummaging around for a moment, she pulled out a metal thermos full of water and sat back up. The orange glow was drowned out in another flash of white light, and she counted.

"One-one thousand, two-one thousand, three-one thousand." Rumble. "Little closer now."

Over the next half hour, the weather worsened as the front approached, and the small orange glow disappeared. Rhia listened—to the sound of the wind, the high, thin whistle of the metal rails, the constant spray of water across the bow, the slap of the hull as it plunged over the cresting waves, and the deep rumble of thunder.

From time to time, when a large wave tugged hard at the boat, Rhia would grip the wheel to catch her balance. She estimated the waves to be between six and eight feet high now, and the *Elizabeth Maru* was straining against her anchor. The lightning was nearly constant, with loud cracks of thunder close on its heels. Rain and spray streaked the windows. Taking a deep breath, Rhia closed her eyes and tilted her head back, stretching her neck from side to side. The storm was right above her. She suddenly felt like a tiny piece of cork bobbing in a giant swimming pool and was disquieted by the thought.

BANG!

Rhia leapt to her feet, dropping her thermos to the floor. Her heart beat fiercely in her chest as she scanned the cabin for the source of the sound. A web-like crack had split the back cabin window, and in the sudden illumination of the lightning, she could see something large rolling around the deck. Confused, she stood wide-legged for a moment and stared into the darkness. It wasn't long before lightning flashed again.

"Yep. There is it. Son of a bitch!"

One of the black barrels had broken loose from its tie-down, had slammed into the window, and was now rolling violently around the stern deck. She watched as it hit the back rail and bounced back toward the cabin as her boat rose to the crest of another large wave.

Rhia grabbed the back of her chair to prevent herself from falling and weighed her options. "It's going to break something else." She stared through the back window into the storm. "You're right. I'll do it."

Barefoot, Rhia groped her way through the cabin, nearly

tripping on the thermos, which continued to roll back and forth on the floor. She stopped in front of a tall series of drawers built into the wall and turned one of the small aluminum handles. The boat's motion pushed her into the drawers, then heaved her backward as it crested the wave. She pulled the drawer open. Grabbing a headlamp, she accidentally pulled out several small items tangled in its straps before quickly shutting the drawer again. The bits and pieces clattered to the floor and joined the thermos rolling around under her feet. Half falling, half leaping to the door, she pulled a small coil of line from a hook on the wall, strapped on the headlamp, and headed out into the storm.

The wind blew stinging rain into Rhia's face as she opened the cabin door. Tucking her chin down into the collar of her PFD, she pulled hard to close the door behind her, then wrapped one arm around the top of the port deck rail and crouched as low as possible. She made her way slowly toward the stern, toward the rolling barrel, her balance constantly adjusting to the moving boat beneath her.

Between the strobe-like flashes of lightning, Rhia tried to predict the heavy barrel's movements. Her rain gear provided some protection from the spray of the waves and the rain that pelted her, but, like most of her scavenged gear, it was ill fitting. The jacket she wore over the cinched-up pants was also too big, leaving a puckered gape at the nape of her neck where her PFD compressed it, and within moments she could feel a cold cascade of water trickling down her spine. She held the coil of line tightly in her left hand, unsure how she would capture the rogue barrel or ever hope to retie it. Several times she was forced to brace herself behind the winch for protection as the barrel careened past her.

Shaking her head, Rhia realized she was on a fool's

errand. Even if she could get hold of the barrel that was practically flying around her deck, she'd be unable to wrangle it back into position alone. Her only hope was for it to bounce hard enough to be sent overboard before it did any more damage—a loss for her and the women of her towns. She had just decided to make her way back into the cabin to ride out the rest of the storm when a sudden strong wave lifted the boat. Rhia's feet skidded, and she grabbed desperately at the winch with both hands.

"Shit!"

The boat climbed the wave, yawing awkwardly to port. Clinging to the winch, Rhia was wrenched off-balance. The boat crested the wave and began its rapid descent, and her bare feet suddenly slid sideways. She felt herself lifted off the deck, her legs twisting in the air, as she held tightly to the side of the winch. For a split second, she saw her feet suspended in midair, her body parallel to the deck, and then her left hand slipped. Her head slammed into the cold metal edge of the winch, and through the growl of the wave and the scream of the storm she heard the thunder of the loose barrel bear down on her.

~ Two ~

Rhia woke, jerking and coughing out cold water as the sea roiled around her. The rain pelting the dark water reduced visibility, waves lifted and dropped her body again and again, and pain radiated from her chest like fire. In her confusion, she became suddenly and illogically afraid that her soaked PFD was pulling her down instead of keeping her afloat. The metallic taste of panic filled her mouth, and she writhed in the water, trying to swim backward, away from her fear. Pain bloomed and overwhelmed her. She began to scrabble her fingers over the straps of the life jacket, grasping at the buckles.

Then, through the blinding fear, she felt him beside her, as sure and true as the cold black water and the thumping of her heart. She stopped struggling and lay motionless for a moment, afraid to move or breathe lest she lose him. She knew that if she turned her head, he would be there, but she also knew she didn't have to look.

"Okay. I know," she whispered. And he was gone.

Clarity washed through her brain, driving out panic, as Rhia's breathing slowed. She blinked hard, squeezing the salt water from her eyes before opening them to take in her surroundings. She looked at her hands, the thick orange vest, the waves all around her.

Okay. I'm in the water. This is my PFD. Chill the fuck out, Rhia. Focus.

She tried to take a deep breath, then moaned as pain flared like fire in her chest.

Where's Betty?

She needed to get her bearings. Slowly and painfully, she paddled her arms and legs around her, rotating her body in the water. The storm was passing now, but still-frequent arcs of lightning allowed her to see the dark mass of the shore in the distance. The dim light of dawn was beginning to glow behind the heavily wooded hill that ran the length of the beach. Punctuating the view was the forbidding black mass of the sea stack. She couldn't see the oval eye near the base of Thread the Needle through the whitecaps buffeting her, but its jagged top seemed to hover above the tumultuous water. Far away. The boat must be closer.

Rhia rotated a circle through the water once more, straining her eyes for any sign of the boat. She groaned and kicked her leg hard under the water, frustrated and fearful. *Why didn't I turn on the floodlights?*

After several minutes, she began to feel her fingers and toes tingle in the cold water, and knew she had to head to shore. Her loose rain pants billowed around her, making her legs feel like they were pushing through sludge with every kick. She struggled awkwardly to loosen the rope that held the waist and wiggle out of them. Lying on her back, held up by the PFD, she kicked. The pain in her side was too great to do the backstroke, and it was slow going, but every few minutes she paused to check her progress. The growing light on shore seemed to be getting closer.

After what felt like an hour, the loud sound of waves crashing told Rhia she was nearly there. Glancing over her shoulder, she saw a massive wall of rock. She spun around onto her belly. The sea stack loomed large to her left, its ancient concretionary sandstone horizontally layered like a giant slice of cake. To one side, the arched hole eroded in the rock created a window through which water flowed—the eye of the Needle.

Rhia struggled away from the arch on her stomach, battling against the waves that threatened to suck her into the stone. Her legs kicked, but she couldn't seem to move. Desperate and exhausted, she screamed out in pain as she reached her arms forward and, with several strong strokes, thrust her body past the arch and away from its pull.

The lee side of the sea stack was calmer, but there were still at least forty yards left to get to shore. With great effort, Rhia kicked and pulled, sucking in air and spitting out water until she felt rocks and sand scrape her fingertips. She clambered to her feet, falling twice as she was knocked about by the surf, and finally collapsed onto the rocky beach. The wind roared around her, and the slowing rain washed the salt from her face as she slipped back into the silence of unconsciousness.

~

Rhia flickered her eyes open, saw bold strokes of pink and orange in the brightening eastern sky, and closed them again. Gravel and sand scraped over her bare legs, and strong arms wrapped around her. Her body was lifted, and her mind surrendered to numbness and confusion. Her chest ached, and she felt the strange staccato of her breathing—short, rapid intakes and outputs of air, painful, through her clattering teeth. Unable to focus, she drifted back to sleep.

~

Rhia woke to a ceiling of faded green canvas above her. For a few moments, she struggled to make sense of the situation. Then, blinking hard, she tried to sit up. Pain seared through her right side. Her head felt like leaded cotton, heavy and muffled, with a deep throbbing ache above her eyes. She lay back down, closed her eyes, and tried to breathe deeply.

After a while, Rhia opened her eyes again and looked around. She was lying on the floor of an old tent. The door in front of her was zipped closed, but sun streamed in through a mesh window behind her. Two large backpacks lay on either side of her, their flaps unzipped to reveal tightly bundled clothes, bits of metal, and small, stuffed canvas sacks. Shocked, she realized she was naked inside a dark-blue sleeping bag, and she instinctively pulled the material up to her chin. Feeling the hot sting along her right side again, she slowly moved her left hand and bumped her fingertips over her ribs. About two inches below her right breast, she felt the scream of a cracked rib. Pressing lightly on the others, she surmised that two more ribs were at least bruised.

Rhia was moving her hand to her throbbing forehead when she saw a dark shadow loom outside the tent door. Holding her breath, she listened to the rapid clicks of the zipper as it was pulled open from the bottom and tugged around the top curve of the door. The flap folded in and a large man squatted before her.

His hair and beard were thick and dark, his bushy eyebrows heavy above deep-set eyes. For a moment he stared at Rhia, chewing one side of his mustache at the corner of his mouth. Finally, he cleared his throat and said, "You woke up."

Rhia tugged the edge of the sleeping bag tighter to her chin. When the man didn't say any more, she mustered the courage to ask, "Where am I?" Her voice sounded scratchy and dry.

"You're in our tent. We found you on the beach. We brought you here."

"Who are you?"

"No one important."

Rhia's chest heaved. Her eyes darted around the tent and past the man to the woods outside.

"Your jacket's almost dry," he said gruffly as he stood and turned. "I'll bring you some water."

Tears sprang to Rhia's eyes as she watched him walk away. She was too tired and achy to move, and overwhelmed by her incapacity. Alone, with a strange man who could be one of the raiders she'd heard so much about, naked, and helpless. She squeezed her eyes closed and tried to stifle her growing dread. To show fear would be to give this man power. Her mind still foggy, she couldn't think of any way to escape. Even if she could get out of the tent without him noticing, she wouldn't get far while injured.

The man returned a moment later with a small metal cup

in his hand. He slipped off his worn sneakers and crouched carefully into the tent, cautious not to tread on any part of the sleeping bag that held Rhia. He knelt beside her and awkwardly moved his left hand toward her head.

"Um, I guess you'll want to sit up to drink this." He slipped his warm, rough hand behind her neck and slid it several inches down the back of her spine.

Rhia's whole body tensed at the feel of the man's wide palm pressing against her skin, but she tucked her elbows beneath her and let him help lift her torso. He braced her back and put the cup to her lips. She drank the cool water timidly at first, but finished it greedily. When it was empty, he gently lowered her back to the ground, and she pulled the sleeping bag back to her chin.

"Do you want more?"

Rhia shook her head.

Nodding, he took a deep breath and crawled out of the tent, zipping it closed behind him.

Rhia lay in the tent listening to the movements of the man outside. She could hear the crackle of a small campfire, the snap of small branches and twigs as he walked around, and the quiet clunk and clang of pots and pans. After a time, she began to smell food cooking, and her appetite caused her stomach to gurgle and ache.

A new noise came to Rhia, faintly at first, and she tilted her head to hear it. The snap of twigs grew louder as the noise got closer, and she realized another person was walking toward the camp. When she could make out the subtle sound of the new footfalls around the tent, she heard a gruff whisper, "Hey there."

"Hey." It was a woman's voice, quiet and subdued in the surrounding forest. "Did she wake up yet?"

"Yep. Gave her some water a bit ago."

"Did she tell you what happened?"

"Didn't say anything."

Rhia heard the woman sigh, then saw her shadow darken the tent door. The woman slowly unzipped the flap and crouched down in the opening.

"Hello. Peace to you." She was petite, with long sandy-brown hair tied in a ponytail down her back. Rhia could see streaks of gray around her temples and forehead. Her unbuttoned long-sleeve flannel covered a faded blue T-shirt with the flaky remnants of words across the chest. Rhia's now-dry rain jacket was included in a bundle tucked under the woman's arm. She smiled, and there was kindness in her pale-brown eyes.

"Peace to you," Rhia replied.

"You probably want these." She set the clothes down inside the tent. "You were only wearing the jacket and your PFD. I added one of my T-shirts and a pair of shorts, but they'll be snug. You're a lot taller than me. We made some cattail-leaf sandals, too. Nothing fancy, but . . ." She pushed a stray lock of hair behind her ear. "How are you feeling?"

Rhia hesitated. "How did I get here?"

"We found you on the beach this morning. You were soaking wet and half-frozen, so we brought you here."

"Where's here?"

"Our camp."

Rhia cleared her throat and tried to push herself up onto her elbows again. She winced with the pain, but managed to prop herself up a bit. "I'll get dressed and head out. I don't want to be any trouble."

"You aren't any trouble, and I don't think you should leave today. You took a pretty bad blow to the head."

"I'm all right." Rhia tried to roll onto her side, reaching for her clothes, and yelped as fire tore through her side. Defeated, she lay back down.

The woman shook her head and said, "Look, I know you must be scared—you don't know us—but you're safe here. John and I aren't going to hurt you." She took a deep breath and added, "I'm Carol, and my mate is John. What's your name?"

Fighting back tears of frustration, Rhia's voice quavered. "Rhia."

Carol smiled again. "Peace to you, Rhia. Do you want me to help you get dressed, or would you like me to get you some dinner?"

"Dinner?"

"You've slept all day."

For the rest of the day and through the night, Rhia faded in and out of sleep, her head still throbbing. During wakeful times, Carol would come to the tent to check on her, bringing small bits of food or warm tea that tasted of peppermint and lemon balm. Nauseated, Rhia couldn't stomach much, but she was grateful for the tea.

The following morning, Rhia woke to the diffuse light of the first rays of sun through the trees and canvas. Her mind was clearer, and her full bladder told her she would have to muster the strength to venture from the tent. As quietly as possible, she rolled onto her uninjured side and slowly pushed her way up onto all fours. She had to pause there for a moment to quell the dizziness, before tugging at the door zipper. In the stillness of the forest, each click sounded loud, and she cringed. She crawled out of the tent and saw the couple sleeping nearby. They were huddled together in one sleeping bag near the remnants of the campfire, John's front to

Carol's back, his arm curved over her body.

Rhia glanced around the small camp. A thick carpet of decomposing cedar and pine covered the ground, and heavy brush and trees surrounded it, sheltering it from the wind. In the silence, she could faintly hear the sound of the surf. The beach must be close. Her orange life jacket hung from a branch above John and Carol, immobile in the calm morning air.

Rhia took a deep breath and slowly stood. Her side hurt if she moved her right arm, so she kept it tucked close to her body and used the large muscles in her thighs to push herself up. Once vertical, she paused for a wave of nausea, and she reached out to steady herself with the top of the tent. It was little support as the earth below her feet began to turn. Suddenly, strong arms encircled her waist, and she was guided to a large fallen log about ten feet away.

"Hold on there. I've got you." John whispered the words close to her ear as he set her gently on the log. "Carol, she's up."

The woman was out of the sleeping bag in an instant and moved to Rhia's side. "Slow down there, lady. You need to take it easy."

"I need to pee."

The couple exchanged a quick glance, and Carol said, "Help me get her to the bushes and then you can rekindle the fire."

A few minutes later, Rhia and Carol returned to camp. John looked up from the freshly crackling fire, and Rhia saw him scan her body, with the quickly concealed look she'd seen in men before. She tugged at the bottom of the T-shirt Carol had given her, conscious of how small it was and the way her belly showed along the bottom. She walked to the edge of the fire, and John handed her a small metal bowl and a carved wooden spoon. Mushy gray gruel steamed in the bowl.

"What is this?"

"Mostly bulrush."

"It's edible?"

"Sure," Carol said. "Most native plants around here are. You can dry the rhizomes, seeds, and pollen and crush it into flour. There're also Jerusalem artichoke tubers in the mix, pigweed seeds, shepherd's purse, dandelion root. Sunflower kernels. It's not too bad."

"This is all stuff you foraged?"

"Yes."

Rhia tasted the porridge and was surprised at its peppery bitterness. It was hot and thick, and she was hungry. When she had scraped the last of the mush from the bottom of the bowl, she looked up to see John watching her. He held out his hand, and she passed him the bowl. He scooped himself a serving of food, and began to eat.

"Why are you two camping?"

Carol ate her food slowly, cradling the small bowl in her hand and savoring its warmth in the early morning. "This is how we live."

"You mean always?"

"Yes."

"Don't you belong to a neighborhood?"

"No."

Rhia was silent for a moment. "Why not?"

Finished, Carol set her bowl down beside her on the log. "We left about two years ago. We decided we'd be happier out here on our own."

"But, why? I mean, without a neighborhood, how do you trade for supplies?"

Carol smiled. "We manage. What about you? How did you wind up washed up on a beach?"

"My boat . . . There was a storm, and I got knocked overboard. My boat is anchored a ways offshore. I need to get back to it."

"Not sure how you're gonna do that." John's voice was deep and quiet, little more than a rumble in the stillness of the tall trees surrounding them. "From the looks of you, you've got a concussion and maybe some cracked ribs. I remember what that feels like. You won't be able to do much for a while."

"How far from the shore are we?"

"Quarter mile to the bluff."

"Can I walk there? I want to see my boat."

John looked up from his bowl. "Okay. After we get breakfast cleaned up, I'll help you."

"Carol can take me."

John sighed and looked out into the trees. After a moment, he said, "No. She won't be able to pick you up if you fall. If you're going, you're gonna have to go with me. The fact is, I'm bigger and stronger. I'll take you."

They walked side by side on the overgrown path where the trees were far enough apart, and Rhia in front of John when it was close. His arm was always ready to steady her if she felt dizzy or had to stop to rest. With Carol's help, she had wrapped a pair of John's patchy canvas pants around her torso and snugged it enough to support her ribs without restricting her breathing. Their footsteps were muffled by the thick ground cover of fallen leaves and mosses. The sun, now higher in the sky, cast long dappled streams of light down through the branches overhead and made strange shadows in the tangled bushes and brambles they passed.

When they reached the edge of the sandy cliff that fell away to the beach below, John said, "You can see your boat from here." He pointed out to the calm expanse of water.

Rhia shaded her eyes with her left hand and saw Thread the Needle, dark and ominous even in the daylight, its base nearly exposed now in the low tide. She saw the arch that had seemed to pull at her in her exhaustion and confusion two nights before, and she saw Betty, small and shining, like a point of light in the distance. She was still anchored in the deep water, and barely bobbing on the gentle waves. It was far. Injured, she couldn't make it there without a boat.

"Any chance you can swim out there and pilot her over here?" Rhia asked.

"Sorry. Not much of a swimmer."

"All right. We can head back." They walked for several minutes before she thought to add, "Thank you."

Back at camp, Carol was busy washing clothes in a large pot of boiling water that was perched on three rocks along one side of the fire. She used a thick stick to put in each shirt and stir it before lifting it out, steaming and dripping, and draping it over a low-hanging branch. When each piece was cool enough, she used her hands to squeeze out the water, leaning in to keep her feet dry. Beads of sweat stood on her face and neck. She looked up and smiled when Rhia and John returned.

"Thought I might as well do some wash if we have to camp here a while. How'd it go?"

"Fine," Rhia said. "My boat's still there, but it's pretty far out. You were right. I'm sorry, but I don't think I can get to it yet."

"John and I talked about it last night. You can stay with us for a few days until you're stronger."

"That's very kind of you, but I know that would be a

burden."

"Rhia, it's what good people do. They help each other out."

John took Rhia's arm, led her back to the log, and helped her sit before moving to Carol's side. Wordlessly, he took the big stick from her, dipped it into the pot, and pulled another shirt from the boiling water. Rhia watched them for a minute, their movements as choreographed as a dance.

That night they sat around the fire after a dinner of dried salmon with a salad of wild mint, rosehip skins, and dandelion greens. The pain in Rhia's side had dulled to a deep ache, and her head, though it felt a little better, was still very tender above her ear.

"If you want, I'm happy to sleep outside tonight," Rhia said. "It's not fair to kick you two out of your own tent."

"No. We're fine." Carol was sitting on the ground, nestled between John's legs. His back leaned against the log, his chin tilted up to look at the web of branches above.

"Well, thank you."

They sat in silence for several minutes, listening to the crackle and pop of the flames, watching the small sparks that drifted skyward, dancing in the white smoke. Finally, Rhia asked, "What made you leave?"

Carol raised her bare arms in a stretch above her head and draped one arm casually over John's thigh. "Well, we decided we didn't want to live like that anymore."

"Like what?"

"Like slaves." John's voice was barely a whisper. Carol's arm squeezed a little tighter around his leg.

Carol continued, "We didn't agree with some of the new rules."

Rhia shifted on the log. "Lots of people don't agree with

all the rules. Not everybody leaves town entirely, though."

"Let me ask you something," Carol said. "Have you ever been in love?"

Rhia looked into Carol's light eyes. "No."

"Ever loved anyone at all? Your mother? A sister?"

"My father. He was the one who raised me. He died a while back."

"Well, didn't you want what was best for him? Didn't you want him to be able to live happily and fully? To feel like he was just as important to the world as you are?"

Thoughts of her father swelled in Rhia's mind. The way his eyes would sparkle when he taught her about engineering, electrical systems, fishing, and boating; the way his face would darken when he taught her about the postwar restrictions women created under the banner of peace and harmony.

"Look, I understand what you're saying. I know men don't have the same opportunities as women. Fifteen years ago there were hardly any men around, because we lost a whole generation of them to the Last War. Women got used to doing everything themselves. When men did start to return, the women didn't know what to do—and I'll admit it, there were a lot of mistakes. But isn't it harder to live out here with nothing? No support? No help?"

"But in town, John would have no support. No help. No chance. Once the women took over, they started a campaign that preyed upon all our fears about men. All we hear these days is how men are dangerous and violent, how they have innate differences that we need to be scared of." Carol's hand squeezed John's leg. "The politicians spend all their time inventing laws designed to keep the men down, when they should be promoting the equality we've all been hoping for."

Rhia shook her head. "So, you try to make it work. You

don't just leave. Those laws got passed because we had to take drastic action to stop the fighting and repair everything that was broken. Everybody was just trying to survive then, but things are different now."

"Don't be naive," John said, cocking his head to one side.

"I'm not saying everything's perfect."

"Then don't pretend the New Way rules were just trying to fix everything. In the beginning, we all hoped it could work, that we could finally have peace. Even I was willing to go along with it. Then things evolved. No, devolved."

He sat up a little straighter and leaned his elbows on the log behind him. "Look, I can accept that women took over because they thought they could do a better job than men had done. And with the shithole this world became during the war, I could certainly see their point. But those original rules changed pretty quickly from 'Let us take over for a while and fix things' to 'Let's make laws that guarantee we can keep all the power.' It was retaliation—for the years of the Family Focus Acts, for every bit of misogyny and inequality women had ever faced. They wanted to show us how it felt for them all those years."

It was more than Rhia had heard him say in two days, and she could hear a thinly veiled anger in his voice. Tentatively, she said, "I agree with you. But we're moving beyond that. My town leaders are always talking about how to fix it, and I'm sure other towns are, too. And it's not all bad. We hear every day on the news about cities that are thriving again, women and men working together for the common good, and all the advances in transportation and communication—"

"Yeah, but that's government news," Carol interrupted. "Of course they're going to make it sound good. They need to justify the laws oppressing almost half of their population."

Rhia shook her head. "Maybe. But, regular people understand that they have to do what's right, even if there's a law against it."

"Yes," Carol said. "Regular people try to do what's right, but regular people don't have any power anymore, do they?"

"Sure they do. I'm a runner for a couple towns that have lots of women who know the rules are wrong. In Miranda, women and men work together a lot more now. And all women have the power to treat the men in their lives with kindness and fairness."

"In their own homes." John shook his head. "Sure, Carol and I could do whatever we wanted in our own house, but I would still have to be submissive once I stepped outside, or I'd be accused of trying to take charge. I'd have to pretend to be weak to keep the women comfortable."

"Women don't need you to be weak to be comfortable." Rhia struggled to keep the hostility out of her own voice. "Women are just as strong and smart as men."

"Do you really think that's true?" John leaned forward and met her eyes. "You can't create some theory of equality based on the idea that women and men are the same. We're not the same. Look at my body." He held out his hands, palms up, and sat up straight. Rhia saw the coarse hair that covered his thick, bare arms, and the subtle outline of the curves of his chest through his thin shirt.

"Do you really think you have the same muscle mass as me?" John said. "That you can lift as much as me or carry as much?"

"Maybe not."

"Definitely not."

"*Maybe* not, but I have survived just fine on my own for years—without a man. Survival doesn't depend on having huge biceps. It's about knowledge and wisdom."

"Sometimes it's about being stronger. Survival of the fittest."

"Survival of the fittest to survive. And adapt. And work together." Rhia leaned forward and felt a thrill at the confrontation. "If a woman can't lift a heavy log, she can ask her friends to help her, or she can build a pulley. Simple instruments have been around for thousands of years to overcome a single person's lack of strength. Even the ancient Egyptians knew that ramps and pulleys could—"

"I know how a pulley works," John interrupted.

"Then you should know that it takes more than muscle mass to get things done."

Carol held up her hands. "Okay, look. This isn't about who's bigger or stronger. It's about rules written based on the notions that women are inherently kinder and more compassionate than men, and that men caused all the wars in history and couldn't be trusted with peace. It's about the rules that prevent John from speaking his mind at town meetings out of fear that some women will feel threatened."

"And I told you, I agree with you." Rhia pointed at John. "But he just said he's better than me just because he's stronger. He can't expect me to agree with that."

"Not better," John said, his voice rising. "Different. Different strengths, different weaknesses. Why is it so bad to think women might be gentler and softer than men? Why can't a man be strong and stoic? So what if I don't want to cry, or talk about every little thing in my head?"

Rhia's left leg began to bounce lightly on her toes. "No one's forcing you to cry, or talk."

"Haven't you seen what they're teaching boys in school these days?"

"Yes, finally, for the first time in history, boys are being taught that it's okay to show their emotions. But before the Last War, boys were groomed by society to be barbaric caricatures of manhood. 'Be strong, take charge, don't be a pussy!' From the time you were a little kid, you were told to hide your feelings, and that to show emotion was to show weakness. And that only women were weak."

John laughed. "Can't you admit that there might just be innate differences between women and men? Can't you admit that a man's brain just doesn't work the same way a woman's does?"

"Even if that's true," Rhia scoffed, "and I'm not saying it is, but maybe all those gender differences you claim are innate are really because of societal pressures. The first thing people say when a baby is born is 'It's a girl!' or 'It's a boy!' The first thing we do is label a person with gender, and from that moment on, society places expectations on them."

"Nature versus nurture?" John threw up his hands. "Even if you're right, and there are *no* natural differences between male and female brains, what's your point? We can't raise babies in some weird gender-neutral society."

"Why not?"

"It's human nature to want to label people. We need to categorize things to see how they fit into our scheme of survival." He looked around at the forest surrounding them. "If I didn't label the plants in the woods, how would I know which ones were safe to eat? If I didn't label the fish in the water, how would I know the best ways to catch them? Labels are good, Rhia. And people are different."

"Of course people are different, but not because of their gender. There might be coho, and sockeye, and king, but those are all salmon. In the same way, you put ten people in a room, and you'll find differences in them, but they're all people. People are different because some of us understand that women can do *anything* a man can do, and some people, like you, seem to think that attacking women and telling them they're weak is the manly thing to do."

John leaned back on the log again and took a deep breath. "Rhia, I'm not attacking you. I'm sorry if you felt like I was." He rubbed his beard with his right hand, scratching at the thick tangle of hair there. After a moment he added, "Maybe that's the whole problem. Maybe women will always be scared of men. That's why they made up all those rules to keep us down after the war. That's why they punish men who still scare them."

"Men were scared of women." Rhia tried to calm her voice, but her knee continued to bounce. "That's why they made up all those rules to keep *us* down before the war. All the rights they took from us—it was because men were afraid to admit that women were just as powerful as they were."

John began to chew the corner of his mustache and his gaze settled into the depths of the fire. They sat in silence for several minutes, Rhia feeling unsure how to break the tension that had grown between them.

Carol was the first to speak. "I wish we could have more arguments like this." Rhia looked at her, puzzled.

"No, really," Carol continued. "Arguments are good. Think about it—if you care enough to argue, then you'll realize the other person must care, too. Sure, maybe you won't agree right away, but you'll think it over and maybe come to a compromise later. Arguments can help people understand. Arguments can heal. But, Rhia, under the new laws, only half the population is welcome in the conversation. Men aren't allowed to say what they think at town meetings, and even some women are scared to speak." An uncomfortable laugh played in her throat. "You know there's always at least one person in those meetings who supports the rules so strongly they feel the need to try to convert everyone else. And they feel powerful because the official rules back them up. It's whoever talks the loudest that always gets their way. Maybe if more people felt comfortable talking about this stuff, maybe things could change." She leaned back into John and wrapped her arms around his legs.

"Conversations are good," Rhia said quietly. "Arguments don't help."

"Rhia," Carol said. "I've known John for over twenty years. He's a good man, and even if he's not great at conversation, I want you to know he's never hurt a woman in his life. He's all for equality and fairness, and we left because we couldn't go along with where society was going." She looked into Rhia's eyes, and there was a hint of pleading there. "I don't want you to be scared of him. You should know, you can stay with us as long as you want."

Rhia smiled weakly. She was angry with herself for jumping so quickly to defend New Way rules that, in her heart, she knew were wrong. She was disappointed in herself for not having the right words to express her thoughts, and for not having the courage to stand up to the system the way John and Carol had. Rhia hated that an argument about the New Way Forward could still leave her feeling so confused.

That night, as she lay in the warmth of her borrowed sleeping bag, Rhia heard Carol and John whispering outside the tent. She strained her ears to hear their muffled conversation over the soft rustling of the leaves. John's voice was inaudible, too deep to carry more than a low grumble, but she could pick up bits of Carol's part of the conversation.

"I know, but she can't move yet . . . There hasn't been any sign of guards. I haven't seen any movement on the road . . . I don't know. What if she comes with us . . . You're right. We have to keep moving . . . Two more days." A long pause, and then Rhia heard the deep bass of John's response followed by Carol saying, "Okay. Night, my love."

By the following afternoon, Rhia's dizziness had subsided, and she was able to move more easily. She found that if she didn't bend her torso or move her right arm much, she was able to help a bit around the camp. John had gone to the beach to fish, leaving the two women to tend the fire, wash up the lunch dishes, and scour the surrounding forest for edible plants and herbs.

Carol stayed close to Rhia as they crossed a meadow toward a small stream they could hear bubbling nearby. She pointed out the plants she saw, describing the seasonal changes in each and which parts were usable or toxic.

"This one with the lovely white flowers is yarrow. It's best if you harvest it in the late spring or early summer. You can use the leaves as a poultice right on a wound to stop the bleeding, or drink it as a tea when your lungs are all goopy. It's been in your tea the last couple days as a pain reliever, too."

"Do you need more?"

"No, I've got a decent supply now, so we don't need any today. What I'm really looking for is some stinging nettle. John wants to make a pesto out of the leaves, for the fish tonight. It's found all over the place, so let me know if you see a light-green plant—about this high with heart-shaped, seriated leaves. It'll stick to your pants if you brush by it."

"You must have had a good botany book in your neighborhood."

Carol laughed. "I learned a bit while we lived there, of

course. When food is scarce, you have to find things to eat. But once we decided we were going to leave, we started studying everything we could find about survival in the woods. We had to gather supplies and figure out how to travel light. We probably packed and repacked about twenty times before we had it right. And we had to be careful so our town leaders didn't get suspicious. But we managed all right."

"When you left . . . I mean . . . did anyone try to stop you?"

"They would have. We left at night."

"But, people can move from town to town. Why would they stop you?"

Carol shrugged her small shoulders, wiped a line of sweat from her forehead, and turned away. "Here, look at this. This is wild asparagus. See the old, feathery stalk from last year? The new stalks are getting too big and woody now, but two months ago they were wonderful to eat." She laughed again. "We got pretty tired of it, actually."

They returned to camp about an hour later, their canvas bags full of plants and berries. It was Carol who first heard the noise. She stopped suddenly on the path, and Rhia nearly bumped into her.

"Shh," Carol whispered.

Rhia cocked her head to one side and listened. After a moment she said, "What is it?"

Carol's hand shot up to silence Rhia, and she leaned forward, trying to see through the thick tangle of bushes and branches that hid the old tent beyond. She made her way forward carefully, placing each step heel-toe to minimize the noise of her footfalls. Reaching the final curve in the path, she slowly poked her head around a thorny blackberry bramble. Rhia felt the fear flood out of Carol a split second before she heard her scream.

~ Three ~

"Get away from him!" Carol's scream cut through the silence of the forest. The canvas bags she held were dropped to the ground as she barreled into camp, her arms reaching toward the three armed guards that surrounded John. "Get away! Leave him alone!"

Rhia clutched her right arm tight to her side and hobbled forward as she watched the small woman shove her way between the men in light-gray fatigues and fall to her knees beside her mate. John sat quietly on the ground near the fire, his legs crossed in front of him, his arms bound behind him. Tousled dark hair hung over half his dirt-streaked face, and a fresh welt was growing over his left eye. He looked at Carol with sadness and defeat.

"It's all right, Carol. It's all right." He crooned the words as she wrapped her arms around his neck, sobbing.

"What's going on here?" Rhia called to the guards, forcing her voice to sound firm. "Why are you arresting this man?" She took several steps closer, stretching herself to her full height.

Two guards continued to point their small stun guns at John while the third holstered his and pulled out a small, palm-sized machine. Without a word, he bent down to Carol and, twisting her right thumb, forced her to release her grip on John's neck. He pressed her fingers onto the front pad of the machine, and a second later it beeped. Glancing at the screen, he said, "Carol Mueller, suspected recruiter, breaking and entering, attempted arson, acts of aggression." He slid the machine into its case on his hip and reached into another section of his pack for a length of nylon rope.

"That's bullshit!" John shouted. Struggling against the ropes, he watched helplessly as the guard twisted Carol's arm further and shoved her facedown onto the ground. "Don't touch her! Get the fuck off her!"

Carol thrashed and yelled as the guard pressed his knee to her back and roughly bound her arms behind her.

Rhia ran toward Carol, a mixture of nausea and fury filling her belly, but was grabbed from behind and spun off-balance. Her ribs screamed as she fell to her side. Looking up, she had just enough time to see a fourth guard, a woman in dark-green camouflage, before jerking her face away from the guard's swinging leg. There was a deep thud as a boot connected with the back of her shoulder.

Rhia heaved herself to her knees and crawled several feet to the side of the group before flipping over and sitting on the soft carpet of cedar needles. She looked up at the guard who'd kicked her and, dizzy, watched the dappled colors of the green uniform swirl and meld with the forest all around.

The guard folded her arms across her hard chest. There was a tightness about her, as if her ropy muscles were never relaxed, but always poised to spring on her prey at a moment's notice. Her hair was shaved short, dark-brown bristles showing beneath the green cap she wore on her head. "Who do we have here?"

"Leave these people alone! Who are you?"

"Captain Arlyn Banks." The woman spoke quietly but tersely. Her eyes traveled slowly over Rhia's body, taking in her long dark legs and the exposed front of her shoulder where her borrowed T-shirt had ripped. "Who are you?"

"My name is Rhia Malone, and I'm an official runner for Miranda, New Hope, and Campbell, and I asked you why you're arresting these people." Rhia's breath came out in short gasps, and she felt the salty sting of sweat in her eyes.

The woman looked at Rhia for a moment, her black eyes cold and calculating. "Check her." She jutted her chin at the guard who had restrained Carol, and the man moved to crouch at Rhia's side.

Rhia didn't struggle. She kept her eyes locked on Captain Banks, her lips pursed and defiant as the guard pressed her fingers to the pad of his machine. When it beeped, he read out, "Rhia Malone, runner, suspected recruiter, suspected thief."

Rhia swung to face him and felt her heart thud in her chest. "That's not true." She struggled to keep her voice authoritative. "I've never done anything wrong! That's not true!"

The guard motioned for one of his partners to toss him a rope. Glancing back at the small screen, he added, "Says here she got a whole load of supplies three days ago that never showed up at their destination."

"Everything's on my boat. I was knocked overboard in the storm and these people saved me. I can show you if you—"

Captain Banks smirked as she cut across Rhia's words with a wave of her hand. "No need to show us, honey. Of course we believe you. A beautiful woman like you? I bet nobody ever believes you do anything wrong." Turning to the other guards, she said, "Let's wrap this up. Take them all."

"What? No, you will not take me. You won't take me anywhere." Rhia howled in pain as the man pulled her to her feet. "Keep your hands off me! I'm an official runner! You have no right—"

"Woman, I have every right," Captain Banks suddenly yelled. Her face hardened. "You are with known criminals and you stole from the towns you were supposed to help. The women who were relying on you to—"

"I didn't steal anything! I told you—"

Captain Banks took several quick steps forward and slapped Rhia hard across the face with the back of her hand. Rhia saw a flash of light, and her head twisted to the side from the force of the blow. She slowly turned back to the captain, whose face was contorted with disgust. She could feel the warmth of a slow line of blood as it began to trickle from the corner of her mouth, and she flicked her tongue over the wound.

Captain Banks stepped close, leaning her face to within inches of Rhia's, her hot breath sour and moist. "Not another word out of you," she whispered.

Rhia stood as straight as her painful ribs would allow and met the woman's gaze. For a moment they stared at each other, then the captain pulled back, shook her head, and turned to the guards. "Let's go."

They marched a short distance through the forest until they reached a dilapidated road. Plants and young trees encroached on both sides, and weeds and grasses grew knee-high through cracks in the blacktop. Two of the guards led the way. Rhia, John, and Carol followed single file. The captain and another guard brought up the rear.

They walked in silence for nearly an hour before reaching a larger road. Two small gray pickup trucks were parked in the middle of the intersection, with several guards, three men in gray and one woman in green, lounging nearby. The truck beds were covered by dark-gray caps, on top of which long lines of rollable solar cells were latched. When the procession approached, the three male guards leapt up from the ground and stood at attention.

"Anything?" Captain Banks asked the other woman.

"Nothing. But it looks like you ferreted out something good."

"The male criminal was alone on the beach. The two female criminals were camped with him."

"Pig."

Captain Banks smirked. "They'll sort them out at the Center." Turning to the guards hovering around the prisoners, she added, "All right, let's get these three loaded up and head out."

John was led to the back of one truck. Rhia and Carol were led to the other. A guard opened the door of the cap, then lowered the squeaky tailgate before ushering the two women inside. Without looking at them, the guard closed the gate and slammed the door shut. They heard John being loaded into the second truck, and the quiet electrical hum of the engines starting.

Rhia looked at Carol, sitting opposite her, hunched over

on the hard wooden bench that ran the length of the truck bed, tears streaming down her cheeks.

"Carol, I'm sorry." It was all she could think to say, and she wasn't surprised when she got no response.

They drove for hours, their bodies lurching as they bounced over the ruts and heaves of the broken roads. Twice they passed through neighborhoods, and each time Rhia pressed her face to the grungy window behind her. As the trucks rolled slowly through the gray and anemic-looking towns, children in faded clothing scattered out of the way and stared at the buzzing vehicles. Women, hanging wash on the line or scattering dried corn for the chickens in their front yards, averted their eyes or subtly huddled their children closer to their bodies. The only bright colors to be seen were the banners that hung from several houses, calling out the slogans of the New Way Forward—banners like those Rhia had seen at the trade just days before.

Only once did Rhia see a man. He worked alongside a woman hoeing a wide field near the edge of the second neighborhood. As the trucks rolled by, he stopped his work, stood up straight, and watched silently until he disappeared from Rhia's view around the next bend.

The sun was edging its long way down the western sky when the trucks stopped. Rhia craned her neck and saw a high chain-link fence that stretched the length of a long field. The dry summer grass was cut short for about fifty yards in front of the fence, a barren swath butting up against a tall, swaying golden meadow. The trucks paused for a minute, their engines going silent while a gate was pulled open and then buzzing again as they continued up a steeply sloping drive.

On the other side of the gate, Rhia saw dozens of rusted metal freight containers lined up in the fields along both sides of the drive and packed as tightly together as they would have been on the trains that had once carried them. Faded slashes of white graffiti, painted with large curving letters, were scrawled across the sides of many of them. The few she could make out said things like No New Way or Not Equal. Looking through the back window of the truck, she watched the scene swing around and disappear as they curved around a tight turn.

At the top of the hill, the road flattened out and followed a straight path for several seconds, then the truck coasted to a halt. The engine was turned off, and the guards piled out of the front; two moved quickly to the back, pulled open the gate, and herded the women out. As she rounded the side of the truck, Rhia's steps stuttered at the sight of a massive white brick building looming heavy in front of her. The low sun shone from behind in the deepening light of the long summer day. In the shadows, the main entrance was fronted by four tall columns that held up a portico over a wide stairway.

The two wings of the building reached in opposite directions from this colonnade, like outstretched arms. The east wing was punctuated with small, barred windows evenly spaced along both of the two floors. The west wing had larger, decorative windows in one high-ceilinged story. There were no trees up here, and Rhia looked around to the wide, empty, grassy field that stretched across the top of the massive hill then fell away into an invisible valley beyond.

"No," Carol whispered.

Rhia quickly turned and saw the other truck continuing down the road. John's forehead was pressed against the back window of the truck cap that held him. His eyes stayed fixed on Carol until the truck rounded the side of the building and disappeared from sight.

"Let's go, gorgeous." Captain Banks set her hand firmly

on the small of Rhia's back and pushed her toward the entrance. Other guards were scurrying around the truck, some unloading equipment, some reaching to the top to unhook the solar cells. One guard tugged at a long, yellow, plastic-coated cable that was mounted on the side of the building; the whir of its spool whizzed through the quiet evening. Reaching the side of the truck, the man popped open the cap and plugged the cable in to charge the vehicle.

As they stepped into the shadow of the tall structure, the temperature dropped, and Rhia breathed the cooler air as deep into her lungs as her injured ribs would allow. At the top of the stairs, two large doors yawned open, and the women were led into a wide entrance hall. Ceiling fans turned slowly above, swirling dust motes in the shafts of light that fell through grimy rectangular windows near the top of the wood-paneled walls. Six wooden rocking chairs were lined up along one side of the hall, and Captain Banks gestured to the women to have a seat, then stepped up to a long, ornately carved reception desk tucked into the opposite side of the hall. Three women dressed in pale-blue scrubs sat on stools behind the desk, their fingers tapping and swiping across thin screens in front of them.

"Peace to you, Captain." The head nurse stood and placed her forearms on the long desk, smiling wide as Captain Banks approached. "Back from your week in the field? I'm afraid you've already missed dinner."

Captain Banks smiled and leaned her body against the top edge of the desk. Her muscles softened and bent, her hip curving out to one side. "I'm sure I can find something. After a week out there, a month on duty here will feel like I'm being pampered."

"What have you got for us?"

"We found these ladies in the forest today." Her voice

was kind and gentle, her whole demeanor changed from the brutal cruelty Rhia had experienced only hours before. "Poor women were camping out there with a man who's a known criminal."

"That's not true!" Rhia said. "I'm an official runner and this woman saved my life when—"

"Hush now." Captain Banks's voice was soft and snakelike. She shook her head, a sad expression on her face even as her hand moved to the stun gun at her hip. "From their records, looks like they've gotten tangled up with the wrong sort of man, if you know what I mean." She lifted a device from her pocket similar to the one the guard had used to fingerprint the women earlier, and tapped it against the back of the nurse's computer screen. "Here's their info."

The nurse's shoulders slumped as she looked at Rhia and Carol, sitting rigid in the rocking chairs. She studied them for a moment before looking back at the captain. "Did you capture the man, too?"

"Yes. He's headed to the Village."

The nurse sighed deeply. "Well, don't worry, Arlyn. They're in a better place now." With efficient movements, she tapped her fingers on her computer screen, then rotated the thin unit so it faced Captain Banks. "Just need your print here, and credit for three will be posted to your account."

Captain Banks pushed her thumb onto the blank line. "Thanks, ladies. It's good to know they'll get the help they need. I'll leave them in your capable hands."

"Thank you, Captain. Go get yourself some food."

"Yep." The captain turned away from the desk and looked one last time at Rhia. She winked before walking briskly out the open front door.

When she'd gone, Rhia walked to the desk. For nearly a

minute the nurse worked without looking up, filling out the required forms, before she finally glanced up with a deep sigh.

"Yes?"

"There's been a mistake. I'm not a criminal. I was washed overboard in the storm a few nights ago, and my boat is sitting out in the water right now. If I could just—"

"I understand your frustration, Ms. . . ." The nurse checked the screen in front of her. "Ms. Malone. But I'm afraid I have no power in this matter. I just admit people. You'll have to talk to Ms. Tumwater. She's the justice liaison for the region."

"Okay, then let me talk to her."

The nurse smiled. "Ms. Tumwater's only here on Mondays, so I'm afraid you'll have to wait."

"Today's Monday."

"She's already left for the day."

"What? I'm not going to stay locked up here a week waiting for—"

"I'm sorry, dear. As I said, there's nothing I can do."

Rhia's jaw dropped. "Who's your supervisor?"

"Miss Deacon is the warden of this Center."

"So get her."

"You'll meet her tomorrow. Now please have a seat." The nurse turned back to her screen.

"I haven't done anything wrong. You need to let me—"

"Ms. Malone," the nurse said in a stern voice. "Please don't make me call Captain Banks back in here."

Giving up, Rhia turned in a slow circle and looked around the entrance hall. In the middle of the east wall, near the row of rocking chairs, were closed metal double doors with thick glass peep windows three-quarters of the way up. A carved wooden sign above the doors read To Wards. A heavy silver metal handle in each door held a deadbolt and a lock. Two more doors stood in the center of the west wall, to the right of the reception desk. A similar sign above them read Offices, Treatment Rooms, and Facilities. The doors to the west wing were made of dark oak, but had the same industrial-looking metal handle as the eastern doors.

Her jaw clenched tightly, Rhia looked out the front door. The truck was still parked in the drive. The hot air in the hall was stifling, her body ached, her lip was swollen, and she was filthy. Completely overwhelmed and exhausted, she resisted an urge to simply lie down and rest on the cool cement floor beneath her feet.

"Okay, ladies. Someone will be right up to help you." The nurse went to sit back down on her stool, but stopped when she saw Carol hunched forward in her chair, her back shaking with silent sobs. The nurse smiled kindly once more and said, "Don't worry, honey. It's going to be all right."

~ Four ~

Rhia heard the low gong of a bell through the deep haze of exhaustion. She rolled over on the small bed and pulled the coarse blanket up over her head, subconsciously hiding from the painful truths that waking would reveal. A moment later, a gentle hand touched her shoulder, and she heard a woman's voice, quiet and close.

"You need to get up now. That's the morning bell."

The memory of the previous day flooded into Rhia's mind as her eyes opened. She watched the woman walk across the dim room and stop to squat above the low toilet in the corner.

Rhia averted her eyes and pulled her sore body up from the thin, lumpy mattress. She was cautious to avoid banging her throbbing head on the empty metal bunk above her own as she set her bare feet on the cold, heavily stained cement floor. Her tongue played at the corner of her mouth, testing the crust of dried blood that covered the small gash there, while the bile of anger rose fresh in her belly.

"Looks like you're our new roommate." A topless young woman pulled on faded orange pants as she spoke, then set her hands on her narrow hips. Her long amber hair was draped over her right shoulder, partially covering one of her pale, firm breasts. "I'm Ruth."

"Rhia."

"I'm Charlotte," the first woman said as she stood from the toilet and pulled up her pants. She had a pear-shaped body and a long salt-and-pepper braid hanging in front of each shoulder. "Peace to you, and good morning. You're going to want to hurry, though," she said in a motherly tone. "The door opens in four minutes."

By the time the buzzer sounded and the door swung open with a clunk, they were ready. The three women filed out into the hall, joining a steadily swelling procession of women, all dressed in faded shades of orange, that poured out of identical beige metal doors along the cement passageway. They streamed down a wide staircase, careful to avoid broken sections of railing and crumbling bits of wall, until they reached the main floor. The cafeteria's large swinging doors were propped open, and with Charlotte whispering instructions behind her, Rhia followed the line to breakfast. She picked up her tray and received a glob of hot oatmeal, a few lukewarm orange slices, and a steaming mug of peppermint tea.

Rhia sat at one of four long tables and glanced around at the other women. Twenty-six, she counted. Her eyebrows knit together when she saw Carol sitting hunched near the end of another bench, her eyes fixed on her breakfast. She knew she was the reason they had been caught. She'd distracted them, slowed them down. Guiltily, Rhia began to stand, trying to think of ways to apologize.

"Are you okay?" Charlotte whispered.

"Fine." Rhia looked once more at Carol, then sat back down.

Paper posters were hung all along the pale-yellow cafeteria walls, and colorful pictures of smiling women and men stared mindlessly from each. Each poster contained a phrase meant to encourage the inmates in their journey at the Center. Together We Thrive! Modern Women Cooperate! Let Go of Your Fears! New Men Know How to Love! And the ever-present Grow More, Use Less! Large speakers hung from two corners of the room, and recorded voices calmly and smoothly spoke those phrases every few minutes.

"After breakfast, we have twenty minutes back in our room, then Daily Circle, then whatever's on your schedule. We rotate time working in the gardens, but most days we head to class." Charlotte sipped her tea.

"What class?" Rhia bent over her tray, and her eyes continued to dart around the room.

"Depends on the day. Monday, Wednesday, and Friday we have three hours of Modern History—the teachers lead us through the male-led politics of the 2040s and the Family Focus Acts that slowly eliminated women's freedoms. They talk about the big companies that caused the energy crisis that led up to the Last War, and they help us understand how women finally joined forces to rise up and take charge to fix it all. Oh, Rhia! You'll really examine your beliefs and emotions during this class! You're going to love it!"

Rhia smiled faintly.

Charlotte beamed and continued, "Today and Thursday

it's morning class work on sustainability, agriculture, clean energy, or green building techniques. We get to apply the theories of what we learn in Modern History to real-world problems we'll face in our towns."

"What about afternoons?"

"After lunch each day we have practicals, then group discussions until dinner."

"Practicals?"

"Hands-on work. Laboratories. Either in the fields, in the hangars, or in the Village."

"The Village?"

"Where the men are housed—in the shipping containers." Charlotte turned to Rhia and smiled kindly. Deep crow's-feet framed her eyes like bookends. "Don't worry. You'll figure it all out soon. I remember it was pretty confusing when I first got here, but it gets easier."

"How long have you been here?"

Charlotte's eyes sparkled with pride. "Seven months now." She sat up tall and looked around at the women sitting in long rows beside her. "I can tell who the new people are. I can see it in their eyes and the way they hold themselves." She leaned closer to Rhia. "When they're new, it's like they're closed up. Their bodies are so hard and hunched. They don't trust anyone and they never smile. But after a while, they start to understand how lucky they are to have been brought here."

"Lucky?"

"Yes! Rhia, before I came to the Center, I was like a lost wanderer in the desert. I was so confused about all the troubles of the War and the times that followed. I used my own misfortune to try to get others to feel sorry for me, and I acted out with aggression and anger toward the very people who were trying to help me. I just didn't understand how much progress we've made since women brought balance to this country."

Charlotte laughed lightly and let her spoon rest on her tray. "You know, every morning when I wake up, I silently thank President Asakawa and all the women leaders of this country for everything they are doing. I'm so glad I've had the privilege of coming here and learning all about it."

Rhia stared at her, unsure how to react. "Um, okay."

"Don't worry. You'll understand soon enough."

Charlotte went back to her breakfast, a pleasant smile playing at the corners of her mouth. Rhia glanced around at her other tablemates. Most sat silently or spoke quietly to each other, but when Rhia looked across the table at Ruth, the young woman met her gaze and held it. After several seconds, Rhia lowered her head and ate.

~

They sat around five round wooden tables that were clustered together in the room. Sunlight diffused through a south-facing wall of tall block windows. Most of the women had a notebook and pencil in front of them and were speaking quietly to their neighbors. Two tables over, Rhia saw Carol again, still scowling and sitting low in her chair. She looked small and defeated in the baggy orange uniform, her eyes red and swollen, and she gently rubbed at the rope burn that encircled her wrists. Again, Rhia wanted to go to her, but she couldn't rise to the challenge of inventing platitudes or instilling confidence she didn't feel about John's safety. Instead, she slouched lower in her own chair, hoping the woman who had saved her life and helped her in so many ways during the past few days wouldn't notice her.

The heavy door opened with a loud squeak, and a tall, middle-aged woman strode in. Her light-blond hair was trimmed just above her shoulders, and soft curls bounced around her face as she moved quickly to the front of the room. She wore a stark white dress that was hemmed several inches below her knees and contrasted with the thick blue leather belt wrapped around her waist. Small white buttons lined the front of the bodice and stretched to cover her ample chest.

Every inmate stood quickly and faced the woman as she passed, and Rhia followed suit.

"There she is!" Charlotte's voice was high and breathy.

"Who is that?"

"Miss Deacon. She's our warden, our teacher, and our guide. Rhia, she's the one person in this world who'll be able to shepherd you through your pain."

"The only pain I feel is from a cracked rib."

Charlotte shook her head and smiled.

When the woman reached the front of the room, she turned to the group and said brightly, "Peace to you, and good morning, class."

"Good morning, Miss Deacon," everyone replied.

"Welcome to Daily Circle. Please sit, unless you are one of the two new travelers with us today." As the others sat down, Miss Deacon looked at Rhia and Carol and opened her arms in welcome.

"Let me be the first to say, we are glad that you are here. I am sure these first few days will be confusing and frustrating for you both, but know this—we are all here to help you." The subtle lilt of her voice rose and fell like waves on a white-sand shore. "Your time at Re-education Center Number Three will be an intellectual and emotional journey, and as such, we like to think of you as travelers. There will be hills and valleys, rocks and thorns along your path, but I promise you—you will soon understand the glorious new life that awaits you when this journey is done."

Several of the women in the room called out "Yes!" or "Amen!" Rhia noticed Charlotte nodding beside her.

"Now," Miss Deacon continued. "Let us all rise and say the Daily Affirmation. And say it nice and loud so our new travelers will hear every word!"

The women rose and folded their hands across their chests, facing the front. In a rhythmic singsong, they recited the words each had heard every day since her arrival at the Center. Words most of them knew by heart, and many of them now believed.

"I have been put on this Earth to do good for all people. I have been given this life to make the Earth a safer, healthier, more nurturing and prosperous place for all people. I have made mistakes in the past, but I promise to work harder in the future. I believe that all women and men deserve the chance to reach their full potential. I believe that the Last War was the result of an imbalance in the system and the dominance of masculinity, greed, and aggression. I believe that it is my duty and honor to struggle against the oppression, fear, and hatred of those who cannot see these truths, and I believe that Re-education will help me achieve my goals."

They sat once again under the beaming countenance of Miss Deacon. "Excellent, women. Excellent. Your positive attitudes will take you far in this world!" She pulled a tall stool from the edge of the room and sat down.

"Today I would like to discuss something quite near and dear to my heart." A gentle sadness washed over her face, and her right hand rose to her chest. "Today we will be talking about marriage. Now, as many of you already know, I was once the *wife* of a very powerful man." Her voice dropped as she spoke these words, becoming a whisper that hissed in the deference of the room. "This was before the Last War, before people joined together as equal mates, and before women were granted their rightful place in society. I married him when I was only twenty-three years old, thinking that he was the Prince Charming my mother, my movies, and my society had always told me about—that he was the man who would love me, and guide me, and protect me, and support me throughout my life, and that together we would build a home and a family."

Miss Deacon sighed. "Now, as I said, my husband was a *powerful* man, but he was not a *good* man. He believed that increasing his bank account was the same thing as increasing his manhood. He believed that the weak and the impoverished were only so because of a failing in their constitution. He believed that he was above the common rules of law and that his job was to exploit the here and now without concern for the future of others. And my husband believed that women were put on this Earth to please him. He believed that there should be no consequence for his philandering, his womanizing, his flirting, and his bragging. And he believed most of all that I would always be there to support him, and worship him, and clean up his messes after he was done!"

At this, many of the women in the room booed and hissed, shaking their heads and clucking their tongues. Miss Deacon rose up from the stool and took several steps toward Rhia's table. She seemed to glow from within her lily-white frock, and her eyes smoldered with intensity.

"And, my friends, do you want to know the worst part of all this? I cannot place the blame entirely on this man! I have been forced through my years of soul-searching and heartfelt meditation on this issue to acknowledge the fact that I, myself, was just as guilty as my husband in the perpetuation of the whole mess! I now know that a part of me wanted him to ride in on his proverbial horse and take care of me. I wanted to be the kind of woman who had beautiful things—beautiful clothes, beautiful parties, beautiful children, a beautiful house—and I knew, deep in my heart I knew, that I was willing to trade my very soul for these things." She tapped each of her fingers as she went through this list, then balled her hands into tight fists.

"I was once the kind of woman who was willing to trade her freedom for security and dependability. I was willing to trade my intellect and my ingenuity—to stay silent when men around me asserted their opinions even though I disagreed with them. I was willing to allow the men around me to take charge of my finances, my education, even the construction and maintenance of my home and my vehicle. And I was the kind of woman who allowed my husband to destroy my self-confidence, to chip away at my courage and my strength for years, to the point where I truly believed I would die or rot away a desiccated, wrinkled, lonely old maid if he ever left me."

Rhia watched this woman with a mixture of fear and awe. Small drops of spittle flew from Miss Deacon's lips as the tempo and volume of her speech rose, and her cheeks now burned red.

Miss Deacon continued. "Now, I know from talking to you all that there are many in this room who have experienced the same sort of relationships in your lifetime. There are women here who have been coerced by men, subjugated and oppressed by men, raped and beaten by men. But I am here to tell you all that you will never have to live like that again!" She opened her arms wide to the room, a benevolent smile tugging the corners of her full lips. "Under the guidance of the New Way, the men of this world are being taught how to *truly* love a woman. They are being taught how to respect and care for women as equals, and they are being taught how to finally acknowledge their own strengths and weaknesses without fear of ridicule or rebuff. Here in Re-education Center Number Three, we are working to lead both women and men into the bright new future where they no longer have to abide by the stereotypes and societal regulations of the past, and they can finally achieve their full potential.

"Marriage is no longer a contract that gives a man dominion over a woman!" Miss Deacon continued. "We have moved beyond the Old Testament ideas of 'Wife, submit to your husband!' We have moved into a new realm of beauty, and peace, and understanding. When you find the woman or man with whom you want to share your love and your life, you are no longer required to give up a piece of your spirit and your soul to please them. You are no longer required to call anyone the head of your household, because you will finally be able to find a person willing to be your partner, your collaborator, your mate. Right now, at this very moment, the men in our care are learning how to treat you with the dignity and the respect that you deserve. They are learning that you are strong and powerful, intelligent and brave, and that they need not fear your beauty, your mysticism, or your wisdom.

"If you and your mate wish to commit to each other, you need not bow down before the yoke of an antiquated patriarchy. Rather, you must simply agree to love, honor, respect, and uplift each other in the great and glorious New Way Forward, seeking always to overhaul and amend the errors of our past, working together as equals to build up our new society, our new life together. The New Way Forward is a quest to help the women and men of this world understand that the old ways of anger, and fear, and greed, and inequality, nearly led to the destruction of us all. Continue to follow the quest for these truths, and you will surely be raised up into the light of the New Way Forward!"

Miss Deacon made eye contact with several women around the room. "Go out this morning and glory in the wonder and beauty of the day. Go out and learn new things, examine old beliefs, and look within yourselves for the truth. Above all, know always that you are loved, you are supported, and you are welcomed into the light and love of the New Way Forward!"

At this, several women stood, their arms raised above their heads, and began to laud Miss Deacon.

"Come to me, my friends!" Miss Deacon called out to the group. "Come to me with open hearts and open minds! The New Way Forward can save us all! Come to me and leave your past behind!"

Women streamed to the front of the room, their arms outstretched as they gently touched and praised Miss Deacon. She beamed at them as they came, bestowing a gentle touch to the cheek of some and a brilliant smile to all. The audience's admiration of this rapturous finale was not universal, however. Rhia saw several women who stayed in their seats and seemed to be applauding only out of a sense of duty or courtesy. She also took note of one who did not clap—Ruth, her roommate, sat across the highly polished table from Rhia with her arms folded across her chest and her long legs stretched out in front of her. She leaned back in her chair and glowered at the charismatic woman before them all.

Rhia watched Ruth, curious about the mix of condescension and disgust she saw etched on her face. Ruth, perhaps feeling Rhia's eyes on her, turned her head. They looked at each other for a moment, each trying to gauge the other's thoughts, before Ruth raised her eyebrows and cocked her head slightly to the side. With a covey of women flocking beyond her to reach the outstretched arms of Miss Deacon, Ruth leaned across the table and said, "I think that woman is full of shit."

~

"Miss Deacon has changed my life! Under her guidance I've finally realized why I had so much sadness and difficulty in my life, you know? If you can believe this, before I came here I was working as a recruiter with my sister, Ethel. We did everything we could to convince people that the government was hiding things and that men were being treated unfairly. We even thought—"

"I'm going to get more water." Rhia rose from the lunch table, interrupting Charlotte.

"Oh. Of course. Do you need any help?"

"No. I've got it."

Rhia walked slowly toward the line, and was pleased to see Ruth leave her own place at the table and head in her direction. She stood behind Rhia in the queue, close enough for both the sound and the breath of her whispers to reach Rhia's ear.

"Looks like you've made a friend in Charlotte."

"Yeah, I guess so."

"She's quite a convert."

Rhia kept her chin down, moving only her eyes to glance around the room as she spoke. "Yep."

Ruth laughed quiet and low in her throat. "Well, I guess

that's one way to go."

"What do you mean?"

"Nothing. It's probably good for you to be her friend. Lots of women realize it's easier to just go with it and agree to everything they say. If you decide to just turn off your brain and let them take over, I'll understand."

"Excuse me?" Rhia turned to Ruth, her eyebrows raised.

"Or maybe you won't. Maybe you're one of the strong ones. Time will tell. Not everyone falls quite so hard for Miss Deacon and the system. Some of us see what's really going on."

Rhia turned sideways as she shuffled forward in the line and saw Ruth out of the corner of her eye. "What's really going on?"

"You'll see."

They had reached the front of the line, and Rhia held out her mug for a ladleful of water. She peeled away from the line and slowly headed back toward the table. Charlotte was waiting for her, and began her one-sided conversation where she had left off.

~

The sun was high in the sky by the time the women walked to their afternoon classes and laboratories in the hangars. Rhia took deep breaths of the hot, fresh air, grateful to be free of the sharp vinegar smell that clung to the stained cement walls and floors of the east wing, and frustrated to feel the sting of her ribs as they struggled to heal. She followed the crowd of women across the flat grassy field behind the building, glancing back to try to locate the tiny barred window of her own shared room among the dozens that winked out at her in the glare.

Lining the top of the building were six large speakers, and out of each came the same calming, reassuring voices uttering the phrases printed on the banners and posters hung around the cafeteria. Grow More, Use Less! New Men Know How to Love.

With a sinking feeling, Rhia realized her conscious thoughts had already stopped registering the recordings. They were like white noise.

Reaching the far side of the field upon which the main building stood, Rhia stopped short. Before her was a long slope, devoid of trees, that opened up to a wide flat valley. Five groups of rusted metal shipping containers were laid out in a grid, with six boxes in each group. Men were stepping out of some of the containers, sliding the heavy metal doors shut behind them, and moving toward the four huge gray hangars that stood to the north. From this height, she could see an expansive half circuit of tall fence bounding the property that made up the Center. Around the perimeter stood ten tall lookout stations, and Rhia noted two people stationed in the small shelters at the top of each, watching all that moved below. Most guards wore the same gray camouflage as the men who had captured her in the woods. The few female guards wore green.

"That's the Village." Ruth sidled up next to Rhia, her arms crossed over her chest. "The men stay there most of the time, but they have to go to the hangars for classes and to the Big House for sessions."

"Sessions?"

"If their crimes include any violence against women, they undergo Feminine Empathy Sessions. FEmS." Ruth looked at Rhia's face and added, "Wait until you see it. They inject them with Psilocox. It's a hallucinogenic chemical that's supposed to help them be kinder to women somehow. It's completely barbaric."

"Well, if they were violent to women, I can't say I have a lot of sympathy."

"Agreed. But remember, that's a pretty broad category these days. We're not talking about rapes and murders—those criminals aren't sent to a Center. This could be something much smaller, and is sometimes just a bullshit excuse. A woman in your neighborhood accuses you of intimidating her, you're suddenly sent here."

"That's the sort of stuff the neighborhood leaders are supposed to sort out. They're not going to send someone away just because—"

"You don't believe me? You don't think innocent people can get sent to a Center?"

Rhia looked away. "I'm not saying that. It's just . . . that's not right."

"I agree." Ruth tugged on Rhia's arm, and they began to walk together toward the hangars. "But that's not the worst of it. Ten percent of the men are selected to get false pregnancies."

Rhia spun toward Ruth and stopped, ignoring the women who had to veer around her on the path. "What?"

"They're chemically and physically adjusted to experience what pregnancy feels like. An expanding balloon is surgically inserted into their abdomen, and it's filled up with saline over the next nine months."

"Come on," Rhia said in disbelief.

"You don't believe me? You'll see for yourself. Trust me, things here are far worse than the rumors we all heard before."

Rhia wanted to like Ruth. She could be a friend, about the same age. But this couldn't be true. She would have heard about it, even if it were only a whisper in the stories that circulated about the Centers. "They can't do that," she said. "They can't just inject drugs and balloons into people against their will."

Ruth shrugged. "Sure they can. They're the law, Rhia."

"But the politicians and regional leaders must—"

"They know all about it. Deacon has even given tours, bragging about the emotional results she gets. Break them down and then rebuild them the way she wants them to be, to act, to think. She's a real hero. As long as she isn't castrating them or lowering their breeding potential, Deacon can do whatever she wants."

Both women went silent as they followed the worn path down the hill toward the hangars. Signs over each building told what classes were inside—Engineering, Physics and Mathematics, Hunting and Preserving. Rhia and Ruth continued past these to Botany. Ruth pulled the small metal door open and held it open.

The temperature dropped as Rhia stepped into the darkness of the barnlike structure. Overhead, heating conduits, vents, fans, and strips of industrial light fixtures crisscrossed the arched ceiling. Long, thick, black wires hung down from junctures in the electrical system, and huge fluorescent panels directed their stark glow down into four partitioned rooms. Rhia and Ruth made their way down the long central hallway to room 3 at the back.

Rhia sat beside Ruth in the back row. In the front of the room was a long rectangular table upon which stood glass beakers, sample jars, and small, stuffed canvas sacks. A wide chalkboard was mounted on the front wall, and a white canvas screen hung near it.

The door behind them continued to swing open and

closed as women filed in. Rhia glanced at each of them as they passed, silently trying to gauge which would be zealous supporters of the Center like Charlotte and which would be as opposed to it as Ruth. Then she sat up straight in her chair. A tall man had entered the room, clothed in the same plainly styled T-shirt and pants as the women, but in faded red. He didn't look up from the floor, but walked quickly and quietly to the seat on the other side of Ruth. Most of the women in the room ignored him, but she saw Ruth raise her elbow and nudge him subtly as he sat.

Ruth leaned over to Rhia. "Some of the men get to come to classes when they're close to getting out of here. This is William." And to the man, she added, "Rhia's new. Just arrived yesterday."

He leaned forward and ticked his chin upward for a second, barely glancing in Rhia's direction.

"She's with us," Ruth continued. "She's only been here a day and she can already see how fucked up this place is. Rhia, when you work in the Village, try to get in William's group. He's one of us."

Rhia watched the man through the corners of her eyes, trying not to stare. He was ruggedly handsome, with dark eyes and full lips. His dark hair was shaved close to his scalp, and a thin scar cut across the back of his neck. It started just below his right ear and etched its way downward before disappearing below the back collar of his T-shirt. He sat tall, his straight spine held an inch or so away from the back of his chair; his muscular arms were tensed. She could see the tan line just below his sleeve, his skin a darker shade of brown where exposed to the summer sun. In his right hand he held the same small notebook and pencil the women carried.

Over the next several minutes, seven other men joined

the class, each finding a seat among the women. Rhia watched each of them enter, but her eyes were drawn back to William, to the strong curve of his jaw and the way his chest rose and fell below his thin shirt as he breathed. His hands rested lightly on his thighs, and yet something in the tension of his legs made him look like he could jump up and run at a moment's notice. He must have felt her watching him, and suddenly, for the first time since walking in, he turned his head and looked directly into her eyes. She felt a sudden flush in her cheeks and quickly looked away.

Once everyone was seated, three women entered through the back doors wearing the same pale-blue color as the nurses who had admitted Rhia the night before. Instead of scrubs, however, they wore canvas pants and short-sleeved, button-down chambray shirts with several pockets.

"Those are the botany teachers. Ms. Brakille's the short one. She's the lead teacher," Ruth whispered.

Rhia jerked in surprise—she recognized one of the teachers. Laura Decker, a young woman from Miranda she'd known most of her life, the daughter of one of her closest friends. Rhia hadn't seen Laura since she left for college six weeks ago. Why would she be teaching in a Re-ed center? Struggling to regain her composure, Rhia watched the three teachers walk down the center aisle and take their positions behind the chipped and worn table in front of the class.

The teachers first busied themselves taking out books, papers, and chalk, then the oldest of them, Ms. Brakille, looked up. "Is there a new student here today?"

Rhia slowly stood, her eyes still fixed on Laura. "Yes."

"I brought you a notebook. You'll use it for notes and tests, and hand it in to us every few weeks to check, so don't lose it." Reaching into her bag, Ms. Brakille pulled out a small notebook and a pencil and handed it to a woman in the front row. "Please pass these back. Your name is Rhia Malone?"

Laura looked up from her papers, her eyes scanning the crowd. When she saw Rhia, her face went pale and her hand moved to the edge of the table for support. She stared, incredulous, for a moment before blinking once and dropping her gaze.

Clearing her throat, Rhia pulled her eyes from her friend, looked at the head teacher, and said, "Yes. Um, thank you."

"I'm Donna Brakille, and I'm the head botanist here at the Center. My interns are Nadine Montgomery and Laura Decker." She motioned toward each of the younger women at the table. "We've been talking about medicinal plants native to the Pacific Northwest, and we'll start today with a brief quiz about the properties of the bitter roots we discussed last week. Do your best to catch up." She turned to the wide chalkboard behind her and began to scribble dusty white questions across its flat green surface. "You'll have ten minutes to answer these from the time I've finished writing."

Rhia took the notebook as it was passed to her and sat down. She opened to the blank front page and stole glances at the head table, at Laura standing there. The young woman's golden-brown cheeks had flushed pink, and Rhia could tell that Laura was purposefully avoiding looking in her direction.

When the head teacher had finished writing, Rhia scanned the questions and began to write her answers on the rough cream notebook paper.

After an hour of lesson, Ms. Brakille announced a ten-minute break, and the students all stood to stretch and chat. Rhia had watched Laura during the entire class, trying unsuccessfully to catch her eye, and she took this opportunity to probe Ruth.

"How long have these teachers been here?"

"Hmm? Oh, some of them have been here for years, I suppose. Ms. Brakille has been here at least as long as I have, but I'm not sure how long, really."

"What about the assistant teachers?"

"Ms. Montgomery has been here about six months now. So far, she seems decent." For the first time since Rhia had met her, a subtle smile fluttered across Ruth's face, and Rhia was surprised at the softness that flashed in her eyes. "You can tell she would rather be doing her research than teaching us about making sore-throat tinctures from Oregon grape, but she tries to be patient."

"What about the other one? The one with light-brown hair?"

"I don't know much about her yet. She's only been here a couple weeks, but she's okay. Quiet." Ruth's face hardened. "Give her a year and she'll be as bad as the rest of them."

The class was called back into session, and Ms. Brakille once again stood in front of the chalkboard, now freshly wiped. "Now that we've finished talking about calendula, we're going to begin our discussion of the Pacific yew—*Taxus brevifolia*."

Laura stood behind Ms. Brakille and wrote the common and Latin names out in large letters on the board. She picked up a small black remote control and turned to the white screen draped against the wall next to the chalkboard. When she pushed the remote, the class heard the clicking of an ancient slide carousel as it rotated to its first slide.

Ms. Brakille said, "This is an important medicinal tree that is widely distributed throughout the Pacific Northwest and can be found in moist, shady areas. Although the red *arils*, or berries, are highly poisonous to humans, the dark, scaly bark contains a chemical compound called taxol, which is known to inhibit several types of cancers, including breast, ovarian, testicular, lung, melanoma, head, and neck cancers. It was also used in the early years of this century as a secondary treatment during the AIDS epidemic."

The words *taxol*, *cancer*, and *AIDS* were spelled out on the board as well, and Laura clicked through slides showing close-ups of the tree.

"This tree is usually less than forty feet tall and resembles a large shrub. It can be distinguished from the western hemlock by its orderly needle arrangement. The needles grow spirally but lie flat; they are dark green above and light green below—never white—and are pointed, but not sharp."

Rhia scribbled notes for the remainder of class, her eyes often darting to Laura, her mind racing with potential excuses to talk to her after dismissal. But when the lecture finally ended, Laura was at Ms. Brakille's side and whispering in her ear.

Ms. Brakille looked up at Rhia. "Ms. Malone? Would you please come to the front?"

Rhia wove through the herd of women and men heading to the exit at the back of the room, gliding between strangers' shoulders, to make her way to the front.

Ms. Brakille said only, "Ms. Decker will ask you some questions to see what you know," and she packed up her bags and left without another word. The other assistant, Ms. Montgomery, stayed close to Laura.

"Do you want me to stay, too?"

Laura shook her head and smiled. "No, Nadine. Go ahead. I'll meet you in the lab."

The young woman hesitated, then left.

As soon as the last student left and the door closed, Laura

threw her arms around Rhia.

"What are you doing here?" Rhia demanded in a low whisper.

"Me? What about you? Why aren't you back in Miranda?"

"Your mom said you went to college in Olympia. That was weeks ago."

Rhia pulled away from Laura and held her at arm's length, examining her.

"Never mind that! Jesus, Rhia, why are you in a Re-ed center?"

"I shouldn't be! You've got to help me."

"Where's Betty?"

"She's anchored offshore, about thirty miles north of the trade. I was knocked overboard in the storm a few nights ago. This couple helped me, but then guards found us and brought us here."

"Why would they arrest you?"

"They're saying I stole my shipment and ran off with recruiters."

"What?"

"Laura, you have to tell them I didn't do it. You have to tell them to let me out of here."

"Of course! They can't just lock you in here without letting your prove your innocence. You don't want to be in a Center, Rhia."

"I know that! I have to meet with the justice liaison, but she only comes on Mondays, so I'm stuck here until next week!"

"But all the stuff on your boat—"

"Will be ruined," Rhia finished. "Laura, tell them I didn't do it. Tell them to let me out of here."

Laura stared at Rhia, her mouth open as if about to speak.

After a moment, she turned away and began to pick up her things and stuff them into her bag. "I don't know. I mean . . . Rhia, now that I'm thinking about it, I don't think that would help at all."

Rhia felt her skin grow cold. "What?"

"Only the justice liaison can let you out, and you just said she's not here until Monday. You said that yourself. I don't have that kind of power."

"There's got to be somebody you can talk to! The director, or the teachers, or someone. What about Ms. Brakille?"

"She's great. She's very sympathetic to the inmates here, but she can't get you released."

"But if you go to the warden, to Miss Deacon . . . If you tell her you know me . . ."

"I just got here. I don't think I have any . . . I'm only eighteen. I'm just interning here to get credits so I can go to school."

"But your mom said you got in. Kate said you started this term."

"She thinks I did."

"What do you mean?"

"Margaret got in, of course. She was always the smarter one, and they accepted her right away. But they wouldn't take me. They said I would have to prove my intent by doing an internship for a year first."

Rhia's shoulders slouched. "But your mom thinks . . ."

"I know." Laura shook her head. "I applied to internships at all the regional schools, the labs in California, and nobody wanted me." She seemed to grow smaller under Rhia's disapproving glare. "Rhia, you can't tell my mom. You know she wouldn't let me work at a Center."

"Of course she wouldn't! How can you be working for these people? They brainwash people! Jesus, Laura. You've heard the stories as much as I have."

"I'm not brainwashing anybody! I'm just working. I have to do this."

"You can't do this. It's not right."

"It's just a job."

"It's not about a job. It's about justice. Re-ed centers were built to keep people from questioning authority. This place was built to silence anyone who disagrees with the rules. You know that. Jesus, Laura, you should be fighting to shut this place down. Your mom and Michael would die if they knew you were supporting it."

"I'm not supporting the Center. I didn't have a choice."

"There's always a choice. You could choose to fight. If good people refused to work here, they wouldn't be able to hide under the guise of education."

"It's people higher up than me doing the bad stuff. I'm just working. I'm using them to get someplace better. That's my way of fighting the system." Laura pulled a small length of fabric out of her hip pocket, knotted it, pulled it over her head, and tucked her shoulder-length hair behind the headband.

"Rhia, my family has no money and no power, and as much as I love Miranda, it's just a tiny neighborhood. I didn't get into a school, so I have nothing. When I finish my year here, I'll go to school and get credentials." She sighed.

"Look, even if I wanted to shut the Centers down, no one's going to listen to someone like me now. You have to be powerful to change anything. You know that, Rhia. What can I do to change anything?" Her voice wavered. "I had to take what I could get. Besides, Donna Brakille is amazing. She knows so much. And wait until you see the lab! I'm part of an amazing research team here—we're really doing great things. I get to study—"

"But you're part of the machine! You can't claim innocence when you're working at a Center, Laura. It just doesn't work."

"And you're a runner. You take all the stuff we grow and make and deliver it to them."

Rhia stepped back as if she'd been slapped. "That's not the same. I take goods to the trade and get my towns things they need. I barter for things you need."

"Isn't that being part of the machine?"

"Laura, that's different. I'm not working for the Center!"

"I didn't have any other choice."

"There is always a choice."

"No. Not this time." Laura's dark eyes were set. "I want to be a biochemist. I want to help people who are sick. I want to find medicines that will prevent kids from dying, and this was the only way I could do it."

"Laura—"

A lump formed in Rhia's throat. She thought about the visits she'd made to Laura's home three years ago. Laura's twin sister and her brothers had already been moved to a friend's house to keep them from getting infected, but her parents, Kate and Michael, had stayed behind, nursing their young son as he struggled to fight off the disease that was consuming his body. Laura's baby brother, barely two years old, with tiny fingers and tiny toes, tiny sinuses and tiny lungs, so infected with tuberculosis that near the end his every breath was a wet and sloppy rattle. Rhia had delivered food, medicine, and supplies to the edge of their property, and had watched from a distance as the family struggled to tend and soothe the boy, seeing him get weaker by the day. When he finally succumbed, she saw the white smoke rise from their yard as they burned him with his sheets and clothes.

"Laura— I know this is what you want to do. But not here. Not in this place."

Laura looked down at the table and said, "I'm sorry, Rhia. It's the only way."

Rhia sighed. "Look, help me get out of here and I'll try to figure something out. I've got connections with some of the other runners. Maybe I can—"

"Rhia, what can I do? I can't do anything to help you."

"Are you kidding me? You can tell them I'm not a criminal! You can tell them you know me and that I—"

"I don't have that kind of power! They wouldn't believe me, anyway. Besides, I'm sure you'll be able to prove you're not a criminal. Just tell them the truth and they'll listen."

"Laura Decker, don't you dare cop out on me. I've known you your whole life. You're strong, and smart, and—"

"There's nothing I can do!" Laura interrupted.

"Don't you stand there and tell me you're not willing to help me."

"Rhia, it's not that! I'm just saying nothing good will come of it if I start making waves. And what will they think of me if they know I'm friends with you? You said yourself, you're only in here until next Monday. If I start causing trouble, they'll hate me, and I'll never get into a school."

Rhia felt as if the floor had shifted beneath her feet, as if the world she had trusted had suddenly tilted out of balance. When she'd seen Laura at the front of the class, she'd been so sure of her imminent freedom. To have it stolen away so quickly made her heart ache.

"You shit."

"Don't say that. What is it, like five days until you get out?

You're asking me to risk my whole career. My whole life! Besides," Laura said, "this way, I can be your friend on the inside. I'm here if you need anything, and I'll do my best to help you in any way I can." She stuffed the last of her papers into her bag without looking at Rhia. "Look, I need to get to the lab. Um, I know you know a lot of this stuff already—I'll tell Donna you have a solid basic botany background and need lots of lab time. That way I'll get to see you again on Thursday." She smiled, trying to seem confident, pretending she didn't understand the fate to which she was sentencing Rhia. "Besides, I'm sure you'll be out of here as soon as the justice liaison comes. Just tell them the truth. They'll let you out, and you'll be back home in no time."

Laura slung her bag over her shoulder and walked to the door. As she was about to leave, she turned back. "Better get to your next class, Rhia. Come find me if you need anything."

~

The thick rubber seal squelched as Laura pushed open the door to the laboratory. A maze of long white tables covered with beakers, test tubes, and tarnished equipment wove through the brightly lit room, and there was the distinct smell of bleach. She set her bag down at her small desk in the corner and began to flip through the stack of papers piled there.

"Everything okay?" Nadine pulled her eyes away from a microscope, pushed her rolling stool back, and spun to face Laura. Her hair was pulled back into a tight bun at the nape of her neck, and she had lab goggles pushed up on top of her head.

"Yep. Fine."

"How's the new woman?"

Laura looked up. "What do you mean?"

"Did she know anything about medicinal plants?"

"Oh." Laura pawed through her papers again. "Um, yes. The usual. She's got a good handle on the top twenty. Could use more work on bitter herbs."

Nadine watched her silently for a minute, then in one strong move rolled her stool down the long aisle to Laura's desk. She sat with her hands in her lap, waiting for more, and when Laura said nothing, she leaned far forward and put her face in front of Laura's. She smiled kindly. "What's up?"

"Nothing. Just busy."

Nadine crinkled her eyebrows. "Hey, you okay?"

Finally, Laura set down the file she was holding and looked up. She saw the concern in Nadine's face, and though she tried to feign everything was fine, her own sadness and fear swelled inside her. "NayNay, do you ever wonder if we're doing the right thing here?"

"Of course we are. Our work is going to help prevent and cure illnesses. Some day, you and I are going to discover the plant that will save a million lives."

"No, I don't mean that. I mean, do you ever think we shouldn't be working at a Center."

Nadine let out a long sigh. "Hey, I know it's not the greatest. That centrifuge is so noisy it will probably explode one of these days." She swung her chin around the room. "But we're learning so much."

"I'm not talking about the equipment. Do you ever wonder if we're working for the wrong side? Some of the things we do here just don't feel right."

Nadine leaned back and raised her eyebrows. She pulled the goggles off her head and swung the band around her hand for a moment. Finally, she said, "You know I don't agree with everything that happens here, but we have to do what we're told."

"I know."

"We just have to stay a year, and then we'll get into a real school."

"But, *we* process the hallucinogens that make up the Psilocox. I don't care what Miss Deacon says about it expanding people's minds, I don't think I'd want a friend of mine to go through that. Think about your brother—if he were here would you do that to him?"

"My brother would never do anything to get sent to a Center." Nadine bristled at the idea. "Besides, it's not illegal—"

"Because Miss Deacon says it's worth it."

"And if it was so bad, why would the colleges accept us after interning here? Even Ms. Brakille says they aren't really hurting anyone."

Laura propped her elbows on the desk and rested her head in her hands. She rubbed her forehead in wide circles with her palms and sighed. "I don't know."

Nadine pulled herself next to Laura and set her hand on the small of her back. "Laura, the chemicals in the Psilocox are just a tiny part of what we do in here. Look around. We have a dozen experiments going on, and all of them are about trying to help people. Sure, if we could do all this in a lab that didn't have anything to do with a Center, or a prison, or a containment facility, it would be great. But we don't have any choice right now."

"I know."

"Hey." Nadine gently tugged at Laura's stool and turned it until they were face to face. "I'm going to get into Olympia in six months, and then six months after that, you'll join me. I've heard that Dr. Clark is amazing, and they're doing groundbreaking work there. It's all going to be worth it." She leaned in close to Laura and wrapped her arms around her back. In a quiet and reassuring voice she whispered, "I promise."

Laura looked into Nadine's eyes and couldn't help but smile. When she had failed to get in to school, she'd seen all her hopes and dreams disappearing. The Center was her last resort, but she'd had to make up an alternate story for her family. The lies she told about where she was going had made them happy, and yet, each one felt like a nail driven into her heart. She had almost convinced herself that the Center wouldn't be so bad, until she arrived and saw the way the inmates were treated and the power that Miss Deacon held. She knew she'd made a terrible mistake.

How lucky she'd been to find a friend like Nadine in such an awful place. Nadine understood that there was a price to pay to get what you want. Nadine didn't make her feel guilty for being here.

Laura lifted her hand and touched Nadine's cheek, lightly combed her fingers through the untamed wisps of fine hair above her ear. They leaned in close to one another and rested their foreheads together. Nadine tilted her chin slightly to the side and, lifting her lips to Laura's, softly kissed her.

"We're in this together," Laura breathed as she pulled her body closer.

"All the way."

~

After dinner that evening, four guards herded Rhia, Ruth, and Charlotte, along with five other women from neighboring cells, down the long cement hallway of the first floor. When they passed the closed doors of the darkened cafeteria and came to the end of the hall, one guard inserted a key that opened the wide metal doors to the entry hall and shuffled the women through. They passed by several nurses sitting behind the admissions desk before being goaded through the other set of wooden double doors, across the hall.

There was a distinct change in the feel of the hallway in this wing of the building. Instead of cement floors and barren, yellowing walls, old wood paneling lined the length of the hall and wooden floors creaked below their feet. The effect was probably originally meant to be warm and welcoming, but Rhia felt a claustrophobic tension in her chest. The dark walls leaned close, and she felt she could smell the slow decay of the old, brown wood surrounding her. Dryness filled her nostrils, as if the wood itself was sucking the moisture from the air.

Halfway down the hall, a guard opened a heavy door and ushered them into a wide-open tiled shower room. As the four guards watched, dead-eyed and spiteful, the women hung their clothes on metal hooks in the wall and took a small sliver of milky-white soap from a bucket on the floor.

When all eight were lined up in front of the skinny showerheads, the water was turned on. A blast of cool water sprayed Rhia with stinging force, and she hurried to wet her body. All around her, women rushed through the job, their elbows bouncing up and down and side to side, their legs and arms bending and contorting as they lathered their skin and hair. Five minutes later, the water turned off, and they each grabbed a thin gray towel from a rack and rubbed the coarse cloth over their bodies.

Dressed, they were led back down the long, dimly lit wooden corridor. Closed doors lined both sides of the hall, some with tiny glass windows embedded in the center. Many of the rooms were dark, but a blue-white glow came from one room on Rhia's right. She slowed and looked inside as the other women streamed past her, and her breath caught in her throat.

A man lay naked on a table in the center of the room, his pale skin sallow and taut under the harsh lights. A cloth gag was tight between his open teeth and tied behind his head. His arms and legs were strapped down and an IV tube wound its way from the inside bend of his elbow to a metal pole nearby. A nurse in light-blue scrubs stood beside him, monitoring the blinking machines assembled behind his bed and marking information on a chart in her hand. Another nurse was hunched over the man, a permanent marker in her hand. The man began to struggle under the bonds, his hips bucking against the table and his genitals flopping uselessly from side to side. The nurse leaned one arm across his torso to steady the man and began to scrawl thick black lines across his thin belly.

A guard shoved Rhia from behind, sending her falling forward, off-balance. She grabbed for the wall, but twisted and sprawled painfully onto the worn floor. The pain in her ribs flared.

"Keep moving," the guard growled.

Rhia slowly pulled herself up and hobbled down the hall, hearing the high, muffled shouts of the man in the room.

After the lights had been turned off in her cell, Rhia lay on her back in her bunk. She was grateful for the darkness, which seemed to be the only thing that stopped Ruth and Charlotte from arguing. It frightened her how Charlotte so fervently supported everything Miss Deacon did and said, but

Ruth's vehemence also seemed extreme.

The building hummed in the night; Rhia thought she could feel the vibrations of the electrical systems through her thin mattress. She cringed each time one of her roommates coughed or sighed and silently cursed her confinement in this smelly, crowded place. With a deep exhale, she closed her eyes and tried to remember the feel of her boat rocking below her, the smell of the saltwater spray as she sat on the deck, the expansive freedom of watching the sunset turn the clouds pink and gold on the horizon. As tears streaked down her cheeks, Rhia thought of Betty, alone on the water, waiting for her to return, waiting for her to come home.

~ Five ~

After breakfast on Wednesday morning, Rhia returned to the large room where she had listened to the disturbingly rousing sermon Miss Deacon had given the day before. Once again, all the female inmates seated themselves around the polished round wooden tables, many of them with expectant and joyous looks on their faces. Rhia scanned the room and saw Carol sitting alone near the far wall, her arms folded tightly across her chest. An empty chair was beside her, and Rhia walked to it.

"Carol," Rhia said.

Carol looked up with a scowl. "What do you want?"

"Look, I wanted to say . . . I want to apologize. I feel like it's my fault you're in here. You were helping me, and maybe that's why they found you." Carol didn't reply, and Rhia added,

"How are you? Are you okay?"

"You don't even know, do you?" Tears welled in Carol's eyes. "You don't even know what you've done to us."

"I'm so sorry. I . . ."

"This is what we get for being nice to you?"

"We just have to wait until Monday . . ."

"Go away. Leave me alone." Carol turned away.

Rhia waited a moment, then turned and made her way to the table where Ruth and Charlotte sat.

A few minutes later the doors swung open, and Miss Deacon swept into the room with powerful confidence. The buzz and chatter of voices crescendoed momentarily before fading to silence. When she reached the front of the group, she turned and leaned back on one of the tables. The sun shone through the windows behind her, haloing her light-blond hair and revealing the curve of her long legs beneath the thin fabric of another white skirt.

She smiled. "Peace to you all. Welcome to Daily Circle, my friends! Let us join together in the Daily Affirmation." The women in the room rose and spoke in unison. When finished, they quietly retook their seats.

"Today I want to talk to you about evolution," Miss Deacon began. "Not about worms turning into lizards who turn into monkeys who turn into men. Not that kind of evolution. I will leave that to the scientist. I am talking about the evolution of the human woman and man. We all know that cavemen during the Ice Age had to go out hunting for woolly mammoths while their wives back in the cave would tend to the children, gather herbs and berries nearby, and cook the food. Men were the bosses, and if women did not submit to their will, they would bonk them over the head with a club and drag them back into the cave."

Several women laughed, and Miss Deacon smiled brightly.

"We all know this, right? We used to learn this in school. This was thought to be a requirement of biology. In every species there are differences between female and male, and humans are no different. Men grow bigger and stronger and are better at physical activities like hunting and fighting. Women bear children and nurture and tend to the nest. This is the way women and men were designed, right? So why try to fight it?

"Well." Miss Deacon leaned forward. "What if all this was wrong? What if everything we have been taught about our ancestors was wrong—a fabrication by modern men to reinforce their wishes for the way women should behave in a modern society?" She paused.

"Think about it, my friends. For thousands of years, men were in control of all the official learning. Men were the only ones who could go out and study ancient artifacts, archaeological sites, archaic writings. And men were the only ones who were allowed to disseminate what they had learned—usually to other men. Don't you think that sort of one-sided study would result in some major biases and, dare I say, errors? Don't you think that men might have selected the texts, the evidence, and the ideas that would most benefit their own way of thinking? History is written by the victors, my friends, and for a very long time, the victors were men." Miss Deacon raised one eyebrow and scanned the room.

"It's only within the last two hundred years or so that women have been allowed to enter into scientific study and allowed to report on their findings. And even then, many, many men refused to believe the results simply because a woman had written them. When women were allowed to become professors and became renowned scientists, the world began to change. The whole *world* changed, my friends.

"When women were finally allowed a voice, they started to question everything the men had been telling them for so long. They started to ask themselves, 'Do I have to get married and have a baby as soon as I am physically able? Do I have to do things the way they have always been done? Do I really believe all the stories from the Bible if men wrote all those stories? Do I really believe all the rules of society if all those rules were written by men?' And these brave, strong women began to believe differently, think differently, and act differently from women before them. We became highly educated, took important jobs, began making new policies and new laws—and we began to expect the rest of the world to respect their women as much as we did in this great country!

"And that was when it all started to go wrong." Miss Deacon pushed herself up from the table and walked slowly across the room, winding between the tables while the seated women watched her, rapt with attention. "When women started to show men that they were strong and smart and brave and did not need men in the same way anymore, some men got very frightened. Oh, now, my friends, I understand this fear." She nodded. "I understand how scary it must be to have your whole world change in the span of just a couple generations. And I understand how scary it must be to have your power, your long-held power and dominance, chipped away from you.

"So the men of the world started to fight back. It began with the enslavement of young girls and women in the Middle East. Girls as young as seven or eight would be stolen from their families and sold to men who would rape them and beat them, all the while justifying it with their religion. And as wrong as we all knew that was, even our great country did nothing to stop it. *Why?* Why would our government turn its back on whole countries full of women who were being enslaved?"

Miss Deacon held up her index finger. "*Maybe* it was politics that held us back. *Maybe* it was greed that held us back. *Maybe* we were so dependent on oil and gasoline and cheap goods that we were willing to allow atrocities to spread like a virus across the globe. Then again, maybe women and girls just didn't matter enough. Maybe women and girls just weren't worth fighting for." She shrugged.

"Oh, how they told us we were wrong to think ourselves equals! They told us we didn't deserve to be paid the same for a job, even though we were doing the same work as a man. They told us we were going against biology, evolution, and the very fiber of humanity itself when we said we didn't want to marry and tend to children as homemakers dependent on a husband who would be the breadwinner!" She pointed at women around the room as she listed her grievances. "They fought back *emotionally*, telling us that strong women were not attractive, that feminists were ugly, and that egalitarians were weak. They fought back *spiritually*, telling us God wanted women to be submissive to men. They fought back *politically*, pouring millions of dollars into campaigns to defeat strong female candidates. They fought back *financially*, making laws that taxed single women at a higher rate than single men or married couples. And they fought back *physically*, by engendering and tolerating a culture of sexual harassment and rape of women in colleges, universities, militaries, businesses, and industries around the world."

Miss Deacon raised her hands above her head and closed her eyes. "Oh, yes, my dear friends, we were nearly beaten back into submission by men who were so afraid of our feminine power that they would stop at nothing to destroy the few advances we had made in our country! We were nearly beaten back, by their ideas and rules and laws full of fear and anger and hatred for women who had the courage to stand up and say, 'We do *not* want you to dominate us anymore! We do *not* want you to beat us with your club and drag us back to the cave! And, most powerfully of all, we do *not* believe you ever had the right to do these things to us in the first place!'"

Her hands clenched into tight fists and she banged them down onto the table below her. One of her soft curls had bounced out of place and hung over her forehead, partially covering one of her seething brown eyes. "Do you really think that cavewoman would have stayed if that caveman had treated her poorly? Do you really think she would have kowtowed to him?" She shook her head. "This was a strong woman who knew which plants she could safely eat and which ones would poison them all. She knew how to skin and preserve the meat that fed her family, and she knew how to trap and hunt and kill. She also knew how to raise children, sew clothes, and keep everyone alive through the long winter. If that caveman injured her, who did he think would do all these things? If he killed her, what would become of him? And if she left, there was undoubtedly a caveman next door who would have taken her in.

"No, my friends, even a caveman from thousands of years ago knew the value and power of a woman! Even that caveman understood that only by working together and sharing the work, successes, and triumphs of the cave could the whole family thrive. If a caveman did go out on a dangerous hunt, the cavewoman had to know how to survive if he didn't come back again that night."

Miss Deacon breathed in deeply and stood up tall. "So, here we are! We have survived the stifling Gender Rules of the first half of the century and the Family Focus Acts. We have survived the devastating Last War and the constant threat of sexual slavery. We have survived the famine and the cold and the darkness of the years that followed the war, and we have finally learned that only by sharing our work, successes, and triumphs can our own cave really thrive!" She pounded her fist into her palm. "*Never* let a man tell you that you are weaker than he is. *Never* let a man tell you that you cannot do everything he can do. *Never* let a man tell you there are historical or evolutionary precedents for his attempts to squash you, to subjugate you, or to bonk you over the head with his club. *Never* believe these lies again! The men who wrote the textbooks for a thousand years have lied to you. Men wrote all of our history. The *future* will be written by women!"

No, Rhia thought. *That's not right.*

Rhia watched the women around her leap to their feet, and thunderous clapping erupted throughout the room. Miss Deacon smiled as women congregated around her, touching her, hugging her, patting her. After soaking up this adoration, she looked up and scanned the room. Seeing Rhia near the corner, she called out, "Ah, Ms. Malone! Come see me in my office after Circle."

~

The room was bathed in soft light that saturated the lacy curtains hanging from the wide bay window behind the desk. Rhia sat stiffly in the thin wooden chair opposite and looked around, at the lushly carved wooden panels that lined the walls, the deep green of the two spidery plants that billowed from tall, decorative planters, and the framed photographs and awards on the shelves. Everything was so neat and tidy, she got the sense that Miss Deacon had arranged her belongings with purpose. She imagined the woman holding a ruler, measuring distances between items and checking every angle. Even the articles on the desk in front of her were methodically arranged. Rhia's left knee bounced up and down as she stared at the trim group of pens, meticulously lined up alongside a large manila folder. She yearned to reach across the desk and nudge just one of those pens out of position.

The door behind Rhia swung open, and Miss Deacon billowed into the room, her long white skirt and the scent of rosewater trailing behind her. As fluid as silk, she moved to Rhia's side and stood, her arms held out for an embrace. Awkwardly, Rhia stood and allowed the woman to encircle her. Miss Deacon's arms were plump and strong, and Rhia felt the air squeezed from her lungs for a brief moment before she was released.

"Welcome, Rhia Malone." Miss Deacon swept away from Rhia and moved to the other side of her desk, sitting down in the well-padded leather armchair there. Metal casters squeaked as she pulled the chair forward and slid her legs beneath the heavy wood. "Thank you for coming to visit me this morning."

"I didn't know I had a choice."

Miss Deacon's eyes darted up to Rhia's, and there was a flash of something not quite traceable there. Just as quickly, it disappeared. A broad smile curved across her fair face. "My friend, you always have a choice. Your whole life has been full of choices—some well made, others not so—and all those choices have led you here, to my office. And now that you're here, I would like to invite you to take a good look at those choices you've made, and to explore the reasons and the rationale behind them."

"But I haven't done anything wrong," Rhia began.

Miss Deacon held up her hands. "My friend, please let me continue. I meet with each and every one of the women and men who come to Re-education Center Number Three, and I can assure you, they all claim they have done nothing wrong." She inhaled deeply. "It's a claim as common as the air we breathe, and as pervasive and pungent as the dirt beneath our feet. But when they have been here a while and are allowed to delve into the very depths of their souls, they all begin to realize there is room for improvement in their lives. They all realize they've made poor choices in the past, and they all begin to desire the ability to make good choices in the future. I've invited you here today to welcome you. To offer you the opportunity presented here. And I hope with all my heart that you will accept it."

Rhia spoke quickly, trying to squeeze in words before Miss Deacon began talking again. "Who do I need to speak to about getting out of here, because I've been wrongly accused and need to get back to my boat and my job?"

The soft smile on Miss Deacon's lips flickered. "Well then, let's see." She looked down to the beige folder on her desk and opened it wide. Rhia's face looked out from the top of the stack of crisp white papers inside. It was the photograph from her official identification badge, given to her by the regional director of runners four years ago. In the picture, she had shoulder-length dreadlocks, which framed the proud smile on her face. Several paragraphs were typed below the photo, and the words spilled over to the second page. Miss Deacon scanned the file quickly, obviously already familiar with its contents.

"Hmm. Well, Ms. Malone, I see here you were found fraternizing with two known criminals for whom we have been searching for quite a long time."

"I can explain that. They—"

"It also says here," Miss Deacon interrupted, "that you used tradable goods from your assigned neighborhoods to purchase a large quantity of other goods, and then you disappeared without delivering said goods."

"There was a storm. My boat's still out there. If you would just let—"

"My friend, these are very serious crimes."

"Yes, but I didn't do any of those things!"

"Were you with the two criminals when the guards found you?"

"Yes, but—"

"And did you deliver the goods you promised your neighborhoods?"

"No, but—"

"Well then, my dear! I'm not really clear what the confusion is here. And I would urge you to abandon your futile pleas of innocence immediately and begin working toward a new chapter in your life. Did someone convince you to do these things? Is there a man in your life who has been manipulating your thoughts and feelings? The man John, with whom you were found?"

"Of course not—"

"You are safe here. You are finally able to throw off the shackles of his oppression and—"

"I'm trying to tell you that—"

"Join with your sisters in the New Way Forward. Rhia Malone, this is your opportunity to become the woman you were born to be! With our help, you will no longer need to fear the men in your life, and you will become strong and independent."

"I don't fear anyone!" Rhia shook her head and breathed,

"Jesus, Ruth said that—"

"Ah, yes. I have heard that you have been consorting with Ruth Bailey quite a bit. Perhaps we shouldn't have put you in with her." The index finger of Miss Deacon's right hand waggled. "Hmm. Well, I certainly wouldn't presume to tell you who your friends should be, but I would like to give you a gentle warning about Ruth." Miss Deacon looked kindly at Rhia. "You see, not everyone who comes to Re-education Center Number Three is able to overcome the fears and frustrations of their prior life. Ruth has been here quite a long time, and I'm deeply saddened to say that she has repeatedly raised emotional barricades against every effort we have expended to help her." She sighed, then smiled again. "Of course, I hold hope that Ruth will come to see the error of her ways at some point, and will join with us in the freedom of a clean conscience. But until that time, I fear that your own journey may be hindered by her lack of progress and her deep negativity."

Miss Deacon glanced back down at the file. "Now, in a case such as yours, I would recommend intensive group discussions with Ms. Archer. I think you will really connect with her, and—"

Rhia stood up suddenly, knocking her chair backward. "You're not listening to me!" Her face was hot, and she felt her hands trembling. "You just keep talking, but you don't let me say anything! I'm trying to tell you that I didn't do anything wrong! I was knocked overboard during the storm last week, and I nearly drowned. John and Carol found me and helped me. That's all! Ask them!"

"Ms. Malone, I would not take the word of a known—"

"And if you would let me out of here, I could get back to my boat and fix all of this. This is insane! You can't just lock people up in here without letting them prove that they haven't done anything wrong. You can't just keep me here when I could so easily show you I'm innocent! That isn't the way the system works, lady."

Rhia shoved her hands onto her hips. "Contact the leaders from my neighborhoods. Ask them. They'll tell you I've never done anything wrong in my life, and I can assure you, the second I get out of here I am going to appeal to the regional officials to overhaul this whole fucked-up place."

Miss Deacon's hands were folded on top of Rhia's folder. Her expression had changed from mild surprise, to irritation, to an eerie pleasure by the end of Rhia's pleas.

"Oh, yes. I can see that you are going to be quite a challenge."

Miss Deacon inhaled deeply and exhaled loudly through her widening smile. The leather of her armchair scrunched as she stood up very slowly, and she placed her hands flat on the desk and pushed herself up to her full height. When she spoke, her eyes shone and her voice was quiet.

"Rhia Malone. I'm very sorry that you are so worked up about this. If you are convinced of your innocence, I'm sure the justice liaison will be able to help you on Monday. We would never want to falsely confine anyone without just cause. Unfortunately, I'm unable to release you until such time as the liaison informs me that it's proper to do so. And so, my dear," her voice became oily and deep, "you are completely in my care until that point." Her lips curled into a smile of perverse pleasure. "I'm looking forward to this."

A heavy drop of sweat trickled down Rhia's spine, and she felt her flesh crawl.

~

"The thing that pisses me off the most is when they call themselves egalitarians." They were walking across the field, and Rhia had to hurry to keep up with Ruth and Charlotte.

Ruth continued, "There's nothing equal about what they believe. It's like they're trying to commandeer that word and redefine it. I swear, I think that was the devil's greatest trick—to change the definition of *egalitarian* into 'man-hating.'" She threw her leg forward, kicking at a clump of grass and sending bits of green flying into the air.

"Ruth, no one here hates men," Charlotte said. "The teachers are trying to help women and men get over all the anger and fear of the past. If you don't study the history of oppression in the last centuries, how are you going to avoid repeating the same mistakes?"

"That's exactly what the women in power are doing, Charlotte! It doesn't matter if it's women or men in charge. The bosses always find a way to screw the little guy."

"So what are you suggesting? Nobody in charge? No decisions ever get made?" Charlotte rolled her eyes.

"People should be able to make their own decisions!"

"So, no rules. No laws?"

Ruth hesitated and looked at Rhia. "Fuck them. Fuck Deacon. Fuck her and her goddamned mouth. I swear, Rhia, one day I'm going to shut this whole fucking place down, and I will personally smash Deacon's ugly face into a cinderblock wall."

Rhia felt small beads of perspiration break out on her brow. "Uh-huh." She swiped her hand across her forehead and wiped it on her orange pants.

"And they call that brainwashing session this morning a class?" Ruth continued. "Modern History? I feel like I've just spent three hours in some weird test tube where they are mixing up all kinds of crazy."

"Ms. Archer was only trying to explain the trouble with the oversexualization of young women in the early twenty-first century." Charlotte patted Ruth on the arm.

"The worst part is that they cushion everything in these confusing ways," Ruth said. "Yes, women were encouraged to show off their bodies with skimpy clothes as an act of empowerment, and there were popular celebrities and leaders who told young girls that they could finally own their own sexuality, but Ms. Archer's in there telling us it was all this intricate male conspiracy? Like, men were really holding the puppet strings, saying, 'Yes, ladies, strong women show the world their breasts and love to have sex all the time with many different men!' I mean, how convoluted are their brains to believe that? Rhia, don't tell me you believe that shit?"

Rhia shrugged. "I don't know, Ruth. I mean, there are all those studies about male sexuality. They say men think about it all the time. And for so long, men were in control of the media and education . . . Could it be true that they were manipulating everything?"

"That's not the point," Ruth said. "Everybody wants to have sex."

"Then what's your point, Ruth?" Charlotte asked.

"My point is, there have always been good men and bad men, and there have always been good women and bad women. Why can't we figure out what's wrong and deal with it without blaming a whole gender, or race, or religion?"

"I don't know." Rhia sighed. "After three hours of this, my brain's so fuzzy I'm not even sure what I believe anymore."

"That's the point, Rhia. You've got to fight it. They have it down to a science. No one would buy into all their crazy shit if they just came straight out and said, 'Let's brainwash you to do our bidding,' or 'Let's beat men into submission.' Deacon's too clever for that. She's handpicked the teachers so that they all follow her lead. She's the ultimate evil."

Rhia stopped walking and faced Ruth. "Look, when you get out, you need to go to the regional director. You need to tell them what you've seen and heard here so they can—"

"I'm never getting out."

Rhia hesitated. "What do you mean?"

"You don't really think they would let me out, do you?" Ruth's mirthless laugh crackled in the midday heat. "Rhia, they know I know everything. I've even heard the voices under the recordings they play all day long."

"What?"

"Not the voices again." Charlotte groaned. "I have to get to class. See you at dinner." She walked away.

"Don't you hear them yet? In all those phrases the speakers are always blaring out? Listen closer, Rhia. You'll hear whispered voices just underneath them. I haven't been able to figure out what they're saying yet, but I've heard Deacon's name a few times."

Rhia cocked her head to the side and focused on the phrases being broadcast even then over the large speakers attached to the main building. For a second, she thought she could hear something, just below audible levels, but then it disappeared. She knitted her brow. "It's too hot for this."

Ruth said, "They know I've seen what they do. They could never risk letting me go out and tell everyone about it."

"You're not the only one here who doesn't believe it all," Rhia said. "I've seen a few other women at Daily Circle who don't seem to buy into Deacon's sermons. Some, they don't even clap. Obviously not everyone is going to become a zealot like Charlotte. I mean, it's not like the Center can just keep you here until you're converted."

"Oh, honey," Ruth said. "That's exactly what they do." She gave Rhia a pitying smile, as if she were explaining to a child.

Rhia watched Ruth walk away toward the hangars. *I shouldn't even be here!* she thought. *Just get to Monday. Just talk to the justice liaison. Just get the fuck out of this place.*

Alone, Rhia tromped down the grassy slope toward the village of converted shipping containers. She would spend the rest of the afternoon assisting in the transformation of a barren, hollow rectangle of metal into a prison cell for men condemned to live at the Center.

Nearing the grid of already-refitted containers, Rhia took a chance and looked up at the tall watchtowers surrounding the Village. At the top of one she saw a man and a woman, each holding a long rifle. They patrolled the small balcony of the tower, back and forth, gazing down with expressionless faces at the people working below.

The black guns and the metallic smell of the shipping containers all around her reminded Rhia of the terror of the Last War. By her ninth birthday, her father had become one of the missing masses of men and boys pulled into the fighting. She lived, if it could be called living, on the outskirts of Miranda, scrounging for the little available food and hiding whenever the dreaded sound of marching boots was heard. She had seen the blood and the death those boots left in their wake, and she had felt the white-hot pain of brutality the one time she'd been caught. Even now she could remember that metallic taste in her mouth, the blood that flowed from her broken lips, and the sight of the black gun that lay next to her body as they took their turns on top of her.

And then, nearly four years into the war, the black guns that had been the symbol of death became the symbol of rebellion. After hundreds of millions of men had died, women ended the fighting. They marched peacefully at first, resistance spreading across India, Europe, and the democratic countries that still remembered a time without war. When their own government bombed a thousand protesting women and children in London, American women joined the cause. The female population outnumbered the men three to one by then, and seeing their advantage, women began to work together. Reluctantly, they picked up the guns and bombs of the bleeding and broken soldiers scattered upon their very doorsteps, and they rebelled against their own military as well as against the invaders. The war about oil became a war about peace.

The women added to their ranks as they passed through each neighborhood and fought en masse against the weary and war-tired troops of old men and young boys that were the pathetic remnants of the armies that had battled too long, for long-forgotten or long-expired reasons. Many men were willing to lay down their weapons in hopes of the peace the women promised. By the time the new army reached the major outposts, the women soldiers numbered into the thousands and easily overcame the exhausted and unprepared forces there.

The war ended with the glorious ascension of President Lydia Harris to the newly built capitol building in New Chicago. As her first act, the weapons of destruction and brutality were melted down to create building supplies to aid the resurrection of broken cities and infrastructure across the country. The New Way Forward, a promise of peace and harmony from the matriarchal government, had begun.

How happy people had been in those first months after peace was declared! How sure they had been that the changes would benefit them all, now that women had restored balance. And how soon the new government realized that being in charge meant staying in charge, and staying in charge meant keeping the *other* group down. The New Way Forward was supposed to light a path to equality, prosperity, and fulfillment, but the women in charge soon found ways to strip men of power in order to hold on to their own. And fifteen years later, Rhia found herself in a Center where women and men were once again surrounded by guns.

"Where're you going?"

The smooth voice came from right behind Rhia, and she pivoted to see Captain Banks only a step behind her. The woman had on the same green camouflage she'd worn the day she found Rhia, Carol, and John in the forest, and her jaw was set in the same hard line.

"The Village." Rhia took a step backward.

"You scheduled to be there today?"

"Yes."

"I'm glad. I wouldn't want you to get lost now." Her hand rested lightly on the stun gun at her hip. "How are you adjusting to your new life at the Center?"

Rhia felt her heart pounding, and bile began to rise in her throat. Anything she might say could be a mistake. Instead, she stood silent, trying to hold the gaze of this woman from whom cruelty seemed to ooze like oil.

"You know, you don't *have* to wallow in the mud with the rest of these pigs." Banks jutted her chin in the direction of the Village. "Women like you aren't built for the shit jobs. I've read your file. A runner by age twenty-one? That means you must at least be smart enough to use your looks to get what you want." Banks ran her hand across the dark stubble on her head. "Maybe you should think about who can help you in here. If you play your cards right, you might become a guard one day."

"I'm not a guard. I'm a runner."

Banks raised her eyebrows and shook her head. "Well, you never know. You might just change your mind. If you do, you be sure to let me know, okay?" She tilted her head to the side and smirked. "I see that pretty mouth of yours is healing nicely."

Rhia turned to go.

"I'm stationed here a month. Let me know if you need anything." Captain Banks laughed loudly as Rhia hurried across the field. "Don't worry, honey. I'll keep my eyes on you."

As Rhia neared the shipping containers, she spotted William with a small group of people. Her pace slowed as she watched him. He passed a long piece of dark-gray rebar to a woman who knelt on the ground and held it straight and firm on the grass. William picked up a heavy sledgehammer, lifted it high above his right shoulder, and swung it forward, making contact with the top of the rebar. He took two more swings at it, driving it several inches into the ground. The woman tied a long piece of string to the top, stretched it three feet out, and tied the end to a second piece of rebar, then handed that to William. He walked around the center post, using the end of the bar in his hands to scratch the outline of a six-foot-diameter circle in the ground.

The woman who'd held the rebar headed toward Rhia as the others picked up shovels and began to dig inside the circumference of the circle. "You're new?" she asked. She was in her midthirties, with olive skin and shiny straight hair pulled into a long ponytail that hung down her back.

"Yes. Rhia Malone. I was told to work here today."

"I'm the forewoman of this section. Ms. Chang, but you can call me Briana."

Rhia watched William turn away from the group of diggers, dark circles of sweat under his armpits and a wet line down the back of his faded red T-shirt. Her eyes traced that line from his broad shoulders to the tight muscles in the small of his back. As he bent to set down the pieces of metal, his shirt clung to his skin, and when he stood again, she could make out the strong V shape of his torso.

"Everyone learns something new here," Briana continued. "Find something you want to learn, and ask people to help you learn it. This isn't the Big House," she jutted her chin toward the building at the top of the hill. "We work together down here and try to help each other out."

Rhia nodded.

"Just keep your head down and don't do anything to attract the guards, okay?"

"Okay."

"Do you have any idea what you want to work on?"

"Um," Rhia stammered as she pointed to William. "I . . . I talked to that man yesterday in Botany. He said he'd help me out."

Briana looked at William, then back to Rhia. "William?"

"Yes."

Briana hesitated. "All right."

Rhia watched the forewoman walk back to the growing pit, then Rhia moved to where William stood next to a pile of tools. She stopped behind him and cleared her throat. "I'm Rhia. We met yesterday in the botany hangar."

William turned and looked her up and down. "I remember."

“Ruth said I should work with you today.”

“Do you always do what people tell you?”

“Excuse me?”

William moved to the edge of the deepening hole in the ground and passed down a pickax, “Briana, they can use this when they hit the clay layer.” Turning back to Rhia, he added, “You need to think for yourself.”

“You don’t know anything about me.”

“And you don’t know anything about me.”

They looked at each other for a moment, and Rhia held his gaze without blinking. Finally he said, “Look, you can work with me if you want. I don’t care. I’m just saying you shouldn’t do it just because Ruth told you to.”

“Forget it. I’ll go someplace else.” Rhia began to walk away.

William reached out as if to touch the side of her arm, but stopped short. “Wait.”

Rhia turned her head and looked at his hand hanging in the air between them. William pulled away and took a step backward.

He shuffled his feet for a second, looking at the ground. “I’m just saying we’ve got enough people working on this. If you dig, it’ll be too crowded.”

“What are you digging?”

“We need a pit for the septic tank—that big thing,” William motioned toward a silver container nearly as tall as he was. “Two can dig the pit, three can work on the drainage field. Once that’s done, we’ll have to haul four yards of crushed rock from the piles by the edge of the field and line it all before installing the tank and the four-inch PVC pipe for the drain. But that’s probably tomorrow.”

“Then I’ll go someplace else.”

"No. Look, Ruth's right. Stay with me until you get your bearings." He sighed. "I could use help in a box today. Do you know anything about floors?"

"A box?"

William took a deep breath and jutted his chin toward a row of six shipping containers nearby. "The boxcars."

Rhia's heel bounced for a moment before she nodded her head. "I know a bit."

"Come on. I'll show you what to do."

Rhia followed William toward a twenty-foot-long blue shipping container that had streaks of reddish-brown rust cascading from each of corner. He kept a step in front of her, and didn't speak. Women and men were working along the bottom edges of the other five boxes, ratcheting thick bolts through the bases into half-inch-thick steel plates embedded in the concrete foundations below.

"The big crane brought these down last week and set them on the concrete pads. Once they're hooked into place, they won't move anywhere. A hurricane could blow through and the boxes would stay put." William slid a heavy metal door sideways along a rolling track and stepped inside the box without looking back.

When Rhia followed him in, she nearly tripped on the wooden joists that lined the floor. Squinting her eyes, she tried to adjust to the lack of light. Between the vertical steel support beams, the wired electrical boxes, and the PVC plumbing tubes that crisscrossed the interior walls, the box was coated with thick sheets of fuzzy gray insulation. The bit of sun that shone through the open door and the single square window cut into the opposite side of the box seemed to be absorbed by the material.

"This is wool?"

"It's a combination of sheep wool and hemp," William said. "It keeps it a little cooler in the summer, a little warmer in the winter. Four men will share this box when it's done, so it'll be set up with bunks along two walls, a table to eat at, a small sink, and a john. What we need to do today is install the three-quarter-inch plywood subfloor over the existing joists."

"How'd you get plywood?"

"The Center can get anything." He rubbed his hand across his flat stomach. "Not that it's really a subfloor. That's all the boxes get. It's not going to look as good as your floor at home, but they don't care about making the boxes look good."

"I live on a boat."

For the first time, William stopped moving and looked at Rhia. "A boat?"

"Yes. I'm a runner."

His mouth opened slightly, and a quizzical look came over his face before quickly vanishing. He cleared his throat and continued, "The plywood's in stacks outside. You'll have to cut it and lay it. Can you do that?"

"Yes."

"So you know what I mean when I say, 'Cut edges along the perimeter of the room'?"

"I've built a house before." Rhia tried to keep the edge out of her voice, but disliked the condescension in his.

"You said you lived on a boat."

"My friend's house was burned down by raiders a few years back. I helped her build a new one." She canted her hip to the side and narrowed her eyes. "And I've helped other women in my neighborhoods, too."

"Fine." He stepped past her and stopped in the doorway. The sunlight framed his body, shrouding his back in darkness as he spoke. "The tools are all outside. Let's get to work."

The heat pressed down on Rhia's shoulders as heavy as hands. She surveyed the piles of materials. A stack of four-by-eight sheets of light-brown plywood stood near gray metal boxes full of nails and a rolling trolley of tools. She selected a retractable measuring tape and a hammer from the trolley and tucked them into the waistline of her pants before going back into the cool darkness of the box. The metal floor below the joists was dotted with rust and small holes through which only the blackness of the cement foundation below was visible. She measured the space, measured again to be sure, and after doing the math, went back outside to find William.

"The first one goes in the center?" Rhia asked.

William had pulled a sheet of plywood off the stack and was walking back toward the box. "Yes. We'll lay them out before nailing. Do you know what size the others should be?"

"Two four-by-fives, two four-by-sixes, and two two-by-eights."

"Right. Start cutting. I'll be back."

Rhia pulled several sheets off the stack. With her measuring tape and a heavy pencil she made notches along the plywood where the cuts would be. She dragged the first sheet through the grass and laid it on two sawhorses.

"I'll hold down the other end. Makes it easier." William moved behind Rhia, his back to her as he leaned his weight onto the wood.

"Thanks."

Rhia flipped the safety switch on the power saw and, with an ear-piercing buzz, the machine tore through the wood. As she neared the other end, William moved away from her to support the two sections. Together they hauled the pieces to the box, fitting them like a puzzle in the dim light. They arranged them to maximize support, the grain of the plywood perpendicular to the joists below.

On hands and knees they crawled around the floor, checking angles and spaces. When satisfied with the position of the sections, William brought a small metal can full of nails into the boxcar and set it equidistant between them. They began to hammer in the dozens of nails that would hold the plywood in place.

"Have you been here long?" Rhia asked.

"Long enough."

"Months?"

"Thirteen months, three weeks, and two days."

Rhia smiled. "Not that you're counting or anything . . ." His reply was only a quiet grunt. "Did you do this sort of work before?"

"Nope."

She let his answer hang in the air for a minute, hoping for more. When he didn't offer anything, she said, "I have to do a lot of maintenance on my boat." Again, she waited for him to speak, and again, he didn't. "It's a thirty-two-footer. Nice big hold, plenty of cabin space."

"Hmm."

"You ever been on a boat?"

William sighed and looked over at Rhia. She raised her eyebrows and smiled, trying to invite conversation. After a moment, he said, "No."

They worked side by side, crawling around the small space. Rhia continued to talk, filling the silent spaces when they would reach for a nail or adjust a board. The deep sound of their hammers echoed off the metal ceiling, bouncing around until soaked up by the thick wool insulation of the walls. She stole quick glances at William, watching the way he worked, the thick curve of the muscles in his forearm as he swung his hammer.

"Ruth acted like you and I were both on her team, or something. I take it you're not a big fan of the Center, either?"

William only grunted.

"Well, she seems to want to take me under her wing. You two are friends?"

"Yep."

"I guess I was just wondering . . ." Without looking, Rhia reached to take a nail from the small metal can between them and brushed against William's hand doing the same. To her surprise, he instantly recoiled, pulling his hand up as if he had touched fire. He spun and backed away.

"Sorry," Rhia said. Puzzled, she saw William's eyebrows crinkle, and he quickly looked back to the floor. Without a word, he turned the can on its side, spilling the nails out into a fan shape across the plywood. He picked up several and popped the ends into his mouth, holding them there until they'd be needed.

Rhia took a nail and, with a final glance at William, went back to work.

Over the next half hour, the still air inside the shipping container grew warm from the heat of their working bodies. Rhia tried to give William space, fearful of the reaction her first inadvertent touch had caused, but there was little room to maneuver. When she was close to him, she could breathe in his dark, earthy scent, and she knew the smell of her body would be filling his nostrils, as well.

"Where are you from?" Rhia asked.

"Heatherton. It used to be called Hermansville."

"Do you have any family?"

"My parents were killed by the bombs. My older brother never came back from the war."

"I'm sorry."

"It is what it is. Everybody lost somebody during the Last War."

"Not me."

William looked at Rhia, his eyebrows up. "You don't know anyone who died in the war?"

"Well, yes. Indirectly. But nobody really close. My mom died a few years before, so it was just me and my dad. He was a communications engineer in the war, but he came back after. He lived with me on our boat until he died, a couple years ago." Under her breath, she added, "Happiest years of my life."

William watched her for a moment, seeming to debate his next words. Finally, he said, "My mother grew up on the coast of Maine. She used to tell me about a little sailboat they had. She and her brothers would sail up to this rocky cove north of their dock and explore tide pools. She said there were sea stars and barnacles . . ." His eyes took on a faraway look.

"She never had a boat out here, though?"

"No. But once, after the government took away her driver's license, she said she was going to go to the coast and sail out to international waters. As if they couldn't touch her there." A low chuckle rumbled in his throat.

"Well, they can't. But it's hard to stay out there. You need to come back from time to time. My dad loved the freedom of it, though. You know, living outside the neighborhoods, nobody telling him what to do."

William raised his eyebrows and nodded. "I can see the appeal of that."

"He was a good man." Rhia's voice broke as she struggled to tamp down the mix of emotions that swelled inside her. Sadness and stress coursed through her veins, alongside waves of loneliness and the desire for a human connection in this troubled place. And now she was alone in a dark room with a man she barely knew, talking about such personal things. Something about the closeness of William's body, the intimacy of the sounds of his breathing, and the rhythmic work they were doing was like a drug that loosened her tongue and relaxed her defenses. Something about him made her yearn for closeness.

She cleared her throat and continued. "He taught me everything I know. It's a shame more fathers didn't come back after the war. Maybe things would have been easier. A lot of those men knew how to do things it took us years to relearn. Maybe they could have helped us figure things out."

"Well, the bombs and the starvation afterward killed off a lot of knowledge."

"My father said the New Way was tough for some of the older men that came back. He said he felt like he'd fought through hell to save this country, only to be told he wasn't wanted once he got back."

William's dark eyes were deep and thoughtful. "You need to be careful what you say," he whispered. "Some people don't like that sort of talk."

"Ah, but you might notice that I said my *father* said those things." Rhia's eyes sparkled. "If I tell you what he said, then I haven't actually said anything wrong." She turned to him, a questioning look on her face. "Just like you said *some people* don't like that sort of talk. That doesn't really tell me what you think, does it?"

"You want to know what I think?"

"Yes."

"I think I have to be careful around you." William shook his head, and a slow, reluctant grin pulled at one corner of his mouth. "I think you're the kind of woman who could make a man's brain feel all fuzzy."

Rhia laughed and lifted the bottom edge of her shirt to wipe the sweat that covered her forehead. She saw his eyes dart to the small triangle of skin that was exposed along the front of her belly, and she held her shirt up just a second longer than necessary. "Don't worry. That's not me, it's the heat."

William raised his eyes to Rhia's, and for the first time, the hardness and fear that had clouded them was gone. In their place was a hint of playfulness. As she watched, he smiled, a slow, small, and guarded movement that she knew in her heart was as generous a gift as he had given anyone in a long time. He shook his head again, looked back down at the floor, and began to hammer.

Rhia watched a moment more, puzzled and sad. She thought about William's thirteen months in the Center, and she feared the ways she might change if she were imprisoned here that long. She looked down at her own hands, the hammer and nails they held, and imagined thirteen months of Miss Deacon's Daily Circle sermons, thirteen months of lukewarm gruel at every meal, and thirteen months of building shared cells out of boxcars.

How much forced labor had the Center extracted from its inmates? How cruel was it to require men to build the very boxes that held them? And how many men would be forced to live in this small shack she was helping to build? Maybe Laura had been right—maybe everyone was just part of the machine.

A trickle of sweat ran down Rhia's right temple, and she rubbed it away. She took a deep breath and sat back on her heels, suddenly looking forward to the stinging, public, yet cool shower in the evening.

"God, I'm hot."

William bent to pick up a nail between them and grinned,

deepening the small dimple in the center of his cheek. "Well, at least you're not humble."

"What? Oh, no. I didn't mean . . ."

For a moment, a light laugh played in his throat, but seeming to remember unwritten rules of conduct, he quickly stifled it. "Sorry. I shouldn't have said that. I apologize."

Rhia waved a hand in front of her face as if trying to dispel the awkwardness of not only her comment but also his reaction. "Don't worry about it. It was a dumb thing for me to say." She looked up to the grimy window. "Does that open?"

"No." William leapt up and pulled the sliding metal door open. "This won't help much, I'm afraid. The air's not moving at all today."

"Where do the men bathe? Do they use the showers in the main building?"

"No, we only go the Big House for sessions." There was an acid in Williams voice as he spoke the last word. "Once a week we use the stream that flows near the west edge of the perimeter."

"There's a stream?"

"You can see it from the top of the hill. Behind the west tower."

"Must be nice."

He shrugged his shoulders. "Nice in the summer. Come out there with me in January and you might not think so."

"Hmm. I bet." Rhia put her hands on her hips, arched her back, then leaned forward and went back to work nailing in the board below her. William glanced at her one more time before bending over his work and doing the same.

Several minutes passed before Rhia paused again. She waited until William stopped to reach for more nails before asking, "The men go to the main building—the Big House—

for sessions?" She tried to sound casual.

"Yes."

"What are they like?"

William set down his hammer. He wiped his hands across the tops of his thighs and then his right hand swept low across his stomach.

"Ruth said . . ." Rhia hesitated, unsure how to continue. "She said some of the men here get injections and things." When he didn't respond, she added, "She said they do things to the men's bodies to make them . . . better understand women."

William pulled several nails from the can and rolled them between his fingers. "Hmm."

Again, she leaned back on her heels and looked at him. "Is it true?"

He picked up his hammer and looked up at Rhia. She could see the muscles in his jaw tighten as he clenched his teeth and knew he was trying to decide what to say. Finally, he said, "Tomorrow's Thursday."

"And?"

"We have FEmS on Thursday. You'll find out for yourself."

Rhia pursed her lips and sighed. "You're not very helpful, are you?"

"I am. I'm helping you build this floor, aren't I?"

Rhia smirked. "Yeah, all right. Helpful with floors; not helpful with questions."

"Sorry if I don't have all the answers. I just know there are some things you have to decide for yourself." A somber wave flashed across his dark face. "You'll see tomorrow."

She leaned toward him, bent low to catch his eye, trying to be playful, trying to make him smile again. "All right. I'll wait until tomorrow then."

"Good."

"Good." Encouraged, Rhia added, "Should I let you know what I decide?"

He looked up, the light gone from his face. "If you want."

Rhia smiled, trying to recover the flirtatious sparkle they had shared, but a subtle shift in William's posture told her he had shut down. The smile faded from her lips as she hunched over her work again.

When it was time for a break, they sat at the edge of the open doorway, each holding a small cup in their hands. All around them, women and men worked on other shipping containers. Some carried PVC pipes, some carried large coils of electrical wiring, others worked in pairs hauling white porcelain toilets or small silver metal sinks to waiting boxcars.

Rhia took a sip of the cool water from her cup. "How many of these things are they building?"

"They want to have a hundred eventually."

"A hundred?"

"Not all for us." William drank deeply from his cup. "Four men stay in one box, so the ten we already have done are enough for us. We're building twenty more permanent ones, and they eventually want seventy built to ship to other towns. These boxes are quick, durable, and cheap. People who don't have a house will be able to use these."

"Do you have a house back home?"

William hesitated. "I did."

"I'm sure it'll still be there," Rhia mumbled. "So, what did you do?"

"What did I do?"

"Why are you here?"

"No point asking that." William set his cup down in the

caked dirt beside him and wiped his hands on his thighs. He arched his back in a stretch and continued, "They could say I'm in here for burning down the capitol building, but that doesn't make it true."

"You think everybody here is innocent?"

"Centers aren't always for people who break the rules. They're for people who disagree with the rules."

Rhia's knee bounced and she twisted the cup back and forth in her hand. "Sounds like Miss Deacon hasn't quite converted you yet."

As if suddenly remembering something, William turned to her. "You know what? I'm scheduled to be released in four weeks. At this point, I'll agree with whatever they say." His words sounded flat in the humid, heavy air.

Rhia recoiled. "Really?"

He watched her for a moment, trying to calculate something in his mind. Finally, he said, "I'm done trying to fight it." He stood up and turned to go back into the boxcar. "Take some advice, Rhia. Just go along with it. It's easier than trying to fight."

Rhia drained her own cup and followed William back into the shadowy box. For a while, they worked side by side in silence. Thoughts swirled inside her mind. If she could just make it until Monday, she would talk to the justice liaison and get out of here. She could get back to Betty and her friends in Miranda and the neighborhoods she served. She would take on an apprentice to help her on the boat. She would be more careful. She would never come back here again.

Even as she thought these things, she feared the slow hardening of her soul that would take place if she lived the rest of her life knowing that innocent people were being locked up here while she chose to pretend they did not exist. She wished she were still blind to the injustice of the Center, wished it were all still just distant rumors and gossip, and wished the women and men trapped and harassed and abused in the name of Re-education were still nameless and faceless.

She thought about the inmates working in the hot sun, their bodies used and their minds controlled by people who claimed to be nurturing liberty and fairness. This wasn't the country her father had fought for. This wasn't the life these people deserved.

When the last board was pounded into place, they began to clean up. William carried the tools outside and checked them back in with the guard at the toolshed while Rhia collected the few nails that littered the floor around the small metal can. When he returned, he stood in the bright doorway, silently watching her. His long shadow covered her as she squatted to drop the last nails into the can, the cool umbra of his body draped over her back, but she didn't turn around.

"Looks good." William's deep voice resonated in the small space.

The smallest hint of a smile tugged at Rhia's lips, and she turned to look at him. "You mean the floor?"

His eyebrows crinkled together for a second, then he quickly looked away. "Of course. The floor."

"Step out of the doorway. You're blocking my light."

William walked inside, his tattered shoes clunking across the newly lain floor as he moved to Rhia's side. He squatted beside her, held out his hand for the can, and nodded at the floor. "Good job."

Rhia sat back on her heels and wiped her brow. "You too."

"Yeah."

Rhia watched him as he continued to nod, looking around

at the floor, the nails, the walls, everywhere but at her. Once his mouth opened as if to speak, but closed again, his lips pressing together. She couldn't figure out if he wanted to praise her work and was hesitant to say too much, or if he thought he should say more but couldn't think of anything. She waited, hoping he would look into her eyes again.

Finally, he cleared his throat, stood up, and walked to the open door. "We'll be working on the plumbing in here soon. You can either help with that or move on to the next box to do another floor."

Rhia followed him out the door and was glad when he turned back to look at her. She stood straight, her shoulders back and her head lifted.

"It's up to you," he added.

"William," Rhia said softly. "Where are you going to be?"

"I'm doing the plumbing."

"Then I'll work here, too."

William stared at her for a moment. He blinked, his broad chest expanding with a deep inhalation. Cocking his head to one side, he studied her intently, perhaps trying to gauge her meaning and wondering if he dared reciprocate the affinity she was suggesting. His dark eyes flitted quickly down the length of her body and back up again to meet her gaze.

Rhia saw the confusion in his eyes, as if he both feared and longed for the companionship she offered. Then there was the slightest softening of his brow, and the corner of his lips curled into the faintest smile. He had made his decision. Rhia smiled.

~ Six ~

Rhia nodded at Ruth and sat down next to her at the large round table. It was only her third day here, and she had already begun to feel accustomed to Miss Deacon's Daily Circle. In fact, a part of her looked forward to seeing the imposing woman sweep into the room, her white skirt billowing around her like her own private cloud, and she had to admit she was curious to see what new topic would be used to whip the others into that fervor that was both frightening and intoxicating.

So when the heavy doors swung wide, Rhia turned to witness the beginning of the show. To her astonishment, however, Miss Deacon was not alone. As she walked slowly and proudly into the large room, four men followed in her wake. They all wore the same faded red T-shirts and pants she had seen on the men in the Village. Two of them walked slowly, their eyes forward, without emotion. They looked like automatons behind this vivid and virile woman.

The man that followed stumbled slightly as his eyes darted around the room. His face and head were shaved clean, and Rhia could see heavy nicks and scratches on his scalp, as if the shaving had been done against his will. His hands were bound behind his back with thick rope, and his feet were bare.

Rhia stifled a gasp as she realized it was John, looking much smaller and paler than she had known him in the woods. Her own eyes darted around the room to locate Carol, who sat straight-backed on a chair near the center of the room. As John processed past her, their eyes met, and Carol nodded tersely. Though she seemed to be trying to give John courage, Rhia saw a look of intense fear in both their faces.

Momentarily distracted by John's presence, Rhia was shocked when she saw William at the end of the line of men. He walked past her without acknowledgment, and continued to the front of the room.

When Miss Deacon reached the front of the class, she turned to face the women and held her arms out wide.

"Peace to you! Good morning, my friends! What a week this is. We have been blessed with the arrival of one new man and two new women into our fold." At this she smiled and nodded to Rhia and Carol. "And we have, as always, the opportunity to explore our long-held beliefs, to re-evaluate some of the ideas and notions that have stuck with us for too long, and to rejoice in the knowledge that we are proceeding on this great and glorious journey together as a family."

Miss Deacon glided between several of the front tables. "And I hope you all *do* know that I think of you as my family—my children, sisters, brothers, even as my parents from time to time, for there've been many an occasion when I've learned something from you." At this, Miss Deacon's smile beamed out across the room full of rapt women.

"Today, of course, we have brought a man to experience the joy and peace that comes with his first Feminine Empathy Session." Miss Deacon gestured to John, who stood apart from the other men. "Before we welcome him into the fold, he must take the difficult and life-changing steps that will start him on a new path in his life. To help him on his way, we have three men whom it has been my pleasure to get to know during their time here at Re-education Center Number Three. These men"—Miss Deacon laughed a light and girly laugh as she swept her arm around, indicating the three who stood motionless and silent behind her—"are men of valor. Men of courage. Men with the mettle to own up to all the abhorrent and repugnant vices so often beset upon their gender. And they have dedicated themselves to spending their time here with us wisely."

Her face took on a strange and coquettish look as she walked slowly to William's side. He continued to stare straight ahead, but Rhia thought she could see the muscles in his jaw tighten as Miss Deacon approached. She stopped close to him and laughed again, her usually resonant voice now a tinkling giggle that made the hair on the back of Rhia's neck tingle.

"I am so proud of the strides you all have made." Miss Deacon seemed to indicate her feeling for all three men, but her face was only inches from William's now. She set her hand gently on his upper arm and let it slide down to his hand. She clasped it tightly in her own, and squeezed it. "When you came here, you were so full of anger and hatred and fear, and I have helped you to become the gentle, trustworthy, and brave men you are today." She spun to face the women and clapped her hands together in an ardent plea. "My friends, it is my hope for each of you that you may someday live in a world populated by men such as these!

"Now, I know many of you have been here to see the journey these men and others like them have been privileged to take, and I know that it hasn't always been easy for you to witness this journey. Our new traveler, John, has only just begun this great odyssey, and I can see the fear that lingers yet in his eyes." Her face darkened as she moved toward John, who seemed to be trying to make himself smaller, while unable to hide in the bright light of the room.

"My wish for this man is for him to take comfort in the fact that he stands here today with men who have made it through the dark times, who can bear witness to the fact that the difficulty he is facing now is but a moment in what will undoubtedly prove to be a rewarding and satisfying long life ahead. Yes, certainly the physical and emotional pain that goes along with such a powerful transformation can be difficult both to endure and to watch. But, I bring Markus, Stellan, and William to you today as shining examples of the consummation of all our efforts here." Her hand thrust toward the three men and she asked, "Men, what say you?"

At the sound of her call, Markus, Stellan, and William snapped to attention, feet shoulder-width apart, backs straight and tall. Their arms instantly became stiff lines at their sides, each fingertip together pointing to the floor. With their chins jutted forward and their eyes straight ahead, they spoke in clear unison to the room:

"My life was a tangle of shadows and fear before I was privileged to come to the Re-education Center. My desires were coarse and cruel, and my heart was full of anger and aggression before I was privileged to come to the Re-education

Center. The Re-education Center has taught me to be a better man, to let go of my pain, to understand my failings. I will be an example to all men of the strength, power, and wisdom that comes through this understanding. I am honored to have been reborn at the Re-education Center, and I will strive to uphold the dignity and honor of my gender."

The rumble of their deep baritones echoed around the large room, hanging in the air with the heat of the day that was already rising heavy and thick. Miss Deacon clapped her hands together, and the women began a round of thunderous applause. Rhia could see the thin curve of a proud smile playing on the lips of Markus and Stellan. Their eyes shone, as if they had achieved something great. William, though he stood as exact as the others and called out his creed with force and precision, held the same tight, stoic expression she had seen since his arrival in the room.

"Beautiful, men! You have made me proud." Miss Deacon stepped quickly to the table at the front of the room and rang a large hand bell that stood waiting. Within seconds, the back door swung open again, and four guards filed into the room. Among them was Captain Banks, whose cold, wide smile made her look like a shark moving in for the kill. Two nurses in pale-blue scrubs followed the guards, and they all marched past the watching women to the front of the room. William, Markus, and Stellan stepped aside as the guards and nurses circled John.

"John," Miss Deacon called out as she moved an empty chair behind him. "You are here today to begin your Feminine Empathy Sessions. You've been charged with four counts of hostile acts toward women, the attempted recruitment of others into the failed militia against the government, two counts of attempted arson, petty theft from two government trade centers, and three counts of direct harassment toward a leader in the town of Bonita." The guards untied the rope behind his back, took hold of his arms and shoulders and pushed him down into the chair. Captain Banks was the roughest of the four, forcing John's right side down hard enough to make an audible thud against the old wood beneath him. She smirked at the sound. Then they wrapped thick leather belts around him, binding his waist, ankles, shoulders, and wrists.

"Get off him! Get away from him!" Carol yelled as she leapt from her chair and charged toward the front, her arms reaching forward in desperation. She was almost to John when Captain Banks swung her leg out hard, catching Carol in the ankle and sending her crashing to the floor. Banks jumped on top, digging her knee into Carol's back and twisting her arm painfully backward. Then Banks's fist rose into the air and, with frightening speed and ferocity, slammed into the back of Carol's head.

"Get off her!" John shouted. "You son of a bitch, get off her!" He writhed under the belts that held him tight to the chair.

With her free hand, Captain Banks pulled the small stun gun from her belt and flicked the switch. There was an instant crackle of electricity in the air. As Carol lay curled up on the ground, her hands wrapped around her head and loud moans issuing from her throat, Banks kicked her hard in the side before plunging the stun gun into Carol's back.

Rhia watched in horror as Carol silently froze on the floor of the classroom. She became as stiff as a board, her arms and legs straight and her neck arched. After several seconds, Banks released the trigger and pulled the stun gun away, leaving Carol limp and trembling on the floor. The silence was replaced by

Carol's childlike sobs and the distinct smell of fresh urine.

"Get her out of here." Miss Deacon hissed with a quick flick of her hand.

"No!" John screamed. "How dare you—"

"Leave them alone!" Now it was Ruth, sitting beside Rhia. "Deacon, you bitch! You'll pay for this! You'll pay for all the men you rape, you stinking whore!"

"Be quiet!" Deacon yelled as Ruth continued to shout.

"Get away from that woman! Get away from them both! How dare you do this to people!" Ruth sprang to her feet, tipping her chair backward as she banged her palms onto the table.

"Ruth Bailey, you sit down!" Deacon's voice rose to a scream as she tried to drown out the curses flying from both Ruth and John.

"Fuck! Leave her alone! Carol!" John strained against the belts.

"Get them both out of here!" Deacon screeched.

"You're a quack! You're a fraud, and this is all going to—"

In a fluid leap, Captain Banks dove over the top of the table and slammed into Ruth. Rhia instinctively threw up her arms and was knocked sideways as the two women sprawled to the floor beside her. The captain raised her sinewy arm and hurled her fist down onto Ruth's face, once, twice, and a third time.

Rhia flailed frantically, pushing herself to sitting and backpedaling as quickly as possible. She watched, horrified, as Captain Banks pummeled Ruth until one of the other guards reached them and pulled her off. The second guard whipped out his stun gun and used it on Ruth, who stiffened and convulsed. When the shock ended, Ruth began a barrage of guttural curses that held little power, as her body lay shaking and weak.

Banks stood and slowly wiped a splatter of Ruth's blood off her chin with the back of her hand. As John continued to shout from the front of the room, the second guard pulled Ruth to her feet and began to drag her toward the door. Banks's chest was heaving, and her hat had fallen off. She bent low to snatch it up and, rising, noticed Rhia watching her from the floor nearby. Her mouth curled into a twisted smile, uneven teeth wet and shining. She winked at Rhia, shoved her hat down onto her head, and turned to go.

As Banks passed the guard dragging Carol, she shoved him aside, and Carol fell to the floor with a thud. Banks squatted, thrust her arms under Carol's armpits, and pulled her out of the room.

John's shouts died away as he watched the heavy door swing closed. He sat motionless, his face contorted in a grimace of despair and fear.

Rhia pulled herself to standing and, with trembling hands, righted the overturned chairs strewn around her before sitting again. A lump stopped her throat, and she fought off the tears that stung her eyes. She stole a quick glance around the room and saw that no one was watching her. All the women stared forward, their attention never seeming to stray from Miss Deacon.

"I must apologize for that interruption, my friends." Miss Deacon sighed as she pushed a wisp of blond hair behind her ear, then flattened the folds of her skirt. "It is always a sad thing to see the women of our group resort to such behavior, and it is especially disturbing when we are blessed to have a man with us who is in such need of our help and support." The opposition removed and her composure regained, she turned to the two nurses and nodded.

They came forward, knelt on each side of John, and began to pull equipment from a leather bag. One hung a stethoscope around her neck as the other pulled a small envelope out of her breast pocket. Inside the envelope was an alcohol swab, which she wiped liberally across the soft skin on the inside of John's elbow. Then she pulled a long section of rubber tubing from another pocket, snapped it straight in the air next to her, and wrapped it tightly around his upper arm.

John threw his weight side to side against the straps in a futile attempt to avoid their touch.

Miss Deacon stood behind John and continued: "John, as I have said, you have gone astray. You have deviated from the path of justice and righteousness, and yet, for all the evil you have done, John, we are giving you the chance to be washed clean! For all the trouble you have caused, we believe that you can be redeemed. Today is the beginning of your rebirth. You poor man." She shook her head as she set her hands on the back of his shoulders. "Years and years ago you were set upon your path of anger and aggression. From the moment of your birth you have been shown only cruelty and masochism. From the moment you were *delivered* from your loving mother's body by a doctor who *wrenched* you free of her grasp and *thrust* you, naked and crying, onto metal scales and plastic boxes under the harsh glow of bright lights, you were taught that a woman could never be strong enough and good enough to deserve you. That simple act of *delivering* you from the evil of your mother's body was your first lesson in the frailty and weakness of women."

She bent her face close to his cheek and he twisted his head away from her. "We are here to show you the truth! We are here to help you remember the ultimate power and wisdom that has belonged to women for millions of years. It is that same power, that mystic strength, that may have been the first reason for a man to fear a woman, but today we will help you let go of that fear and acknowledge the feminine goddess power.

"It began at your birth, John, and it is to that moment we must return!" She snapped back to standing. "You have lived on this path for decades, and surely it will take more than one day to purge the fear and frustrations you have carried your whole life, but today we will begin. Take comfort in the safety of this room, John. Everyone here is on your side. Everyone here will help you on your journey. We are gathered here to bear witness to your rebirth."

As she spoke, she circled John, alternately beaming down at him and engaging the crowd of onlookers. Her long white skirt swished behind her, tumbling over the top of his legs as she passed close to him.

"Now is the time for you to see the error of your ways! Now is the day of your rebirth into a world where women are your friends, your honored companions, and your heroes! Today you will undergo a rebirth full of the glory and beauty and power of womanhood!"

Miss Deacon suddenly knelt before John, grabbed his bound arm, and draped the top half of her body across his lap. Her fingers stroked the inside of his elbow, tracing the thick vein that stood out below the rubber tubing. "John! Through a tiny hole we will reveal to you secrets that have too long been kept from you! Through this tiny hole, your world will expand and grow. Through this tiny hole, the truth will flow!"

Still kneeling, Miss Deacon jerked her chin to a nurse. "The Psilocox."

The nurse pulled a syringe and a clear glass vial from her

breast pocket, and drew up a small amount of liquid. The guards behind John wrapped their arms firmly around his chest, and the nurse pressed the tip of the needle to his arm.

"No!" John growled.

For a second, there was only a puckered indentation on his flesh, then the sharp tip penetrated and pushed deep into the throbbing vein. The nurse glanced at Miss Deacon and, seeing her nod once more, began to inject the fluid.

Miss Deacon smiled rapturously, her eyes closing as the plunger pressed the liquid into John's vein. Then her eyes opened to narrow slits, and she raised her head to William, who watched, stone-faced. Their eyes met, and in a hushed voice she spoke to him, seeming to forget the dozens of people surrounding her. "Do you remember your first time? Do you remember how frightened you were? But I knew. I knew from the first moment I saw you that you would be special." Her chest heaved against John's thighs, and her hand reached up to touch his face, though her eyes remained fixed on William.

"Your fist experience with rebirth was the most beautiful thing I have ever seen, and every time a new man comes to this chair, I hope he will have an experience as powerful as yours." She licked her bottom lip, bit it lightly with her teeth. "As powerful as *ours*."

She looked at John and caressed the bottom of his chin. His eyes were beginning to glaze over, and she spoke directly to him, but loudly enough for the whole class to hear. "John, you have been injected with Psilocox, a serum that will help you remember your past. You need not fear. When you come across troublesome or fearful things, I will be here to guide you and help you. Just listen to my voice, John. I will be here to help you through the whole journey. Don't be afraid, John. I am right here for you. Do you understand?"

John seemed to be struggling to focus. His eyes blinked several times. He began to breathe out short snorts of air. His jaw clenched and he squeezed his eyes shut, shaking his head and groaning.

"Don't try to fight it, John," Miss Deacon crooned. "Right now you are beginning to feel strange and new sensations, but these are all *good* things. I want you to try to remember back to when you were a very small child. Small fingers, small hands, small feet." She touched these parts of his body as she spoke, her voice smooth and calming. "Can you remember that, John? You were just a small child then, and you lived at home with your mother and father in a blue house on Persimmon Street. Do you remember? Your sister, Michelle, was two years older than you, and she used to play with you in the back yard. Think back, John. Think back to the time before you went to Whitman Elementary School, back to the time when you were just a tiny baby." Her hands caressed him, gently touching his arms, his cheeks, his hair.

"Remember back, John. Remember back to the time when you were wrapped in a soft blue blanket. Your mother held you and sang soft songs of love to help you fall asleep. There, in your bedroom, she sat in the white rocking chair near your white wooden crib and held you. Can you see it?" She paused now, waiting for his answer.

His eyes still closed, John's face relaxed momentarily, as if he were beginning to see the visions of which Miss Deacon spoke. A faint smile flickered across his lips, then his brow furrowed again and he arched his neck away from her.

"Can you see it, John? Can you see me holding you there in our rocking chair? My brown hair is tied back in a loose ponytail, and I'm wearing that green dress you loved. It was soft against your tiny cheek as I held you. Can you see me,

John?" She paused. "John? I said, can you see me?" Her voice grew suddenly harsh.

His face contorted, and with a deep grunt, he said, "Yes."

Miss Deacon smiled benevolently again, falling back into the role of mother, repeating more details from the government files and photographs she must have amassed before this session.

"Good. Oh, John, you are such a good baby! I love holding you and rocking you. I love the smell of your downy head as you lie asleep on my shoulder. I love sitting in this white rocking chair with you and nursing you as you drift off to sleep in my arms." She watched his face relax. "There, there, sweet baby. Shh." His head bowed to his chest, and his breathing settled into a steady, peaceful rhythm.

"Untie him." Miss Deacon stood and stepped away from John.

The guards quickly unbuckled the straps, lifting John as he slumped forward. Miss Deacon moved to the front corner of the room and sat on the floor, her back supported by the walls behind her. The guards dragged John to her and positioned him in front of her, between her outstretched legs. She wrapped her arms around his torso, propping him up between her thighs to steady him.

"Here I am, John. Mommy's here. You are just a tiny new baby in my arms. The sunlight is streaming through the windows of your bedroom, and you can hear the soft wind blowing in the curtains behind us. I am rocking you gently in my arms, my sweet little baby. You've slept so peacefully on my chest, but now you can start to wake up. It's time to wake up now, my tiny new baby."

John squirmed in her arms, and his hands began to curl into tight fists. His head moved slowly from side to side, but his eyes remained closed. One of his fists moved in a jerky fashion toward his face, eventually finding its mark and slipping into his rooting mouth. He began to make noisy, slurping sounds as his legs curled up in a fetal position.

"Oh, my sweet baby," Miss Deacon laughed gently. "I know you're hungry. Mommy's here." Again his head began to search, wobbly, rooting around for the nipple that would feed him.

"Ah, John, I know you want Mommy to nurse you now, but I can't give you your milk yet, sweetie. We have to do something together first." His face contorted in frustration. "Don't worry, honey. Mommy will help you. Mommy will take care of you later. John, we need to go back just a few more weeks, my love. We need to go back to the day when you came out of Mommy's belly. Do you remember that?" His head slowly nodded, though his eyes stayed closed.

"Good boy. I knew you would remember. You are always so smart and good. So, here while I'm holding you, I want you to go back to the day you were born, John. I want you to get smaller and smaller until you are only twenty inches long, John. Can you feel yourself getting smaller? You are almost there, sweetie. Almost. You need to be only seven pounds and three ounces, my love. Can you get that small for me?"

Again, his head nodded, and his face twisted from the effort. His body seemed to fold in on itself as she spoke, getting smaller and tighter, his arms and legs squeezing close to his chest.

"Almost there, John. A little smaller. Almost . . . and, yes! You are small enough now. And just look around you! Here you are in Mommy's belly! It's warm and wet and good in here, isn't it? You are so small and folded up so tight, floating in a warm pool of water, soft and protected, surrounded by the muscles of my uterus, where you have lived and grown for over nine months now. You can hear the muffled sounds of the world outside me, can't you? The voices of your father, your sister, and me—but none of those sounds are as constant, and steady, and rich, and beautiful as the deep thrum of my heart beating for you, John. Listen to the sound of my heart, John." She pressed his ear between her breasts. "Lub dub. Lub dub. Lub dub." She tilted her head to the side and rested her cheek on the top of John's head.

"For all your life, I have fed you, and grown you, and given you everything you need to thrive. And now this all must change, for now you must be born! But don't worry, my love. This time there will be no drugs that sting, no stranger's hands pushing and pulling and twisting you, no bright lights or cold, hard tables. There will be no one here to take away your mother's power and usurp her in this moment of her greatest achievement! This time, John, your mother is going to birth you through the mystical goddess power that has been imbued in her. The power of her sisters, and mothers, and daughters, throughout the generations!" Her voice was becoming raspy and deep, breathy with the passion she was trying to harness. "Your birth will be full of the glory that is woman!"

Miss Deacon moaned. "Can you feel my power, John?"

He nodded.

"Can you feel the strength of this woman's body? My muscles beginning to bear down upon you?" She began to squeeze and rhythmically rub his body with her hands, her arms, her thighs. "Do you feel the changes in my blood, the blood that flows through us both, the blood that I have given up for you? This woman's body is making new chemicals, and new hormones, and new triggers that will help you in the difficult journey you are about to take. This woman's body has the power and knowledge to change and stretch and alter its very shape in order to give life to you!"

Miss Deacon threw her head back and squeezed her legs tightly around John. She began to breathe loudly, blowing out air through pursed lips, groaning and shuddering while she hugged John close to her body. Her voice rose in pitch and cadence.

"Oh, I stretch for you! I pain for you! But it is what I must do, and it is what only I can do. No one can give you this birth but me, John! No one can give you this life but me! And throughout your life you will owe me the respect and allegiance due to the giver of your life. I am the goddess of you. I am the creator and sustainer of you. I am the beginning and the end of you. And I, like all women before me and all women yet to come, must be remembered and lauded for this great power."

Miss Deacon's body began to rock side to side, still holding John, forcefully squeezing his body in a deep, pulsing rhythm as she released long and powerful howls. Suddenly, she bent her body forward, rolling herself on top of John's folded shape, positioning him below her and covering his whole body with her own. Her legs straddled him and her arms continued to squeeze him with a vise-like grip.

"Come with me, John! Come with me as I open up like the great flower of birth for you!"

Below her, John began to moan, a strange, sick-sounding gurgle through the saliva that now flowed from his gaping mouth.

"I am the woman who is the bringer and giver of life!"

She began to move her body slowly down his, her hands and cheek pressing hard onto the top of his bare skull, squishing and stretching the skin there.

"I am the life force of the world! I am the ultimate

feminine power!"

Her fingertips formed a tight circle at the top of his skull and pushed as she continued to squeeze him with the rest of her body.

"I am the light and the life of this world!"

She opened her mouth and thrust out her tongue, circling around her fingers, wetting the crown of his hairless skull as she pressed down, groaning deep and earthy sounds.

"Come into this world, John," she yelled. "Come into this world and be born again into the light of the blessed woman!"

With a long and rapturous cry, she slid her circled hands over the top of his head, her body bucking and rocking with ecstasy.

As his head emerged from between her wet hands, John's neck arched forward, his face thrust into view for the whole class. His eyes opened and he let out a tremendous shout. The sound seemed to come from the deepest recesses of his being, and its long and mighty bellow hung in the air, overpowering even Miss Deacon's spectacular howling. Tears streamed from his eyes as she continued to grunt and squeeze and push herself down over the length of his body, over his shoulders, his waist, his hips and legs, until, finally, her fingers momentarily squeezed his bare toes before slipping off with a loud snapping sound.

Miss Deacon fell backward against the wall behind her and slumped there, out of breath and disheveled, her hair in sweaty tangles across her face as her chest heaved. She wiped one arm across her brow and looked down at the man before her. A beatific smile spread across her face. John lay sobbing, curled back into a small ball as his body shook uncontrollably.

After a moment, Miss Deacon pulled herself to her hands and knees and crawled to John, hovering over him as she crooned out gentle words of solace and comfort.

"There, there, my love. It's all done now. I've done it. I have given you a birth into a world where women are honored and glorified. I've done it all for you, my love. It's all better now."

Rhia stared at the spectacle before her, her mouth hanging open in thrilled horror at having witnessed something both grotesque and riveting. Finally able to blink, she tore her eyes from the two huddled bodies on the floor and crossed her arms in front of her chest. She looked down to see a light sweat clinging to the soft hair on her forearms—tiny beads of moisture glinting in the sunlight—and with a strange sense of wonder, she delicately brushed her fingertips over it. She began to notice the loud beating of her heart and the heave of her chest as she tried to catch her breath.

Suddenly remembering the classroom around her, Rhia looked up, searching for William. He had stood in the same place for the duration of John's ordeal, his spine erect, his muscles taut, and his face forward. Now that the ordeal was over, she saw a change wash over him. Sadness seemed to flow from his body as his shoulders slumped, and his dark eyes, when they met hers, swirled with a storm of pain.

~ Seven ~

"Does she do that to all of them?"

"Yes."

"It's disgusting!"

"It's beautiful!"

Rhia and Charlotte were passing through the lunch line, under the banners of smiling women and men at work in golden fields with slogans of New Way harmony arching across their sunlit skies. They paused while a gaunt man in a hairnet slopped a ladleful of gray stew onto their chipped, yellowed trays. It landed with a wet splash, making Rhia crinkle her nose.

"How can that possibly be legal?"

"Why wouldn't it be? Miss Deacon isn't hurting anybody."

"Of course she is!" Rhia hissed. "Did you see his face when the guards dragged him out of the room? He was terrified!"

Charlotte shook her head. "He was overwhelmed by the power of what he had just experienced, but in time he'll come to see what a blessing it was."

"What do you mean?"

"Rhia, didn't you see the other three men? Didn't you see how proud and happy they were? It's because they've gone through the same sessions as John! I remember two of them from when they first came in. They were angry, and full of sadness, but Miss Deacon's sessions have turned them into different men."

Rhia sat down heavily at the long lunch table. Her stomach lurched as she thought about John and the horrors of the morning, and the way she had sat through it all, a passive witness to something she knew in her heart to be an abomination. A movement near the entrance to the room caught her attention, and she looked up to see Carol enter. She limped slowly toward the lunch line, bruises already beginning to form on her chin and forehead.

"Oh, God. Somebody has to stop them," Rhia whispered. "Somebody has to stop this whole thing."

Charlotte sat opposite her and began to eat. "I know it can be difficult to see a rebirth the first time," she said. "My first was hard, too. But Miss Deacon isn't hurting those men at all." She set her spoon down and looked up, smiling. "You saw her. She never hurt him. All she did was help him remember his birth, which can be really emotional for anyone. She unblocked a lifetime of hurt for him. Think about how wonderfully free he must feel after being able to release all that pain and sadness!"

"Charlotte, he was sobbing on the floor. That's not the way to—"

"Of course he was sobbing! Think about all the times you've been hurt and had to stifle your cries. All those times in your life you had to stuff down your sadness and pain and act tough. Every time you do that, it forms a little nugget of distress inside you. It's like scar tissue that builds up over time, and soon you're so full of it that you can't even think clearly anymore."

"She assaulted him!"

Charlotte ignored her. "That man needed a big emotional release so that he could begin to *heal.* Yes, he'll probably cry and cry, but when he's done, he'll feel like a giant weight has been lifted off him. For the first time in his life, he'll be able to feel like he can really breathe! Haven't you ever felt that way, Rhia? Haven't you ever felt better after a good cry?"

Rhia hesitated, confused by the whisper of sense in Charlotte's words. "That's not the point," she finally said. "You shouldn't force someone to cry. You shouldn't force them to relive emotional trauma if they're not ready for it. That's torture."

"Torture! Rhia, how can you think that?" Charlotte leaned forward. "It's torture to live a closed-up life. It's torture to carry that much hurt around with you. It would be torture for Miss Deacon to allow them to stay like that when she knows the way to help them! Did it look like the other men had been tortured? Didn't you see the light and love just shining out of them? That's because of Miss Deacon's sessions."

The image of William standing before the class came to Rhia's mind, and she knew with certainty that he wasn't shining with light and love for Miss Deacon. Part of Rhia understood why he would want to go along with the system just to get out of here in a month, but in some way, the idea of him lying low just to survive bothered her. She wanted to think of William as strong and brave, unwilling to bow to the pressure of this crazy place, willing to stand up against it. How could he just play along? How could Deacon believe that he was some glorious example of the treatment's success? And, more disturbingly, how had he convinced Miss Deacon of it?

She wanted to see William again. She had to talk to him, ask him. Knowing that she would see him at the botany hangar later that day, she attacked her bowlful of tepid mush.

~

On her way to the hangars that afternoon, Rhia saw dozens of small yellow flags sticking out of the ground around the grassy field. Ms. Brakille, Laura, and Nadine stopped the growing crowd of women there and gathered them into a group. Laura looked at Rhia once, then turned her head away. The few wispy white clouds that drifted through the azure sky gave little relief from the sun, and the teachers' T-shirts already had wide, wet armpit rings.

"Hello, class," Ms. Brakille announced. "We'll be doing a practical exam today on the native and nonnative species found in our area. You can see the small markers we've placed in the ground both here in the field and along the perimeter of the compound all the way to the stream. Several markers are located within the Village itself, so you'll need to search there, as well. The tower guards have been alerted to your work today, so feel free to wander, but please stay on this side of the hill. I cannot be responsible for the guards' actions if you cross to the other side." She led the group down the slope with quick, efficient steps. From time to time a man from the

Village would join the group. Rhia watched for William.

"You'll have the full two hours to locate the plants. Write the number from the flag in your notebook, identify the species, say which parts are edible, and write at least two medicinal facts about that plant. The three of us will be walking around to assist you if you need help, but we won't give you the answers. Please work independently." Ms. Brakille turned and began to walk away across the field. The group of women and men lingered only a moment before dispersing.

Laura walked away from Rhia toward another group of students. William wasn't there. With her notebook and pencil in hand, Rhia moved toward one of the flags. Squatting low, she opened the curled yellow triangle and wrote "13" on her paper. The plant next to it was flat and wide, and its green, hairless, egg-shaped leaves grew in a rosette around a main base. She tugged off one of the leaves. As it pulled away from the base, long, stringy, pale-green veins could be seen dangling from the stem. She set the leaf back on the plant for the next person to use.

Setting her book on her thigh, Rhia wrote "Wild plantain" next to the number 13, followed by "Entire plant edible; crush leaves or chew up into poultice to put on insect bites or minor burns; can eat as salad or tea to aid diarrhea." She moved down the hill to the next flag and squatted again. Several beautiful bright-golden flowers grew among grayish-green feathery leaves. Some of the small flowers were still tightly closed; others opened wide to reveal four paper-thin petals with vibrant orange centers.

Rhia wrote: "21. California poppy; whole plant edible when used as a tincture or infusion; use as tea or decoction for anxiety or as sedative, helps bed-wetting; use root extract to slow breast milk production."

As she moved on, Rhia heard footsteps behind her and turned to see Laura trying to catch up. She stopped next to another flag and squatted. Laura reached her a moment later and, crossing her legs beneath her, sat on the ground.

"How are you?" she whispered.

"Well, let's see. I've been hit and shoved, I have to take cold showers with strangers, I eat slop three times a day, and I got to watch a man tortured this morning." Rhia glared. "How do you think I am?"

"Someone hit you? One of the other inmates?"

"A guard, Laura."

Laura dropped her chin to her chest and plucked at blades of grass. "Rhia, I'm so sorry." A faded, wide-brimmed hat shaded her face, but her chest rose and fell heavily. After a moment, she wiped her arm across her cheek and looked up again. There was a sweaty streak through the pale dust that covered her face. "I've been thinking. I want to help you."

"What do you mean?"

"Look, I can't stay here long or people will suspect something, but I've got a plan. You only have a couple days before the justice liaison comes, and then I'm sure you'll be set free, but for the next couple days I'm going to ask Donna, Ms. Brakille, if you can help us out in the lab. I'll tell her you have experience with titrations, and that I really need some extra help." Rhia shook her head, and Laura leaned forward. "It's true. I really could use help, and that way you won't have to do any other work, and at least I'll know you're safe with me. You'll still need to do Daily Circle and morning classes, but right after lunch you'll come to the lab."

"Laura, look, I appreciate your offer, but it's not going to help much. I need to get out of here right now, and being in your lab for a few hours isn't going to stop all the crazy shit they do here." Rhia checked the proximity of the other teachers. "Do you know they inject a drug into the men that makes them hallucinate? That they make them believe all kinds of insane things, implant ideas and mess with their minds? Deacon has power here that no person should have over another. It's horrible!"

Laura's face blanched white, and she averted her eyes. "Psilocox. I've heard about that."

"Have you seen them use it?"

"No."

"Well I did, and it's disgusting." Rhia's voice was a low hiss. "Deacon sort of hypnotizes them and then touches them all over and . . ." Her voice cracked, and she stumbled on her words, unwilling to recall all that she had seen. "Laura, nobody should go through what I saw this morning. I have to get out of here and let people know what's going on."

"And you will, Rhia, but not until next week. So let me help you." Laura was almost pleading.

Rhia wondered how much of this offer stemmed from Laura's desire to assuage her guilt about not speaking up on Rhia's behalf. Maybe Laura was right, maybe there was little she could do for Rhia anyway, but it pained her that Laura wouldn't even try. Or perhaps Laura wanted Rhia to work in the lab so she would understand and accept Laura's job at the Center. She would expect Rhia to tell her mother everything, when Rhia got back to Miranda. If Rhia appreciated her work here, she'd be more likely to convince her mother that it was a good idea.

Either way, Rhia saw this offer for what it was—Laura was trying to make herself feel better.

How could Laura have wound up here? Her family, her neighborhood, her leaders had all made such great strides toward equality and justice. Her mother was strong and supportive of her mate and her sons. Miranda's neighborhood leader was an outspoken supporter of New Way Reform. Just two months ago, Rhia had sat around Laura's family's dinner table, eating, talking, and discussing politics. If Laura hadn't been able to steer clear of the Center, how could anyone?

As frustrated and disappointed as Rhia was, she also felt protective. She was like an aunt to Laura, and had often celebrated her accomplishments and assisted her though tough times. When Laura broke up with her first girlfriend, it was Rhia who had listened to her cry and encouraged her to love again. Over the last year, she'd helped Laura search for information about colleges, and had been hopeful about Laura's future. Now, although their roles were reversed and Laura held the position of authority, Rhia still felt like it was her job to save Laura. If she worked in the lab, maybe she could convince Laura to leave with her.

Rhia sighed. "All right. I'll do it. But, I still want to work in the Village tomorrow afternoon. There are things I need to do. And Sunday is Silent Introspection Day, whatever the fuck that is. So would I come to the lab today and Saturday?"

Laura's eyes brightened, and she smiled. "Oh, thank you! I'm so glad!" She reached out to touch Rhia's arm. "Rhia, it's going to be great. I'll go talk to Donna right now and get it set up." In one fluid movement, she lifted herself from the ground and swept away. Rhia's left knee began to bounce as she watched her go.

A few minutes later, Laura was back. "It's all set up. Come after we break today." She was brimming with excitement. "I have to help everybody else, so I've gotta go." And she was gone again, scurrying back up the hill.

Rhia surveyed the compound. Women and men were

scattered across the slope, squatting or sitting beside small yellow flags in the ground. The Village sat beyond them, rusty, rectangular boxes surrounded by freshly dug dirt and piles of building materials, and a little farther away was the small shimmering curve of the stream. It was snugged up to the tall perimeter fence, at least forty feet behind one of the guard towers, near the farthest edge of the field. The land on this side of the stream had been cleared, and she could see two tiny points of yellow in the ground along the bank. As sweat dripped down her back, she began to make her way down the hill, hoping the water would provide at least a small reprieve from the heat.

She hadn't seen William since he had marched out of the room this morning in the wake of Deacon and the guards. He hadn't looked at her as he passed her table, but the look in his eyes worried her.

When she passed the final row of shipping containers, Rhia felt suddenly exposed and fearful. A watchtower loomed ahead, and though she kept her chin down, her eyes glanced at the guards above her. One man and one woman walked along the open platform, scanning the compound as they paced. The female guard noticed her and, after silently adjusting the heavy gun in her arms, said something inaudible to her partner to get his attention. Her chin jutted toward Rhia, and they both stopped moving to watch her pass.

Rhia did her best to walk casually, but her heart pounded. She lifted the notebook in her hand and pretended to jot down notes about the plants she had identified. Trying to reassure the guards, trying to keep herself calm. She heard their heavy boots clunk along the wooden platform above her. They were moving to the other side to watch her continue on to the stream.

Close to the bank now, Rhia could feel the subtle change in the air. The stifling stillness of the treeless hill was replaced by a hint of freshness. The stream was narrow, barely fifteen feet across. Only a small section of it was within the perimeter of the compound, and Rhia walked to the flag at the most upstream location, knelt, and looked around.

The stream flowed from deep within the woods that lay many yards outside the boundary. The trees and brush had been cleared near the outside of the fence, giving the guards a clear view of anything that approached, though Rhia could think of nothing that could penetrate the twelve-foot-tall barrier or the thick tangles of razor wire that snaked along its top edge. Where the fence crossed the stream, it was attached to metal poles sunk deep into the streambed. Loops of chain link were driven into both banks and curved down into the water itself, allowing the current and small aquatic animals through, but preventing anything bigger than a small fish from entering. Sticks and globs of leaves were stuck to the back of the fence, unable to squeeze through the holes, and she could hear the happy bubbling of the water as it cascaded over and around these obstacles.

The banks on both sides were steep; the stream must flow as a torrent in the heavy spring rains. Just the thought of flowing water made Rhia long for Betty, and her heart felt heavy. She took a deep breath, quickly identified the plant next to the flag near the stream, and walked along the bank to the next marker.

The number 18 was written on the flag that poked out of the grass beside several long wooden planks lying flat on the ground. Rhia looked over the edge of the bank to see five makeshift steps gouged into the soil. This must be the spot where the men entered the stream to bathe. Perhaps they exited the cool water to drip dry on the boards before heading back to their boxes. There were dozens of muddy footprints on the planks, baked dry by the hot sun, and she wondered which ones were William's.

"18," she wrote. "Bidens; whole plant dried and used for tea; reduces irritation and inflammation from urinary tract infections and colitis; shrinks prostates; helps hay fever, sinus headaches, and asthma."

Rhia moved toward the third and final flag, stuck in the mud close to the water's edge farther downstream. The fence passed over the stream again just below this site, delineating the northernmost edge of the Center. The stream sharpened its gentle meander here, curving away from the compound and heading back toward the forest beyond. The slope to the stream was steeper along the cut bank, and she had to make her way carefully down the rocks, sand, and soil to the waiting flag.

She squatted, saw only a thin coating of moss on the rock, and slumped her shoulders. It was a moss, obviously, but what kind? Medicinal uses? She puzzled for a minute, trying to think of something. Finally giving up, she wrote a question mark beside the number in her notebook and started to stand.

Something caught her eye and she stopped, still crouching on her haunches. The fence was only a dozen feet away, and it crossed the water just as it had at the upstream location, but something was different. Over time, the cut bank of the meander had eroded this side of the stream along the curve. Though the metal loops of the fence had been sunk into the bank at one time, there was now a small space between the bottom edge of the chain link and the muddy bank.

Rhia stared at the opening, frozen. She could almost feel the eyes of the guards on her back, and yet every cell in her body wanted to run to that spot and claw her way free. The gap was only a few inches wide, but she knew with the proper tools she could dig it out, make it big enough to squeeze through. Her heart raced. She could visualize herself, muddy and wet, running the short distance across the field on the other side of the fence to the shelter of the woods beyond. And just as clearly, she could visualize the female guard in the tower taking aim at the small space between her shoulder blades as she ran.

Knowing better than to attempt it, Rhia struggled to regain her composure. She pretended to write in her notebook, in case the guards were watching, but her attention was on the small opening that beckoned her. After several moments, she rose and began walking back toward the hill.

~ Eight ~

"You're going to love this!"

Rhia returned Laura's tight embrace. She squinted under the harsh lighting in the lab, adjusting to the chemical smells, the cool air blowing in through the vents, and the constant hum of the machines. Nadine was sitting at a stool near the back. The young woman slowly pushed herself away from the table at which she'd been working and watched them.

"I'm so glad you're here, Rhia. Wait until you see all the work we're doing." Laura sounded breathy and nervous as she pulled away. "Here, look. Nadine is culturing nasal swabs from some of the men to check for MRSA colonization." She went to Nadine's side and gestured to a stack of labeled petri dishes next to an old-looking microscope. "It used to be extremely tough to kill, but Donna Brakille was one of the scientists who developed the PRK antimicrobial therapy before the Last War. Now we can detect it quickly and stop it before it spreads in close quarters like this." She looked at Rhia for a reaction.

"That's great," Rhia said.

Laura exchanged an awkward look with Nadine and continued. "We also do all the lab work for anybody who gets sick while at the Center. You remember how back home Dr. Preston always had to send out samples and wait two weeks for the results? Well, anyone gets sick here—bam!—we have the information almost immediately to help them. Already I've diagnosed two cases of rubella."

"Can't you diagnose that by looking at the rash?"

Laura waved her hand dismissively. "Yes, you can see the rash, but I was able to confirm that's what it really was by the level of antibodies in the blood samples. We quarantined those two people and it didn't spread to the whole herd."

"You mean group."

"We talk about 'herd health' a lot. It just means the whole group of people, or the community. Disease prevention is all about keeping most of the people healthy—doing what's best for the most people." Laura laughed. "Don't worry, Rhia. I know you're not cattle."

Rhia crossed her arms in front of her chest and looked around at the other tables. "So, what do I get to do?"

"I've been working on using usnea, or old-man's beard, to treat gram-positive bacterial infections like strep and staph. You're going to help me dial in the correct doses for effective drug therapy."

"Old-man's beard? That's a moss that grows on trees."

"It's a lichen, actually. That pretty grayish-green one you see hanging off tree branches like, well, like a beard. It's similar to Spanish moss. Nadine harvested a bunch this spring as the weather was just warming, and its metabolism was just starting to fire up again, right?" Laura nodded at Nadine, pulling her into the conversation.

"Um, yes." Nadine wheeled her stool closer and pushed her glasses to the top of her head. "It's best to harvest on a sunny, warm morning. I let it dry for about two days until it's brittle, then cut it into small sections." She seemed nervous about having Rhia in the lab, and she glanced frequently at Laura as she spoke.

"Usnea is a great medicinal plant," Laura continued. "It has antifungal properties, so you can use it to treat ringworm, athlete's foot, candida yeast infections . . . Just apply it right to your skin." She was still smiling, and she moved between the two other women, alternately touching one or the other's arm or shoulder, as if trying to make a physical and emotional bridge between them. "Dr. Preston used it powdered in teas to boost the immune system if we had a cold or flu, too. Remember, Rhia?"

"Okay, but what are you working on in here?"

"Come on." Laura motioned to Rhia, and together they crossed the wide room, stopping near a long lab bench full of burettes, beakers, and flasks. "My main study is testing usnea's ability to inhibit the growth of tubercle bacillus. Multidrug-resistant TB has made it a really difficult disease to fight. It's become one of the most prevalent lethal diseases in the world."

Laura leaned against the edge of the lab bench and looked at her feet. "The disease just consumes you. I mean, you remember how bad it was for my brother. How much he suffered . . ." She fell silent for a moment. "I'm trying to find a way to stop it. I'm trying to find a way to stop tuberculosis from happening."

For the first time since entering the lab, Rhia was reminded of the girl she'd known back in Miranda. She could see the pain flash in Laura's eyes with the memory of her baby brother, and she reached out to touch Laura gently on the shoulder. "That's important work, Laura. If anybody can figure it out, it's you."

"Thanks." Laura took a deep breath and lifted her chin. "So, I'm investigating whether or not something as simple as old-man's beard can help. Usnic acid was once thought to be good at fighting lung infections, like pneumonia, so maybe we can use it against TB. We have to be careful where we collect it, though, because it can accumulate heavy metal pollution from the air. Sulfur dioxide, especially. Sites downwind of the bigger cities, where the Zephyr bombs were dropped during the war, aren't useful. If you try to use usnea from those places, you'd do your body more damage than good. It's also tough to find, because the lichen likes old-growth trees. So many of the forests have been logged for so long, we have to really hunt for it."

"Sounds like Nadine located some, though?"

"She did. She's amazing." Laura smiled across the room to Nadine, who smirked, pulled down her glasses, and bent her head back to her microscope. When Laura looked back at Rhia, her cheeks blushed scarlet, and she shrugged her shoulders in an awkward, guilty way, "Nadine's been the best part about working here."

Rhia whispered. "Are you two together?"

Laura leaned in. "Remember how you said a great relationship was about mutual respect and support with a whole lot of great sex thrown in?"

"Yeah . . ."

"Well, let's just say Nadine's the whole package. She's

great."

Rhia smiled.

Collecting herself, Laura continued. "Anyway, the trouble is that usnic acid can cause liver damage if ingested, so we have to find out the proper dosage to kill the TB, but not kill the liver cells. That's where you come in. In this storage unit, we have samples of liver cells, and in this one," she indicated another cabinet below the bench, "we have dosages of usnic acid. We need to test it to see how much is too much."

"How long will it take to figure that out?"

"I've been working on it for three weeks now, and I expect it will take several months. And that's even before we add the TB cultures into the test. Those take weeks to grow in the lab, and—"

"So, I won't be able to do much to help you."

Laura hesitated.

"Since I'm leaving in a few days, I won't be able to help much," Rhia repeated.

"Well, no. Not the long-term parts of the study. But, like I told you, there is plenty to do right now."

Laura went on to explain the procedure to Rhia, showing her which equipment to use and how to use it. Rhia would keep a detailed log of every test, indicating the date, lot numbers, dosages, and a description of the sample. By the time Laura had explained everything, there was little time left before dinner would be served.

"Come back tomorrow, and you can get in a few hours of work," Laura said.

"I can't come tomorrow. I work in the Village Friday afternoon."

"Wouldn't you rather work in here, though? You don't need to be out there sweating with all those strangers."

"It's okay. I like building real things. That's better than a three-month experiment that might not even work." Rhia crinkled her nose at the rows of glass petri dishes around her, then looked at Laura. "I'm sorry, LoLo. I didn't mean it like that."

Laura laughed easily. "Don't worry. I know lab work isn't for everyone. But I do appreciate your help. While you're here," she added hastily. "And I'm just glad to see you. I know you're angry at me for not being able to get you released, Rhia, but I want you to know I wish I could." Her large, dark eyes looked up pleadingly. "Come in here whenever you can."

"Okay."

"Besides, aren't you worried about working in the Village with all those men?"

"No."

"Are they being nice to you?"

This time it was Rhia's turn to blush.

~

William stood in Miss Deacon's office, preparing for what he knew was coming. He'd been through this so many times before, he knew he had only moments to begin the process of closing his mind, turning off the part of his brain that connected to the sensations of his body. He started by closing his eyes.

He took several deep breaths, and he began to notice the feel of his nostrils as they flared, and the expansion of his lungs. With each breath, he tried to soak in the moments of peace before she arrived, peace that would help to steel his mind before he lost all control of his body.

He had learned to take comfort in the small things he was able to control—things she knew nothing about. Each time the guards shoved him into this room, he moved to the same spot, standing on the brightest of the faded flowers embroidered in the rug. He always stood facing the leftmost pane of the bay window. And he always remembered to breathe. No matter what she did to him, she couldn't control these things.

Several beads of sweat began to swell from William's forehead, but he resisted the urge to wipe them away. He could stay still. He could control his own body.

In the beginning, Miss Deacon had swept into the room for their private meetings the same way she swept into a classroom for Circles or Sessions, but her style with him had changed over time. Now she came quietly, stealthily, as if they shared a secret they didn't want the rest of the world to know. As if these times were sacred to them.

In the silence of the room, he heard the tiny click of the doorknob as it opened and closed again behind him. The deadbolt turned with a metallic scraping sound. His peace had ended. With his final deep inhalation, the scent of rosewater filled his nostrils, and his eyes opened.

"I'm sorry if you've been waiting long," Miss Deacon whispered as she slipped behind him. She touched the backs of his shoulder blades, tracing their curves with the tips of her fingers. "One of the women from the Session needed . . . extra attention this morning. Do you forgive me, William?"

She leaned into him, pressed her cheek into his back, breathed in deeply, and let out a sigh. "I know you do. You know, William, I love when a new man is able to experience rebirth, and I would never begrudge him for it, but it does take so much out of me." Her voice was like a soft purr. "I'm feeling so very tired today, William."

His eyes were fixed on the windowpane in front of him. Though his brain understood that she was there, touching him, speaking to him, he could no longer feel her caresses on his skin. It was like he'd shifted into a different gear—one that separated his physical body from his mind and protected him from her hands.

Miss Deacon stepped lightly around to William's front, her left hand lightly stroking his right arm as she passed. She leaned back against her large wooden desk and set both palms down behind her. Looking up into his face, she said, "I trust that you know how much I appreciate your visits here with me? I trust that you know how much of a balm you are to me, William."

When he didn't reply, she continued, "We've worked so hard to help so many people, haven't we? And we're rewarded for our efforts each time a woman or man is able to leave this place and venture forth, into the world, freed of their shackles and ready to begin the glorious life that awaits them in the New Way." Again, she sighed, and she turned her head to look around her office. "I know we should be buoyed up in this knowledge, that it should give us the courage and strength to continue on in our fight, but sometimes . . ." Her words trailed off, and for a moment she was silent.

"Sometimes it feels like there are so many people against us. Sometimes it feels like we are fighting an uphill battle." She stood again and stepped close to him. "William," she said, looking into his face. "You know I don't condone the use of violence in any form. You know I've struggled against aggression and anger and hostility my whole life. And yet, there are times when a person simply will not see reason. There are times when, after I have tried and tried and tried to help them, they continue to resist me! Well"—she laughed lightly—

"during those times, what recourse do I have?"

Miss Deacon broke away from William, turning and circling behind her desk. As she passed it, she picked up a pen, glanced at it, then set it down again and continued to move. "*I'm* the one in charge of all these people. *I'm* the one who has to keep track of all their progress and report it to the region. *I'm* the one who has to maintain order here!"

William felt his heart begin to beat faster, and he fought to control his emotions. *Ignore her,* he thought. *Block her out.* Though he tried to keep his gaze on the window, tried to focus on the way the sunlight played on the grassy field beyond it, his eyes began to follow her as she walked around the room, as the anger in her built, as her pace quickened. When she swept by him, he could feel the tension in her body vibrating outward.

"I've sacrificed *everything* for this Center, and I deserve to be treated with *respect*! So don't you sit there and tell me I'm crazy. Don't you tell me I'm wrong. *You* are the criminal who was brought here for Re-education, and *you* are the one who continues to fight it. It's not *my* fault you refuse to change! It's not *my* fault you act out during Sessions! And it's not *my* fault we have to beat you to try to get through to you!" As she passed the large potted fern that stood near the window, her hand swept out, knocking it to the floor. With a loud bang, the clay pot broke and sent black soil scattering across the room.

"Do you know how it looks when the regional director comes here and sees that she's still here?" Deacon faced William now, her finger pointed at him. "Do you know how embarrassing it is for me to have to tell them that I still haven't cured her?" Her blond curls trembled as she stomped a step closer to him with each question. "Do you have any idea how disrespected I feel when they shake their heads and chastise me because of *her*? Ruth Bailey is the thorn in my side, William.

She's the thorn in my side as the director hangs me on the cross for not being able to cure her!"

William watched stoically as Miss Deacon seethed. He watched her cheeks redden and her white dress sway as she stepped toward him. When she was only a foot from him, she poked her finger roughly into his chest, but he would not flinch. Staring straight into her stormy eyes, he remained detached from the scene, unfeeling and unresponsive.

"I have awards, William." Miss Deacon nodded, her chin rising with belligerent pride. "I have awards for the work I do here. No one can accuse me of not doing my job, of not giving my all to this cause, of not sacrificing myself for this Center." She blinked, and her mouth suddenly pulled downward. "I'm here every single day, William. I'm here doing my best to help these people. I'm the one they come to morning, noon, and night when there is a problem, and I'm always willing to do what must be done. Do you think I want this constant responsibility?" She searched his stony eyes for an answer. "Do you think I want to be all alone?"

William saw the tension in her face begin to subside. Her shoulders relaxed. The sadness and anger in her eyes were slowly replaced with a soft light, and her lips curved into a gentle and innocent smile. As much as he struggled, he couldn't help but watch as her emotions transformed. Fear began to rise in his belly, and he blinked and looked away.

"Ah, but I'm not alone, am I?" Deacon's head cocked to one side. She lifted her hands to his sides and touched the exposed skin below the short sleeves of his faded red T-shirt. With her fingertips, she stroked his strong triceps, curving her thumbs around to the front of his thick arms. "I'm not alone, because I have you." Her gracious laugh bubbled around them as she stepped closer. "Oh, William. I'm so grateful for you.

I'm so pleased that you choose to visit me."

Miss Deacon leaned toward him, her head still tilted to the side as her face drew near. With her lips only inches from his own, she paused and inhaled deeply. "I thank God for you, William," she whispered. "And I'm going to show you how grateful I am."

Her lips parted as she pressed into his mouth, and her tongue slid between his soft, unresisting lips. Slowly, she circled her arms around his back, pulling him close to her, pressing her body against his. With one hand, she moved his arm around her, then she did the same on the other side, as one would adjust a mannequin. She tilted her hips forward and began to move them in a slow circle.

William could feel the soft fabric of her dress below his fingers, the curve of her breasts against his chest, and the pulse of her warm belly against his own. He closed his eyes for a moment, struggling to resist the unwanted urges rising in his body. Opening his eyes again, he looked down at her face, so close to his. Her eyes were shut, her hair a golden halo all around.

As she kissed him, he looked past her to the window, to the bright daylight. Several birds had landed in the field outside. As she pressed and kneaded him, he watched those birds, saw them hop and flitter in search of seeds or worms in the ground. He counted them, then counted them again.

She led him to the desk, and he never took his eyes from the small flock gathering there. When she untied his loose pants and slid them off his hips, he focused on the largest of the birds. It was some kind of finch, with short compact wings and two long tail feathers. Its head was a beautiful red color that washed down over its neck and chest, fading into the light browns and creams of the rest of its body. It jumped around the others, pecking its curved gray beak into the earth from time to time.

Somewhere in his mind he knew that he was leaning back on the desk and that she had slid her face down his body. He knew her mouth was on him. He knew that his body was responding involuntarily to the way she moved her tongue and lips over him. He knew he couldn't control this woman who held so much power over him, or the way his body betrayed him as she moved and sucked and grabbed at him. So he detached himself from it all. How lovely and happy that small red finch looked as it fluttered about the field.

~ Nine ~

By Friday afternoon, Rhia was really worried about Ruth. She hadn't returned to their shared cell the night before, nor had she appeared at breakfast or Daily Circle. Images of her lying on the floor, bloody and broken at the hands of Captain Banks, had run through Rhia's mind as she sat through three hours of the droning and muddled teachings of the Modern History class. A lukewarm lunch under the banners of beautiful and smiling people had done little to revive her, but rather left her feeling fuzzy and confused.

Rhia looked forward to the afternoon in the Village, working with her hands in the fresh air, free of the constant overt and subliminal messages of the Center. As she made her way down the wide hill that led to the rows of boxcars below, there was a flurry of activity, women and men busily moving supplies and materials to the unfinished boxes, and Rhia stopped to look for William.

She saw several guards patrolling the rows between the boxcars. As the guards passed, people stopped conversations and looked down, at their work or at the ground. When free of direct supervision, the inmates worked together comfortably—women and men both hauled heavy loads; women and men both operated the tools and machines needed for the construction efforts; women and men both directed and communicated and cooperated to get the jobs done. Rhia was struck by the accord with which these people could coexist when the threat of oppression was removed, and suddenly she could imagine a future in which the rest of the world could be like this.

This is what we were all hoping for, Rhia thought. *This is why we agreed to the New Way rules in the first place. How could it have gone so wrong? How could the women in charge destroy the equality they promised? People in power are still setting up laws and systems designed to keep another part of society down.*

Her thoughts were cut short by the sight of the man working at the edge of the boxcar to her left. He was squatting as he measured the length of a board, his back to Rhia. The hair on his head was short stubble, uneven and choppy, as if it had been badly shaved several weeks ago. When he finished measuring, he stood and turned to a nearby sheet of plywood perched on two sawhorses. As he pivoted, Rhia saw the large bulge of his belly. He walked with a waddle, his hand moving to his hip to support his burden.

Rhia stared. The swollen mass inside the man stretched his red T-shirt to its limit, leaving a stripe of pale skin exposed below the hem. His spine swayed to counterbalance the weight in front as he walked, and when he reached the plywood, he had to bend his body forward awkwardly to reach the electric saw lying near the center of the sheet. Standing straight again, he rubbed his big belly with the palm of his hand, pressing and massaging the stretched skin.

"Come to build another floor?"

Startled, Rhia spun to face William. She didn't know how long he'd been standing there, but she could tell he knew she had been watching the falsely pregnant man.

"Um. Yeah. Well, I mean, whatever you need me to do."

William nodded curtly and raised his eyes to the distant forest beyond the fenced boundary of the Center. He squinted in the bright sunlight, and his nostrils flared in a deep inhale. He seemed to be thinking something over. After a moment he nodded again. Without looking at Rhia, he said, "I'm putting plumbing in a box near the back. You can help if you want to."

"Sure. Lead the way."

Rhia followed William through the maze of shipping containers. Some already resembled tiny shacks. Some still looked raw. They turned a tight corner and arrived at a rusty brown box. A shallow wooden roof had been built above it and was now covered by thick black paper. The metal sides of the box had soaked up the sun all day, and Rhia could feel the heat pulsing off the box like waves as she reached the wide, heavy door. William leaned his shoulder into the latch and pushed the door on its track, sliding it open and stepping inside. She followed him into the darkness.

"Close the door."

Rhia shoved the handle, and the door glided shut. Insulation and a plywood floor had already been installed, and her shoes clunked as she stepped toward the center of the box, letting her eyes adjust to the dim light. The air was slightly cooler inside, and she breathed in the scents of freshly cut wood and dust.

William stepped to a pile of wooden two-by-fours, PVC and metal pipes, elbows, and joints nestled along the far side of the box. A simple white toilet bowl and a tiny metal sink lay on their sides nearby.

"We'll have to open it up again when we're gluing everything together, but for now keep it closed. Keeps it cooler in here."

"Okay." She waited for him to say more, but he wordlessly began to pull two-by-fours from the pile and carry them to one corner. She wanted to talk about the day before—the Daily Circle session, the women who were beaten, the sadness in his eyes—but she didn't know how to begin. She wanted to ask how often he'd been injected and abused that way, and how he had recovered from it. And she wanted to ask what other sessions would be in store for John now that he had been reborn under the hands and body of Miss Deacon.

Instead, Rhia exhaled, stepped to the pile, and picked up several pieces of wood. "Um, so, what do we do?" she asked.

"Water comes from this outside line to the sink. We hook up the sink here in a stand we build. That's what the men who get this box will use for drinking and washing. Below the sink is a removable collection tank. After using the toilet, here," he pointed to a spot to the left, "they'll take the tank from the sink and dump it down the hole to flush. So just water in here, water out there."

"Seems pretty simple."

"Yep."

Rhia looked back to the pile of materials. "Why so much pipe?"

"Stored in here. We'll have to haul it to the other boxes after."

"Okay. How many boxes will we do today?"

"Depends how fast we work." William pulled a wrench from his back pocket and squatted in front of a metal water pipe that was poking through a hole in the wall.

Rhia felt awkward. The working space was small, and there were only a few connections to be made. The toes of her left foot began to bounce up and down as she watched William silently turning his wrench to loosen a cap on the water line. Finally, she said, "What can I do to help?"

William sighed and stopped. "I don't know," he said. "Bring the sink over, I guess."

Rhia carried the small metal basin across the floor and set it beside him. She knelt behind William and watched him for a minute more as he began to arrange the two-by-fours into a stand that would hold the sink and collection tank. The longer she waited, the more difficult it became to speak.

Conquering the lump in her throat, she said, "Have you done this a lot?"

William slumped his shoulders and set his forearms on his thighs. His back moved slowly as he breathed, his muscles expanding and contracting.

"Sinks." Rhia said.

"I suppose." William shook his head and picked up an electric drill from the floor beside him. Keeping his back to Rhia, he began to attach wooden boards to the wall where studs had been marked. The buzz of the drill was loud, drowning out the possibility of more questions.

After several minutes, a frame had been installed, and William pushed himself back from the wall. Kneeling beside Rhia, his head cocked from one side to the other as he surveyed the frame. When he mutely reached for the sink, she could stand it no more.

"Okay, I give up." Rhia pulled herself to standing and began to move toward the closed door.

"Where are you going?"

"It's obvious you don't want me here. I'll find something else to do."

"Look . . . I didn't say that," he fumbled.

"No, you didn't say anything." Rhia turned to him, her hands on her hips. "Why'd you ask me to come in here if you didn't want to talk to me? Are you mad at me? I didn't do anything." She struggled to keep the hurt out of her voice.

"I'm not mad at you. I didn't say . . ."

"You didn't say? That's right. You didn't say."

"Rhia, what do you want me to say?" For the first time today, William looked at her directly, and she could see the frustration in his eyes. He sat back on his heels and laid his open palms upward on his thighs.

"I want you to say . . . William, how could you stand there and watch what she did yesterday?" Rhia gulped. "It was horrible! We have to figure out how to stop her."

"What do you mean, we?"

"We have to let people know what's going on in here! We have to come up with a plan to—"

"Rhia, you're in the Center. Who's going to listen to you?"

"When we get out. You've been here longer than me. You know more than me. I mean, does she do that to . . . everybody?"

"Is that what you want to talk about?" William stood. "You want me to tell you? You want me to tell you she did the same thing to me? You want me to tell you I think it's wrong? Jesus, Rhia. Do I really need to say that?"

Rhia could feel the heat rising in her cheeks, could hear

the tremble in her own voice as she continued. "I don't know. I just . . ." She looked around the dark room. "I just don't know what to do. How can this be going on here and nobody knows about it?"

"Everybody knows about it."

"No, they don't! If people knew the stuff she was doing . . ."

"Rhia, are you telling me you've really never heard any of this?"

"Well," Rhia stammered. "We heard some rumors, but nobody knows what's really going on."

William shook his head. "That's bullshit."

"No—"

"Yes, it is. Deacon gives tours of this place. Regional leaders and town leaders have walked through here and seen everything she does. Women from all over have watched those sessions and then gone home and told their neighborhoods what a great job Deacon is doing. Don't tell me you haven't heard all about it."

"Not my town. We didn't know it was like *this*." Rhia took a step backward. "It wasn't supposed to be so bad."

"Are you kidding me?"

"They said they were helping people who were causing trouble. They said it was therapy. I didn't know it was going to be like this."

"What did you think it was like? You thought people were being locked up here, and brainwashed, and tortured, but it wouldn't be *so* bad?"

"I didn't know."

"Yes, you did."

"I didn't know!"

"You knew."

"But I didn't see it! I didn't see it in real life!" Rhia was revolted by what she was saying, but couldn't stop. "It's different now. Before, it was just happening to people I didn't know. It wasn't anybody from my neighborhood." She threw her hands into the air. "I'm not even supposed to be here! I don't deserve to be here."

William stepped toward Rhia, his eyes burning. "You think I deserve this? You think I deserve what she does to me?"

"No, I—"

"You sat back and listened to stories about this place for years and have done nothing. You bury your head in the sand and convince yourself that the leaders must know what's best, or that only bad people are being sent here and they somehow deserve what they get. But guess what, Rhia? Nobody deserves this. I'm here because I wouldn't let them give away my house. My house. My parent's house! I disagreed with someone in power, and they locked me up to shut me up. And now I'm—" William poked his finger at Rhia, but the rest of his body remained frozen in tense stillness. "And now you want me to feel sorry for you? You want me to comfort you and tell you it's all going to be okay?"

"I didn't say that!"

"You come in here accusing me of doing nothing to stop Deacon, when you were out in the world, free, and *you* did nothing." He took a step closer, and even in the dim light of the box, she could see the searing pain in his eyes. "I can't do anything! You're the ones with all the power now!"

"I told you I didn't know."

William suddenly leaned close and grabbed her arm. "You can't make the rules and then complain when they're used against you."

"Let go of me! I didn't do anything."

"Didn't you?"

"No." Rhia tugged her arm free and stood up straight. She was nearly as tall as he was, and she looked directly into his eyes. "They said I stole a shipment, but I didn't. My boat's waiting for me right now, and on Monday, I'm leaving this shithole. So don't act like I'm the bad guy. I didn't do anything wrong, and I don't deserve to be here."

"How can you say that?" William raised both his hands to his head and ran his fingers through his short, dark hair. "No woman can say that!"

"What?!"

"You sat back and watched as half the country had its rights taken away."

"I never agreed with that! I never agreed with—"

"But what did you do? When the president said men had to stay home and couldn't have jobs after the war, what did you do?"

"Look, I—"

"And as a black woman, you should have known better. What did you do when you saw black men being told to keep their mouths shut and work like slaves?"

"What did you just say to me?" Rhia hissed. "This isn't about the color of my skin. This—"

"You let women tell us we were less than human, less important, less valuable."

"Women took over because the men of this world had waged a war that nearly destroyed everything! Look what the world had become—half the planet polluted beyond use; every major city was bombed into the ground; people were scrounging through garbage dumps for food and scraps; women were being raped and murdered as if *they* weren't even human! The New Way might be full of shit, but it isn't about color any more. It's about the shitty job men have done since the dawn of time."

"So you chose to side with white women over black men!"

"No."

"You turned your back on us—"

"You're wrong."

"And then you come in here and say you've never done anything wrong?"

"What was I supposed to do?" Rhia threw up her hands. "Black women have been at the bottom forever, and the egalitarians told us they were going to fix that. They said we were all finally going to be equal."

"And now you feel equal?"

"I know it's messed up! And I don't know how to fix it. I don't even know if it *can* be fixed. Maybe people just need to have somebody to pick on, somebody to feel superior to. Maybe equality is just a fantasy. But how do I fight male oppression, and white oppression, and . . ." Her voice trailed off.

"Look," Rhia said finally. "I'm brown. And you're tan. And Ruth is beige. And so are half the people around here." She shook her head. "So many people are mixed now, how can you say this is about race. We're all beige and brown, William, so where am I supposed to draw the line between who is like me, and who isn't? And if you're mad at me because you think I should be more angry when a white woman oppresses me than when a black man does, then you're the one who's wrong."

"I'm saying women and men should have worked together," William said. "I'm saying you can't rule this country and call it equality when half the people don't have a voice. And I'm saying you are just as guilty as the rest of them, because for the last thirteen months, people like you knew I was in here, and did nothing to stop it."

"I want to stop it! That's what I'm trying to figure out! I want to help you, but I don't know how."

William shook his head again. "No, you just want to get yourself out. You'll get out and you won't look back."

"That's not true."

"Everybody says that, but when you get out, you won't want to make waves and risk getting sent back here. You'll keep your head down and forget about us."

Rhia wanted to scream that it wasn't true—she hated the part of herself that feared that it was. She paused, took a deep breath, and set her hands on her hips. After a moment she said, "Look, I never wanted to be here. You're right. I was happier when I could pretend I didn't know what was going on. But I don't want to forget. I don't want to pretend not to know anymore, but I don't know what to do." She looked into his face, searching for answers. "Help me. You're getting out in a month. Help me figure out how to change it. Help me fix this."

William hesitated. "I don't know how to help you," he said. "I've been in here over a year, Rhia. A *year*." He shook his head. "When I lie in my bunk at night listening to three cellmates snoring or crying, all I think about is getting out and waging a war against this place. Thinking about fighting back, it's the only thing that keeps me going some days. I've watched men and women abused and tortured, and I want to tear the whole fucking thing down."

"Then let's do it!"

"But how can I?" William clenched his jaw. "Rhia, I have

this dream sometimes. I finally fall asleep, and then I dream about home, and it destroys me." He looked down at his open hands. "In the dream, I'm back in my own house, just walking around. I see my bed, my kitchen and my books, and I'm so happy to just be there. I can smell cool spring air coming in through the windows, and it smells like my garden. Fresh leaves, black dirt." He exhaled and dropped his chin to his chest. "I don't know anything anymore. I'm sorry. I don't have any right to accuse you. I can't blame you for not fighting all this. It's so hard to fight. It's easier to pretend. To forget."

"Two of us together," Rhia said, leaning in, "could do more than just one. The two of us together could make a difference."

"It doesn't matter if it's two or ten if most of the people want to just keep their heads down. It doesn't matter if we work together."

"Yes, it does." Rhia took a step toward William. "It matters to me." She met his eyes.

He'd been right—she wished he would comfort her and tell her it would be okay. She wished he would open up and allow the connection she longed for. And as exposed and vulnerable as it made her feel, she didn't want to deny her feelings any longer.

The light shifted in his eyes. She watched the subtle change wash over his face and slide like silk down his body, and for the briefest moment, she allowed an incalescence to kindle in her belly.

Squeezing his eyes shut tight, he shook his head. "Rhia," William whispered. "I know what you want, but I don't have the strength. I shut down that part of myself long ago. Even here, in this dark place, with you so close . . ."

He was no longer talking about fighting the system. He

felt the same desire that flared within her, and she could see him struggling against it. Her chest felt tight, aching, as she watched him pull away.

"Rhia." William spoke her name firmly, standing up straight again. "Women aren't going to listen to me. If anything is going to change, it's got to be women who change it."

Rhia stared, for a moment unable to feel the floor beneath her feet, and grieving for what she had seen flash in his eyes only moments before. She didn't want to ignore the attraction between them. She was hurt that he could.

"So you won't do anything?" she said. "You won't help me? *You'll* get out in a month and forget everything you saw here?" Her words came out with more venom than she had anticipated.

"I can't give you what you want," William whispered.

"Then I'll do it myself." She spun on her heels and yanked at the lever, sliding the door open with a bang. She stormed out into the blinding brightness of the afternoon and into the maze of scorching, rusted boxcars.

~ Ten ~

A hard lump dug into the small of Rhia's back as she lay on her cot that night. It had been under her shoulder the night before. She'd tried to pound it out, smoothing and massaging the mattress, but it only migrated around under the crinkly, waterproof vinyl cover.

Charlotte snored loudly, and Rhia rolled her eyes. She turned onto her side with a sigh, tired of looking at the sagging metal springs of the bunk above her, and tucked her hands under the side of her head.

The conversation with William played over in Rhia's mind, and her disappointment and frustration grew. *What was I hoping for?* she thought. *What did I expect him to say?*

She rarely met men she didn't already know, their jobs and their duties being of lower status than her own, but in the neighborhoods she traded for she had friends who had mates, and she got along well with them. She'd had short relationships with two men in the past herself, but none of those encounters had prepared her for the feelings that swirled in her belly at the sight of William. When he smiled and laughed with her, it made her feel like melted chocolate, warm and smooth.

She wanted to make him melt. She wanted to stand close to him and tell him about her boat, her friends, and her life, and she wanted him to stand by her side and fight against the Center. She let her imagination run to a vision of them sitting together on Betty's stern deck and watching the last rays of the sun playing on the water all around them. She'd take his hand and lead him below deck as the rhythm of the boat rocked them.

No. The mere idea of an idyllic ending to the mess she'd found herself in was ridiculous. What would she do? Search for William after his release? Try to convince him to come to Miranda with her? Recruit her friends to fight the Center with him at her side? She was being naive. She was being a fool.

Admitting that to herself made the warm, chocolaty feeling turn sour.

A deep buzz sounded, and the cell door clicked and swung wide. Light from the yellow hallway streamed in through the opening, momentarily blinding Rhia. She raised one hand to shield her eyes and leaned up on her elbow in the bed as a thin figure stepped into the room. Seconds later, the door swung shut again, leaving them in darkness.

"Ruth?"

"Yes."

Rhia swung her legs over the edge of the bunk and sat up. "Are you okay?" She could hear Ruth's feet shuffle across the small cement floor toward her own bunk, then the high squeaking of the bedsprings. "Ruth?"

"I'm fine."

"What happened? You've been gone so long," Rhia whispered.

"I'm fine. Go back to sleep."

Rhia heard the sound of Ruth's sheets being pulled back, more squeaking springs, and then the covers being tugged back up. She waited a minute more, hoping Ruth would speak, but heard only quiet breathing. Giving up, Rhia lay back down, and closed her eyes.

~

When the low gong of the morning bell sounded, Rhia got out of bed and made her way to the open toilet hole in the corner. As she squatted, she saw Ruth still in bed, her back turned to the room and her blanket pulled up around her head. Charlotte descended from her own bunk and began to hum quietly as she tidied her sheets. When they'd both dressed and prepared for breakfast, Rhia crouched at Ruth's bedside and touched her shoulder gently.

"Ruth, it's time to get up," she said softly.

Ruth rolled over slowly, and Rhia gasped, pushing away from the bunk. Ruth's long brown hair had been roughly shaved, leaving scrapes and scratches across her scalp. Her pale face was a purple web of growing bruises, with a ragged line of stitches running across her left eyebrow and a crust of dried blood clogging her nostrils. One eye was swollen partially shut; the other looked dully at Rhia.

"Jesus," Rhia breathed.

"Oh, Ruth, I'm so sorry." Charlotte stood behind Rhia, gazing down at Ruth and shaking her head. She quickly turned to the small sink, wetting their ragged washcloth with cold water and bringing it to Ruth. She knelt beside her and began to treat the worst of her injuries, dabbing away at the blood, delicate with the scrapes and swellings. "Ruth, Ruth, it's all right now," she crooned. "It's gonna be okay."

Rhia caught her breath and pulled herself together. "What can I do?" she asked.

"Here," Charlotte answered, handing the cloth to Rhia. "Cool this off again."

They tended to Ruth for several minutes, and then the door buzzed, clicked, and swung open for the march down the hallway to breakfast.

"I'll stay with her," Charlotte said. "You go."

"I can stay, too," Rhia said.

"No. I'll be excused. The guards like me. You try to bring us back something to eat. Tuck it under your shirt so they don't see."

"Charlotte, I . . ."

"That's what you can do to help."

Ruth looked up at Rhia and blinked. Her chin dipped downward in agreement.

For all their arguing and late-night bickering about the methods of the Center, for all the times Ruth had called Charlotte crazy and heckled her, Rhia could see that Ruth trusted Charlotte's kindness. She suddenly realized this wasn't the first time Ruth had needed Charlotte to nurse her back to health. With a sinking feeling, Rhia turned and stepped into the hallway to join the tide of women.

~

"I believe that all women and men deserve the chance to reach their full potential. I believe that the Last War was the result of an imbalance in the system and the dominance of masculinity, greed, and aggression. I believe that it is my duty and honor to struggle against the oppression, fear, and hatred of those who cannot see these truths, and I believe that Re-education will help me achieve my goals."

The female inmates sat down again, their attention trained on the front of the room.

"Your affirmation stirs my soul, my friends," Miss Deacon said. "In my own moments of trial and tribulation, your voices echo in my mind and give me the strength I need to carry on." She pressed her hands to her chest and closed her eyes. Her body heaved in a deep sigh.

"What a week it has been!" she continued, opening her eyes and stretching her arms out to the group. "We have seen the arrival of two new women into our fold, and we have been blessed to witness a rebirth—a man made new by the glory and honor of our love, our compassion, and our guidance. Yes, my friends, we have much to be thankful for this week."

Miss Deacon walked among the women, pausing to smile benevolently into the glowing faces of her admirers as she glided between the round tables. "That gratitude is what keeps us going, isn't it? That feeling of appreciation is what propels us forward in our mission. Now, some might say that it is the righteousness of the battle itself that should be our guide, but I disagree. I feel that we must not think of our struggle to help the women and men of this world as a crusade, a holy war. Instead, we must dwell upon the light and freedom that comes through gratitude for all that we have accomplished so far." She stopped at the table where Rhia sat and leaned back against it, her white skirt draped loosely over her legs and her hands folded delicately in her lap.

"Saturdays are meant for gratitude. On this day we are

called to remember all that we have—all the blessings we have, and all the ways our lives are better now than they were only a few short years ago. For instance," and she paused dramatically, "I remember one night before the Last War began when I was still living with my husband. I remember sitting with him at our expensive dinner table in our elaborate home, eating a meal that was surely large enough for twice as many people."

Miss Deacon became quiet and her eyes took on a faraway look. "I can see him there across from me, still wearing his white button-down dress shirt from his day at the office. His tie was red that day—he always liked red ties, said it was a powerful color—and it was still tightly knotted around his neck." She reached her hand up to her own neck and touched it lightly with her fingertips.

"It was three days after Congress had passed the sixth Family Focus Act, banning all women from full-time employment and revoking our driver's licenses. Now, as I've admitted to you all before, I was a woman of privilege in those days. I was the wife of a wealthy man, and he kept me supplied with all the rich pleasures I could want. I didn't have a job, and I was driven everywhere by a chauffeur, so I might not have been bothered by these new rules. Except," she raised one finger and cocked her head to the side, "I had maids. I had housekeepers, and dressmakers, and florists, and stylists, and doctors, and psychiatrists, and a host of other women on whom I depended. And suddenly, these women were gone!

"Now, my friends, trust me when I tell you that I fully understand how trivial these problems seem to those of you who did not come from such comfort and wealth. It's not the loss of my luxuries that I'm trying to stress here. I'm telling you this because for the first time in my adult life, I was shaken to the core by the knowledge of all the work that women do in this world! I was struck by the idea of all those women, millions of them, being told they could no longer do the jobs they wanted to do, the jobs they depended on, because an out-of-work man deserved it more. Yes, in my narrow little world, this new law would cause me terrible inconvenience, but I was suddenly aware of how devastating it would be to all the other women around me.

"My friends!" Miss Deacon stood again and leaned forward on her long, shapely legs. "My eyes were opened that day! And I knew I had to do something about it. So, I spoke to the other women in my circle, all of whom were as inconvenienced as I by this new rule, and together we decided that we must act to reverse it. We must band together and make a change.

"That evening, as my husband sat opposite me eating the dinner that our male chef had prepared and our male butler had delivered, I lifted my chin and I spoke.

"'James,' I said, 'my friends and I have been talking about the new rules, and we have decided that they simply cannot work. Banning women from jobs and not allowing them to drive is simply ridiculous, and will result in the utter downfall of society as we know it. We have decided to protest this decision, and I am hoping you will help me come up with some ideas as to how to proceed.'

Miss Deacon cocked her head to one side. "You see, I had always thought that I had many important contacts and knew many important people in both business and government. I prided myself on that. But when I tried to formulate a plan of attack, I realized that all these important people I knew were really only the *wives* of important people. My social circle didn't include the few women left at that time who were actually running businesses or fighting for change. I would need my husband's support, just as my friends would need the support of all their important husbands.

"Well, I said my piece and sat there at the table, staring across at my husband. He continued to chew for a moment or two, set down his fork, picked up his glass of wine, and took a small sip. And then, without so much as looking across the table at me, he simply said, 'That is not a venture I am interested in.'"

Miss Deacon paused, her chin tilted up, her eyes focused on a spot somewhere along the back wall of the room. She stood silent and unmoving for several moments before finally drawing a great breath and exhaling loudly.

"You see, my feelings and my needs were not important enough to my husband to make him want to risk his own neck. My earnest desire to finally become a help to my gender was not important enough. And there is evidence that he simply did not believe in my cause. Why would he? There were tens of thousands of men out of work at that moment and waiting to take the positions vacated by the women now banned from employment. There were studies, and charts, and graphs that showed the economic benefits of keeping women at home to raise their children. There were psychological and developmental tests that had proven a child's need for a stay-at-home parent. There were estimates of GDP and ROI and XYZ that illustrated the expected growth of society, decrease in criminal behavior, and upswing of global exports if we could only get our women to stop working and get back to the homes and kitchens and bedrooms where they belonged!

"My God! We were inundated with the data! We were barraged with these ideas over and over and over until some women even started to believe it!"

Miss Deacon paced around the room, her steps quickening as her speech found its fire. "But not me! I knew it was a lie. I knew in those first few days that this massive shift in societal policy could not be the truth. One only had to look into the eyes of the woman whose job had been taken away to see it. One only had to ask the woman who had been told to leave her university class if she was happier now. The grave error in these new rules was evident all around us.

"And yet, what could we do? What could we do when people like my husband were unwilling to do anything to help our cause? What could I do when my husband showed his disinterest in me and in the things I found important?

"Well, I'll tell you—I rose up!" She pointed her index finger to the ceiling. "I rose up and found my true calling, my friends! I found others like me, and together we showed him how wrong he had been. I found powerful women who refused to be oppressed, and when the time was right, I joined with them in the overthrow of my husband and all that he stood for!"

She stopped moving, and her gaze drifted to the windows. Quietly, she said, "The war came, and in his cowardice, my husband hid behind his piles of money even while millions of other men fell. But when the war was over, everything he had became mine."

Miss Deacon smiled at the memory. After a moment, she snapped out of her thoughts and looked around the room as if remembering the women listening. "And this, my friends, is what I am grateful for on this glorious summer day. No longer do the women of this country have to ask for help from an elite group of ivory-tower men. No longer are we forced to sit across from them, their pasty, puffy faces dull and lifeless above their starched shirts and blood-red nooses. Oh! How I longed to reach across that dining room table and choke him with that tie!

"Women of this world, we are at last united in the freedom of the New Way Forward! We are at last united in our ability to decide for ourselves what the laws should be, and we are at last united in the courage of our convictions to make this country great again. *We* are the important ones now! *We* are the new leaders! And today I stand before you in deepest gratitude, humbled and honored to be here, in Re-education Center Number Three, where women and men are making great strides toward a great way of life for us all.

"Think on these things, my friends." She nodded. "Ponder them in your hearts today as you work and learn and grow, and dwell upon them tomorrow during your silent reflection. Know that my heart beats in unison with yours, and that we will begin again on Monday with a renewed vigor, a renewed desire, and a renewed sense of purpose. We have come so far from those days of oppression and impotence, and that is surely something to be grateful for."

Women clapped. Rhia folded her arms across her chest.

~

"Remember that time my mom tried cooking fish for Michael's birthday, but she baked so much rosemary right inside it? Oh my God, it tasted terrible! It wasn't even cooked through." Laura giggled as she pipetted a small amount of reagent into a beaker. "We all pretended to chew, and she sat there watching us with that hopeful look on her face, and we really tried to swallow it, but we just wanted to spit it out. Do you remember?"

"Yeah," Rhia said.

"And finally Michael says, 'Kate, thank you for all the work you did,' and he leans over and puts his arm around her. 'And I love you. But, honey, this is disgusting.'" Laura howled with laughter and wiped her eyes with the back of her forearm. "My mom knew he was right. She was so disappointed that for a second I thought she was going to cry. Then we all looked over and saw Jonah sitting there, and he's just shoveling it into his mouth. He was fourteen years old, and I swear, he would eat anything. He finally looks up and sees us staring at him and says, 'What? What's wrong?' And we all just started laughing!"

Nadine stood across the tall lab table, beaming at the story and the laughter that rang from Laura. Between them, a Bunsen burner kept a chemical reaction in a rolling boil. Every thirty seconds, Nadine made a note in the lab book she held.

"Did your brother really eat it?" Nadine asked.

"He ate about three servings of that fish before we all finally had to just leave the table because it smelled so bad. The rest of us went in the kitchen, and Michael made this corn bread thing instead. He used to be a chef, so he just whips up these things without even trying. I think that was the last time my mom tried to cook anything exotic. She just sticks to chicken and soups these days." Laura paused and looked over at Rhia, who sat on the other side of the room unloading trays of samples from a small freezer. "Rhia, do you remember that Christmas pudding he made last year?"

Rhia slammed the freezer door and turned around. "Laura, I haven't eaten anything decent in a week, so can we please not talk about food?"

Sheepishly, Laura dropped her eyes. "Sorry. I was just—"

"I know you want to talk about your family, but I just can't right now, okay?" Rhia's voice was sharp. She pushed the petri dishes around her small workstation. "I don't have the luxury of reminiscing with you. I . . ." Her words trailed off, and she set her hands on her hips and looked at the floor. After a moment, she added, "Look, I'm sorry. I didn't mean to snap at you. I'm just . . . There's a lot going on in my head right now." She looked up and saw Laura and Nadine exchange a worried look.

Rhia groaned and crossed the room to her friend. "LoLo, I'm sorry."

"It's okay. You're right. I should try to be more sensitive. You don't want to talk about home because we can't be there now."

"No, it's not that."

"Is it the work? Do you hate being in here?"

"No, Laura, it's not the work."

"Maybe you were right. Maybe working in the lab isn't really right for you."

"LoLo, no, it's not . . ."

"I just wanted to have you in here because I wanted to know you're safe."

"And I appreciate that."

"If you don't want to be in here, don't feel like—"

"Laura, listen." Rhia took Laura's hand in her own and stepped close. "It's not that at all. I really appreciate that you got me in here. I'm really grateful for that. And I'm sorry I snapped at you."

"Well, what's going on? Did something happen?"

Rhia leaned her hip against the table and folded her arms. "It's just . . . Some things I've seen . . . The way this place works is just . . ." She paused and breathed deeply. "My roommate came back this morning badly beaten."

Nadine raised her hand to her mouth.

"She stood up during the FEmS session on Thursday and

started yelling at Deacon about how wrong it was, and all of a sudden Captain Banks jumped on her and started pounding her. They dragged her off, and she was gone until this morning."

"Well, but," Laura stammered. "What did she say?"

"What?"

"During the session—what did she say that was so bad?"

"That it was wrong to inject those drugs and to assault men like that! That Deacon was evil and that she'd have to pay for all the bad things she's doing here!" Rhia shook her head. "And she's right. I mean, Laura, if you'd seen what she did! And then when Ruth came back this morning, she could barely walk. Her face was all torn up!"

"Rhia, I'm so sorry. I . . . Is she going to be okay?"

"I don't know. I hope so. She ate a little lunch, so I guess that's good. My other roommate's helping her. She hasn't said much to me yet."

Nadine set down her notebook and leaned forward, her arms resting on the table. "Is there anything we can do to help? We have a first-aid kit."

"That's right," Laura said. "It's not much, but there are bandages and antibiotic ointments in there. We have a good store of medicinal plants to help the bruising and pain. Can we give you some to take back to her?"

"I don't know. The nurses stitched her up already. Maybe."

Laura's shoulders sagged, and she sat down slowly on her stool. "What if . . ." She sighed. "Tomorrow's Sunday, so we won't be able to say anything then, but maybe on Monday I can ask Donna if your roommate can come help in here, too. Do you think she'd be good at lab work? Would she be able to help you out at all?"

"Monday I meet with the justice liaison so I can get out."

"Right," Laura said. "Well, your roommate could help me with the work you've been doing."

"I don't know, Laura." Rhia turned over the idea in her mind. She wondered if Ruth would even be willing, to work for any part of the Center. But mostly, she worried about her meeting with the justice liaison. She suddenly felt a nauseating urge to distance herself from Ruth, as if associating with her might hurt her own chances of being released. She was embarrassed at her own cowardice, but she could hardly think beyond Monday.

"If your roommate is hurt like that, she needs a place to feel safe. Or, if she's causing trouble, maybe she just needs some meaningful work to do. Maybe she would have an easier time being here if she was doing something to help people."

"Laura, she got beat up. She didn't deserve it."

"I didn't mean it that way." Laura touched Rhia on the arm. "Let me at least ask Donna. She's a good person, Rhia. She doesn't like some of the stuff that goes on here, either. I'm sure she'll want to help."

Rhia wasn't sure inviting Ruth into the lab was the right decision, but she ignored the foreboding flickering in her mind. "Okay," she said. "I'll ask Ruth tonight."

~

Rhia and Charlotte walked casually down the hall among the throng of women returning to their cells after dinner. When they reached their door, they waited for the others to line up quietly in front of their own cells. Satisfied with the formation, the guards at the end of the hall pushed the wide red button, and they heard the familiar buzz and click of the lock. The door swung open and they stepped inside. When the door thudded closed they began unloading their smuggled food onto the thin brown cardboard cover of Ruth's botany notebook.

Rhia untucked the bottom of her shirt and unrolled the wads of fabric that held several globs of wet, cement-like oatmeal. Charlotte pulled withered carrots and wedges of dried potatoes from the inside lining of her underwear, and they both dug into their thick, institutional-grade bras for the handfuls of raisins hidden there. They set the pathetic feast before Ruth and helped her sit up on her cot.

"Charlotte, if you hid anything up your ass, I don't want it." Ruth smirked, then winced with the pain it caused her torn lip.

"I didn't." Charlotte looked hurt.

"I'm sorry. I'm kidding."

"How are you feeling?" Rhia asked.

"My body hurts, but my mind is clear."

"Can I get you more water?" Rhia reached under Ruth's bed and pulled out the small beaker she had smuggled from the lab that afternoon. Without waiting for an answer, she moved to the sink and refilled it. She was glad to see Ruth drink most of it before setting it on the mattress.

"I think I'll be able to go to breakfast tomorrow," Ruth said. "So you won't have to worry about me anymore."

"Don't rush it, Ruth," Charlotte crooned in her singsong way. "We don't mind bringing you food."

"I know." Ruth chewed the mushy carrot. "But I need to start taking care of myself. I've been lazy for so long, it's about time I start working again."

"Actually, I wanted to talk to you about that." Rhia saw something flit over Ruth's face for a second, and then it was gone.

"About what?"

"Working. See, I've been working in the botany lab some afternoons, and the women in there said they could use more help. So, I thought if you wanted to work in there a bit with me, it might give you some time to recuperate. That way you'd be away from the guards and everything. Just until you're stronger."

"You've been working in the lab?" There was an edge in Ruth's voice.

"Yeah. Ms. Brakille and the two assistants. It's not really Center stuff. They're doing experiments trying to make vaccines for childhood diseases. You don't have to know much, you just have to help out with some of the repetitive lab work. It's not hard."

Ruth looked down at the gray chunks of food in her lap, as if deliberating.

"It's cooler in there, too. They have fans," Rhia added.

After a moment, Ruth nodded her head. "Yes. That's a good idea. I think you're right, Rhia. I think working in the lab would really help me. I need to start doing something to better myself. I need to stop being lazy."

Rhia raised her eyebrows. "I didn't say you were being lazy. You're hurt. I'm not trying to imply anything. If you need a couple more days, that's okay. Charlotte and I don't mind helping you."

"No. That's not what I mean." Ruth looked up at them with an expression that teetered between shame and pride. "Thank you both for helping me out the last two days. But I'm talking about how lazy I've been since I came to the Center." She took a deep breath, as if making a silent resolution. "All this time they've been trying to help me, and I've been too lazy to see it."

"What are you talking about?" Rhia whispered.

"I've lived most of my life being angry all the time. I've wasted too many years fighting against a system that I didn't even understand. Now that I've finally figured it out, I need to start doing the hard work of fixing myself so that I can really start helping people." Ruth's voice was calm and composed. "I'm going to make changes, my friends. I'm going to allow Miss Deacon to help me at last."

Charlotte brought her hands to her cheeks. "Oh, Ruth! Do you mean it?"

"Yes, Charlotte. And one of the first things I need to do is apologize to you for all the trouble I've caused. I know how difficult it's been for you to be my roommate for all these months, when all I've done is fight and rage and complain. And I want to thank you for being so patient with me."

Tears welled in Charlotte's eyes as she leaned toward Ruth. "You are forgiven, my friend. And I'm so happy that you've finally seen the light!"

"Wait," Rhia said. "What are you saying?"

"I'm saying that I understand everything now. I'm saying that I finally understand what I have to do." Ruth's eyes shone in the harsh glow of the overhead light. "These last days with Miss Deacon have finally gotten through to me, Rhia. I now see what I've been doing wrong all this time. When I was down in the cellar with her, she kept asking me what I want—what I want more than anything in this world—and I finally realized what that is." A broken, crooked smile spread across the bruises and cuts on her face. "I want to get out of here."

"Of course, but you don't mean . . ."

"I want to get out of here, and the only way to do that is to admit my shortcomings and reevaluate all the mistakes I've made in the past. I need to take responsibility for all the things

I've done, Rhia."

"But, what about the sessions, and the guards, and the way Deacon brainwashes people?"

"No, Rhia. I was wrong." Ruth shook her head and touched Rhia's hand with cool, dry fingertips. "As Miss Deacon keeps telling me, I've been steeped in anger and hatred and mistrust my whole life, and it's caused me to see everything from the wrong perspective. It's like I've been seeing the world through a lens caked in grease! Miss Deacon has wiped away the sludge of the old world and allowed me to see clearly for the first time."

"No, you can't mean that." Rhia backed away from Ruth's cot until her hip bumped into the metal bars of her own bunk on the other side of the small room. "What did they do to you? Did they inject you, or something? Did they—"

"Rhia, I know you're still new here," Ruth continued, "but take comfort in the knowledge that you're in a wonderful place and you're surrounded by people who want to help you."

"Stop it!" Rhia shouted.

"You have to let them help you, Rhia."

"Stop it!"

Charlotte held up her hands. "Now, women. Let's not fight." She turned to Ruth. "Remember that Rhia is on her own journey. She'll learn everything in her own time, Ruth."

"Yes, you're right." Ruth looked up at Rhia and smiled.

~

The only sounds Rhia heard on Sunday were the simple gongs that indicated the timing of the daily rituals, the buzzes and clicks of the cell doors, and the scraping of benches and chairs in the cafeteria. The repetitive chanting from the speakers around the Center was silenced, as were any conversations among the inmates. Not a word was spoken on the Day of Silent Reflection, but rather women and men meandered through the grounds, stopping to sit in the sun or to gaze at the sky, their minds in deep thought about the choices and paths that had led them to this place.

Rhia slowly made her way down the slope toward the Village, pretending to meander without direction. She passed several women and men lying in the grass or sitting cross-legged under the deep blue sky. Those who seemed lost in the quiet questions they pondered troubled her less than those whose eyes contained little more than a blank stare. She had tried to speak this morning, while still in her cell, and had been silenced when Ruth raised a quick finger to her lips, an eerie look of humility and determination still in her eyes.

As she neared the Village, Rhia noticed that the usual activities and noises of construction were missing. Only a few men moved about, some sitting on the stoop of their shipping-container shack, others rambling around the area. Stealing subtle glances up to the towers that loomed overhead, she saw that this was not a day of rest for the guards—two camouflaged figures continued to pace across each deck. She needed to move cautiously now.

Trying to stroll casually, Rhia passed by the Village and headed toward the nearest guard station. When she was just thirty feet away, she squatted down and examined a plant at her feet. She could hear the heavy boots of the guards on the wood above her. Then, as the deep thuds ceased, she knew they were watching. Perspiration pricked at her forehead, and she had to close her eyes to steady the racing of her heart. *Move slowly,* she thought. *Don't draw attention. Just walk casually.*

After a minute, Rhia stood and continued her aimless

saunter, her arms loose at her sides and her eyes on the ground around her. She wound far to the left of the tower, then doubled back, easing her way toward the stream. Reaching the bank at last, she sat down with her legs long in front of her and gazed at the sparkling water as it flowed slowly past. She began to count in her head—*One-one thousand; two-one thousand; three-one thousand*—on up to sixty-one thousand. Without moving her head, she slid her eyes to the right, to the chain-link fence where it crossed the cut bank. The small hole was still there, exposed by erosion and the merciless trickle of time and water.

Some larger stones were embedded in the dry dirt bank around the hole, and vertical metal support poles were pounded in the ground at five-foot intervals along the fence. She would need a shovel or a pick to make the hole big enough to squeeze through, but she couldn't imagine how to get tools from the locked and guarded toolshed.

Rhia thought she could feel the eyes of the guards burrowing into her back as she sat. She shouldn't attract attention to this spot, but she hated to leave the tiny window of freedom. She longed to crawl to the opening and press her face to the hole, to breathe in deeply—as if the air on the other side of the fence would somehow smell and taste different from the air of the Center. She wanted to dive into the water and magically swim through the twisted metal barrier, pulling her arms through a strong breaststroke that would propel her away from the muddled nightmare inside.

Instead, acting casually, moving slowly, Rhia reached to the ground and picked up a small stone. It was smooth and cool in her palm. She stood up, inhaled the humid air into her lungs, and gently tossed the stone to the stream below. With a plop, the concentric rings of ripples began to pulse outward. Rhia watched them a minute more, silently meditating only on the path of the water as it flowed downstream, out of the Center, and eventually to the waiting ocean below.

~ Eleven ~

On Monday morning, Captain Banks barged into the Modern History classroom, shouted Rhia's name, and commanded her to follow. She didn't even wait for the teacher to finish her thought. She led Rhia down the empty corridor of brittle wood paneling that lined the west wing of the building to the closed door of an office. There she stopped and turned to face Rhia.

"Big day with the justice, I see," Captain Banks purred. She raised her arm and leaned it against the doorjamb, blocking Rhia's path. "I bet you've been practicing batting your eyes and swinging your hips so she'll feel sorry for you, but you can forget it. I've already testified about how I found you out there in the woods. I told her I saw you cavorting with those pieces of shit; about how you'd all been sleeping together in a filthy tent; about how you resisted questioning."

She tilted her head to one side and stared at Rhia. "But, you know," she whispered. "That might not be the whole story. Maybe you really were out there just by accident. Maybe you were just in the wrong place at the wrong time." She leaned forward. "Maybe you and I could help each other out."

"What are you saying?"

Banks smiled. "I'm saying, maybe I saw your boat out in the water when I captured that man on the beach. I bet if I told the justice that, I could get a couple guards to haul a rowboat out there and see if your story checks out."

Rhia's heart pounded. "Of course it checks out."

"Or maybe you were just picking the two of them up, and you were all going to sail off into the sunset with the goods from the trade."

"That's not true."

Captain Banks shrugged. "It's hard to say, I guess. But, if I was to go in this room and tell the justice I believed you, well . . ." A slippery smile spread across her crooked face. "Maybe your chances of getting out of here would go up." She took a small step closer to Rhia, her arm still blocking the door to the office. Her black eyes smoldered. She leaned forward and lifted her free hand toward Rhia's cheek.

In the stifling dry air of the hallway, Rhia could smell Captain Banks's sour, rotten breath. As Banks's hand approached her cheek, Rhia stiffened and pulled her head back. Banks stopped, her hand hovering in the air.

"Be a smart girl," Banks whispered, her face inches from Rhia's. "I could make this go a lot easier for you. You be nice to me, and I'll be nice to you."

Through clenched teeth, Rhia spat, "Don't touch me."

Anger flickered across Banks's face for a split second, then her right eye twitched and she pulled back. With a smirk, she said, "I thought you were smarter than that." She slid her arm off the doorjamb and stepped to the side.

Rhia moved forward and raised her fist to knock. Suddenly, Banks wrapped an arm around her back and pushed a hand beneath the bottom edge of Rhia's shirt. She pressed her pelvis into Rhia's hip and slid her hand up to Rhia's breast. Rhia stifled a cry as Banks squeezed her hard and pressed her lips to her ear.

"You can't get away from me," Banks hissed. "I own this place." She thrust her hips forward, shoving Rhia sideways, and just as quickly as she had attacked, she let go and moved to the opposite side of the hall. There, she stood at attention and watched Rhia regain her balance. "I'll be here when you get out," she whispered.

Rhia's hand trembled as she raised her arm and knocked.

"Come in," a muffled voice called from inside.

The door creaked. Rhia stepped into the dimly lit, wood-paneled office. Unlike Miss Deacon's office, there was only one small window, which was coated in a thick film of dust. No green ferns decorated this room, and the only furniture was a battered desk and two metal folding chairs.

"Sit down." The woman behind the desk wore her long brown hair in a chignon at the nape of her neck and had small, wire-framed glasses perched on the end of her nose. She was in her mid-forties, fit and healthy, with subtle wrinkles in her brow and around her eyes. She held a pen in one hand and a file in the other and was rapidly reading its contents. When Rhia sat in the open folding chair, the woman flipped the cover of the file closed and looked up for the first time.

"You're Rhia Malone?"

"Yes."

"I'm Agnes Tumwater, the justice liaison for your region,

and I'm in charge of your case. I see in your file that you've been here since last Monday, and I apologize that you've had to wait so long. I cover a large area, and I know it's probably been difficult for you. Have they explained what my role is here?"

She spoke in quick clips, as if she had honed her sentences to the most efficient words to save time.

"They said you were the person to talk to about getting out of here." Rhia leaned forward in her chair. "They're saying I stole a shipment, and that I was with criminals, but it isn't true. Everything is still on my boat! I was knocked overboard during a storm and—"

Tumwater held up her hand. "We'll get to that. First, I have to explain my role here." She pulled a rectangle of cream-colored paper from a small pile on her desk and passed it to Rhia. "I'll go over this with you. It's written in legal terms, but I'll paraphrase. The first paragraph tells you what I can and cannot do. I am here on your behalf, and will act as your counselor in all legal matters related to the alleged crimes that brought you here. I'll advise you as to what I believe is the best course of action based on my eight years of experience in this role and my seven years of experience as a defense attorney before that. This is not a trial, and I am not a judge. If I believe you have a good chance of convincing a judge of your innocence, I'll advise you on that process after we have gone over everything today. I would strongly advise you to be honest and forthcoming with me today—I'm extremely busy, and I often have only one shot at helping you. If you are dishonest with me today, there may be little I can do. Do you understand?"

Rhia nodded. "Yes."

"Second paragraph: After we've talked today, if I believe I

can help you, I'll ask you to write down the names and neighborhoods of anyone who can support your claims of innocence, as well as any other details that I can use to investigate your case. Please be as specific and clear as possible." She took a breath.

"Last paragraph: If I determine that there is strong enough evidence to indicate you did commit your alleged crimes, I'll advise you on what I believe is the best course of action. At that point, our meeting will be concluded today, and if you choose, you can make another appointment with me in the future."

Tumwater leaned forward and met Rhia's eyes. "And lastly, if at any point in your confinement here, you feel as if you are under extreme duress or you are being mistreated, you can make another appointment with me. This doesn't include things like a drafty cell or disgusting food. This doesn't include the general prescribed physical and psychological treatments used at this Center. This is to be used only if you feel you are in direct danger, and you need to understand that there may be consequences to your allegations. It's likely you'll have to stay here for a week or more even after you have complained to me, even if your allegations are serious. Do you understand?"

Rhia hesitated, picturing Captain Banks waiting outside the door. Her hands still trembling, she said, "Yes."

"Good. You keep that form." Tumwater sat back at her desk. She flipped open a notebook and clicked her pen. "Now. I've read over the accusations against you. I've also read that you claim you were knocked off your boat during a storm the night of the last trade at Piper Point, and that the two people you were brought in with, Carol Mueller and John Mueller, found you on the beach and were helping you recuperate in their camp. Is this correct?"

"Yes."

"Had you ever met Carol Mueller or John Mueller before that time?"

"No."

"Would they say the same if I asked them?"

"Yes."

"What are the chances your boat is still anchored in the water off Thread the Needle?"

At this, Rhia's stomach lurched. Anything could have happened to Betty in the week she'd been gone. "I don't know. There haven't been any more big storms, and she was secure when I got knocked overboard, so she should still be there. But, if someone happened to come across her, or if someone from shore swam out there . . . I don't know." She looked pleadingly at Tumwater. "That boat's my whole life, my home, my livelihood. I need to get back to her right away, Ms. Tumwater. All the food will be spoiled by now, but there were building supplies in the holds, too. I'll work extra to make it up to my towns. Contact the women in my towns! They know me. They know I would never do anything to hurt them. I can give you their names and they can vouch for me!"

"Ms. Malone, hold on." Tumwater was scribbling in her notebook. "Okay, give me three names of women who would support your claim. Tell me their neighborhoods and what jobs they do there. And, Ms. Malone," she looked over the top edge of her glasses at Rhia, "choose women who are known and respected in your towns. The more powerful they are and the more closely aligned with the New Way they appear, the more weight their opinions will carry."

Rhia named three of her closest friends in Miranda, New Hope, and Campbell. She had no doubt they would all come to her aid and would petition to the highest level of leadership on her behalf. She imagined them hearing the news of her capture with both horror and relief. She'd been missing for days, and surely they would have been searching for her. When they heard what happened, they'd probably march en masse to the gates of the Center and demand her release.

Then Rhia added, "And there's the woman at the trade that I always deal with. She knows I'm not a thief. Her name's Ginny Sisken. I can describe her. She's always working at docks twelve through sixteen."

"At Piper Point?"

"Yes. Ginny always unloads my boat and records my trades. You can check the records and see that I've never even skimmed anything off the top."

"Is her name Virginia Sisken?"

"Yeah, I guess."

Again, Tumwater scribbled notes, then she leaned sideways and pulled a second notebook from a satchel on the floor beside her desk. She flipped open the pages, which Rhia could see were covered in inky black cursive from top to bottom, and thumbed through them until she found the page she was looking for. She read for a moment, snapped the notebook closed, and dropped it back into the satchel. "Virginia Sisken is assigned to docks twelve through sixteen at Piper Point—"

"Then that's her! Ask her if—"

"But you won't be using her for a reference."

Rhia stared. "Why?"

Tumwater breathed deeply. "She's employed by the Regional Investigation Unit to keep an eye on the runners. She works at the trade in order to question runners and seek out information about recruitment in the area. Basically, she's a spy who tries to get women to admit that they are unhappy with the system by baiting them with talk about revolution."

Rhia leaned back in the metal folding chair and raised her hand to her forehead.

"And," Tumwater continued, "she has already pegged you as a possible recruiter."

"You are fucking kidding me."

"She's reported that you are strong-willed and independent, and that you've often mentioned feeling like the trades are unfair to the women in your towns. She doesn't have hard evidence yet, but she's made you a person of interest. That's where this other charge against you comes from."

Rhia leaned her head against the back of the chair. She pressed her palms into her eye sockets, squeezing back the tears that pricked there.

"Ms. Malone, I need you to be completely honest with me now. Have you ever been in contact with recruiters or revolutionary groups, or attempted to begin a revolutionary group of your own?"

"No!" Rhia cried. "Absolutely not! Jesus, the way Ginny talked, I thought *she* was a recruiter! I always tried to steer her away from stuff like that. And she was baiting me? Oh my God." She bent forward and placed her head in her hands, trying to stop the spinning of the room.

"And the women from your towns—the names you gave me—is there a chance any of them would be under investigation? Are these women who fully support the New Way, or do they talk about revolution?"

Rhia didn't know how to respond. There were few women, in any of the three towns she served, who would say they supported all the new rules, and those women were known as zealots. Guards rarely traveled that far north, and her neighbors enjoyed a life of relative obscurity. There had been trouble with some men in the past, debates about how best to keep everyone safe, but most of her friends tried to be reasonable and to live within the spirit of equality that the rules were intended to support. Many women knew that the letter of the law was stifling and unjust to men, but they understood that each person, each family, and each neighborhood worked best in the gray zone of common sense—something laws had lacked for generations. Things were getting better now, weren't they? Women and men were working together again, at least in her towns. At least a bit.

Was there anyone she knew who would say she agreed with *all* the rules? If questioned, would any of them be able to deny that they hoped for change and evolution in the system? Would Rhia be sending an inquisition into the heart of the people and places she loved most? And if they tried to help her, would they become guilty by association? She was baffled.

"I . . . I don't know," Rhia whispered. "I mean, none of my friends are recruiters. None of them are bad people, but do they agree with *all* the new laws? Does anybody agree with *all* the new laws? If you question anybody long enough, you'll find something to accuse them of." She stared into her palms, searching for an answer. "Will I get everyone in trouble if I ask them to help me?"

Ms. Tumwater sighed. "Look. The problem with the system now is that it's a lot easier to prove that a person is guilty than to prove they're innocent. Most women working in the justice system—the lawyers, assistants, the aides and inquisitors—are decent people who are trying to do the right thing. But you're right, there are some who realize they are in a position of power over others, and they use their power in improper ways." She looked around the small, dark room and shook her head. "It isn't up to me who'll be sent to your towns to question your friends. You have to decide if it's worth it to you to bring them into this fight.

"If we can find your boat, and the supplies are still on board, and if the Muellers testify that you were not conspiring with them, there's a good chance we can get the larceny charge thrown out." Tumwater pointed the tip of her pen at Rhia. "That's good. Larceny would have meant sixteen months here and penance afterward. But, you have an official agent who says you've spoken about revolution at the trades. Even if there's no evidence that you're actively recruiting people into a revolutionary group, they're still going to keep you here for at least two months for Re-education."

"What?"

"Ms. Malone, based on what I've read in your file, and what you've said today, I would advise you to request an investigation into your missing boat and the missing supplies, and I would advise that we write to your towns asking for character references, from only the women you believe would be the best suited for this job. Those letters of reference will go into your file and help you, but they're less likely to result in a direct inquiry of the women who wrote them.

"I would also advise you to be as patient as possible during your time here, and to try to think of this as only a brief hiccup in your life." Tumwater's shoulders slouched and her eyes softened. "I know this isn't what you want to hear, and I truly do understand how difficult even two months at a Center can be, but based on your file, I think it's your best bet."

"This can't be happening," Rhia mumbled.

"I know." Tumwater said compassionately. "No one ever thinks it will happen to them."

After several seconds of silence, Rhia looked up. "Betty. My boat. What about my boat?"

Tumwater nodded her head and scribbled in her notebook. "Because you're a runner, you're a valuable member of society. East-west travel has been nearly impossible since the interstates and highways were bombed. The new Safe Rail system the government is hyping is already overloaded and understaffed, and doesn't help along the coast anyway. Even the national directors understand that the mosquito fleet of boats is a major source of transportation out here, for people and for supplies. They'll want you to get back to work after you leave the Center, if possible."

Tumwater set down her pen. "If the larceny charges are dropped, I should be able to make a case for your reinstatement after Re-education. There's no guarantee, but there's a chance your boat can be brought to the nearest port and kept until your release. I can't promise anything, but we can try."

She flipped back a few pages and checked her notes. "I'll be in Julieton on Thursday. Thread the Needle is near there." She pulled her glasses off and rubbed the bridge of her nose before looking across at Rhia. "I'll go to the beach and just see if your boat is out there. If it is, I'll begin the paperwork for an investigation. I'll put you on my schedule for next Monday, and let you know where we're at."

"And if she's not there?"

Agnes Tumwater slipped her glasses back on and began to scribble in her notebook again. She sighed. "Let's just wait and see if it is. I'll question the Muellers today. And I'll get letters to the three women in your towns." She looked back up at Rhia. "I'll do my best."

Thoughts spun around Rhia's head as she stood up from the chair and turned to leave. As she stepped into the hallway, she saw Captain Banks waiting for her. For a second, she considered going back into Tumwater's room to complain, but she knew it would be even worse for her if she did. Instead, she squared her shoulders and walked past Banks toward the Modern History class.

Rhia had taken only fifteen steps when she felt a hand press into the small of her back. Banks had followed her, silently, breathlessly.

"How'd it go in there?"

Rhia could hear the smugness in Banks's voice. The hair on the back of her neck stood on end.

"Guess Tumwater thinks you're guilty, too, huh? Well, don't worry about it, Malone. Not everybody's gonna fall in love with you. It's good news for me, though, isn't it? Now you get to be here with me for a whole month. And it's summer! Everything's better in the summer. When I come get you out of your cell in the middle of the night, at least you'll be nice and warm."

Banks walked beside Rhia now, her hand still pressed into Rhia's spine, guiding her down the hall. She spoke in whispers that were anything but gentle and kind. "We'll walk out under the stars together and the hot summer wind will blow over your skin. You can come up to my guard tower, and I'll have a blanket laid out for us. Hey," she laughed quietly, "maybe we can have a little picnic up there. What do you think? Would you like to eat something other than wet cafeteria slop?"

Rhia kept her spine straight, kept her eyes focused on the end of the hall, on the door to the classroom, and tried to block out the viciousness of Banks's voice in her ear.

"Well, maybe you won't be hungry, huh?" Banks continued. "Maybe you'll want to get right to business. You'll stand there and you'll take off all your clothes, nice and slow. I'm gonna watch you stand there in the moonlight. I'm just gonna look at you. Ah, Malone. I can't wait to sit there on the floor, my legs wide open, just looking at you. I'll have you walk over to me, real slow, and lie down on the floor next to me. I want to watch you lie down. I want to watch you spread your legs open for me, Malone. I want to see everything."

They finally reached the classroom, and Banks leapt forward to open the door. As Rhia passed through, out of the corner of her eye she could see the smile spread across Banks's face.

~

As Rhia torqued on a long wrench, turning the heavy bolts that would secure a shipping container to its cement pad, William squatted next to her. She startled, nearly dropping her wrench.

His eyebrows furrowed. "Sorry. Didn't mean to scare you."

"No," Rhia mumbled. "You didn't." She shook her head and repositioned her wrench.

"I have some wiring to work on today and could use some help."

"I told the forewoman I'd get this done."

"Briana?"

"Yep."

William squinted up at the sky and sighed. "Look, I want to apologize for the argument we had the other day."

"Okay."

"Yep."

Neither spoke for nearly a minute. Rhia continued working. Finally, William said, "So, when you're done with this, if you want to, I'll be in the next section down. If you've got other plans, that's okay." He stood and walked away.

Rhia blinked away the wetness in her eyes and moved to the next corner of the box. Her wrench felt heavy in her hands.

When she finished the job, she put the wrench back on the cart and went to see what else needed to be done. Walking through an aisle between two rows of containers, towering walls of metal on both sides, she felt claustrophobic. She dropped her eyes to the ground when she passed a guard patrolling the area, then she saw Briana up ahead. The forewoman had her back to her and was giving directions to someone else. Just before she reached them, Rhia veered right and worked her way over to the next section. She hadn't known she was going to do it until her feet had turned, but now she hurried, glancing into each open box she passed.

The pale-blue door was open only a couple feet, and Rhia nearly walked right by it, but something made her stop and double-check. She leaned back and peered into the darkness. The bright sunlight outside made it impossible to see anything inside, but she'd only made it a few steps farther when the large door screeched open and William called out, "Hey!"

Rhia turned and saw him leaning out of the opening.

"I'm done with my thing, so I can help you if you want." She said it more quickly than she'd planned.

"Come in."

Rhia put her hands on her hips and stepped inside the box. He closed the door behind her, and she heard the clanking sound of the latch as it shut.

"So, we're working on wiring today," she began as she turned to face him.

William stepped close to Rhia. The filtered light that came through the single window behind her cast shadows across his face. "I'm sorry," he said. His voice was a low rumble that moved through her body like a deep earthquake. He swiped his hand across the bottom of his flat belly. "I said stupid things last time. I'm sorry, Rhia."

The stifled emotions of the morning flooded over Rhia like a tidal wave, and her face melted into tears. She covered her face with her hands and stepped forward, setting her forehead on William's shoulder as she cried. Surprised, he leaned back momentarily, then his body softened. He tucked his chin against the side of her head and slowly wrapped his arms around her. Resting his fingers lightly on the small of her back, he breathed in and out, the air ruffling the hair on the top of her head.

"I'm sorry," Rhia said. "It's just been so shitty."

"I know. I'm sorry." William's words were soothing and kind. "I shouldn't have acted like it was your fault I'm here. You had nothing to do with—"

"No, you were right." Rhia dropped her hands to his waist and pulled him closer. She tilted her chin up to rest on his shoulder and pressed her cheek against his ear. "I should have done more. I knew the Re-education centers were wrong. I just wanted to take care of myself. But, I swear, William, I honestly didn't know it was this bad. I didn't know it was like this."

"I know," William whispered.

"And I really wanted to figure out how to change it when I got out, but now I can't even get out!" Rhia's throat felt tight. "I saw the justice liaison this morning, and she said I'd be here at least two months. Even if they find Betty!"

Her breath was coming out in gasps, and William began to gently rub the middle of her back. "Shh, slow down," he whispered.

"How can they keep me here for two months? How can that be possible? I didn't do anything! And Captain Banks . . ."

The room swayed as fingers of darkness began to creep into the corners of Rhia's vision, and she buried her face in William's shoulder.

"Okay. It's okay. Calm down." He adjusted his arms, holding her tighter, pulling her closer.

"The things she says to me! I don't want to be anywhere near her, but she keeps finding me and saying this shit, and—"

"Rhia, listen to me." William set his hands on her shoulders and held her at arm's length. He looked into her face. "You need to take a deep breath. Just calm down." He wiped the tears from her cheeks then slid his hands down into hers. "Shh, it's okay."

Rhia's chest heaved as she slowed her breathing and tried to regain her composure. "I'm sorry. I'm just really overwhelmed."

"You saw the justice this morning?"

William's fingers squeezed Rhia's palm, and she felt his thumb slide just a fraction of an inch across her wrist. "Yes. She said even if they find my boat and all the goods are there, I'll still have to stay here for at least two months. There's a woman at the trade who said I'm a recruiter." Rhia gritted her teeth. "I'm not a recruiter! I've never been a recruiter! But the justice says they'll keep me here for Re-education anyway. How can they do that?"

"All it takes is one powerful person to say something like that, and you're fucked. That's the whole problem, Rhia."

"But it's not right!"

"No, it's not."

"And that bitch, Banks, is so horrible! What do I do? How can I keep her away from me?"

"Okay, look. If the justice said you're here for two months, there's not much you can do. Tumwater does her best, but once you're in here . . . You need to try to keep your head down and stay out of trouble, Rhia. Just do what they tell you to do."

"But how can I . . ."

"You have to separate it in your head. You have to make a place in your brain, like a box, where you put all the crazy shit that happens here, and then you need to be able to open it when they're around so they think you agree with them and close it when you're alone again. You need to be able to shut that box tight to protect the rest of your brain from getting infected."

"That might work when I have to recite things or pretend to agree, but I can't . . . What if she makes me do things? What if . . ." Rhia stopped.

William hesitated. "What do you mean?"

Rhia shrugged her shoulders.

"What are you talking about?" Now William's voice sounded angry, and he backed away from Rhia. "Did somebody say something about me?"

"What?"

"Did Ruth say something about me?"

"No. What do you mean?"

"Then what are you talking about?"

Rhia folded her arms across her chest. "I just . . . It's Captain Banks. She keeps saying these horrible things to me. Threatening me."

William looked away. "Banks? What did she say?"

"She keeps finding me. And she says she's going to do stuff. To hurt me."

"You're right to be scared of her. She's crazy."

"But how am I supposed to avoid her? How am I supposed to close some box in my brain if I know she can get to me at any time?"

William nodded, his face a blank stare. "That's the worst part, I suppose." He stepped away from Rhia and leaned his shoulder against the far wall. Staring at the rough plywood floor below, he said, "That's how they get to you. You feel like you can never let down your guard, because at any second, they could be there. You're never really safe from them. They have all the power and you have none." He sighed and, after a moment, lifted his chin to the side and caught her eye. "Maybe that's why we have to hold on so tightly to those moments when we do feel safe."

As William crossed the small room back to Rhia, he reached one hand out and touched hers. "She's trying to break you, to take over your mind, so you have to hold on to whatever you can. Find some way to stay in control. If you can do that, then she can't win."

Rhia stepped an inch closer to him, both hesitant and hopeful, feeling the light touch of his fingers on her wrist. "How do I do that?"

"I'll help you."

William slowly slid his rough hands up to the soft skin at the back of her arm. "Banks isn't here now, Rhia. She can't touch you in here."

Rhia wanted to tell him everything—Banks's threats, the touches. She wanted him to comfort her and tell her it was going to be all right. But telling him about the repulsive things Captain Banks said . . . If she were to confess these things, even in this dark and private place, would it repulse him? Would he wonder if she had encouraged Banks in some way, done something to invite it? She felt dirty and vile.

"What's wrong?"

"Nothing. I just . . ." Rhia looked around the room, as if

searching for the right words. "I need you to know, I don't want her to touch me."

"I know."

Rhia stepped closer to him and felt a flush rush to her cheeks, but held his gaze. "But . . . I want you to touch me."

"Rhia, I . . ."

Giving in to her feelings, her words spilled out, honestly, fearlessly. "William, when I look at you, I see more than just camaraderie and commiseration. When I stand close to you, I feel more than just your friendship."

William straightened his spine and breathed in deeply. His face was a troubled mix of hunger and fear. "Rhia," he whispered.

Rhia felt strong and brave. For the first time in more than a week, she felt in control of herself and her emotions. She raised her hand to his elbow and let her fingers rest lightly on his skin. Quietly but clearly, she said, "We've been working together almost every day. I like being close to you."

William swallowed. "Rhia, I don't know what you want from me."

"I want more."

"I only have a few weeks left here." His voice was deep and tremulous.

"We're here now." The front of Rhia's shirt brushed the front of his. She could feel her heart pounding. "Nobody else is here."

"I don't know if I can do this."

"What do you know?"

William shook his head but inched closer to her. "Rhia, I don't know anything anymore. Since you came here a week ago, everything's been different." His voice was full of emotion. His chest rose and fell. "I didn't expect this to happen. I didn't even want it, but I'd be lying if I said a part of me isn't glad that you're here. That sounds selfish, but getting to know you . . . feeling . . . something again . . . Maybe it means I'm not broken yet. Maybe it means this place hasn't destroyed every piece of my soul."

Rhia felt William's fingers slowly slide up her arms. After all the fear and frustration of the morning, she yearned for him to hold her, to help her forget, even if only for a while. She could feel the heat of his body, so close, and she wanted to melt into that fire, wanted it to burn away all the filth and contamination of Banks's words and touches, of the Center and its poison. She set her hand on his hip. She felt his body press against hers, and all thoughts of the world around her disappeared, dispersed like smoke before a strong wind. Banks and Deacon, boxcars and injections all faded away, leaving only a man and a woman alone in a dark and quiet room.

William skimmed his hand across the small of her back. Their lips brushed together gently, tentatively, as if they both doubted that this kind of simple pleasure could still exist. He pulled his head away from her and looked into her face. She saw the weight of the last year etched in the tiny wrinkles of his brow, the heaviness of it all pressing down on his shoulders like a blanket, and she wanted to comfort him, to share a kindness and love she knew he had gone long without. She raised her chin, kissed him tenderly, and felt herself soften as his lips responded.

As they both melted into that honeyed softness, their bodies began to remember the automatic movements of desire. He ducked one of his strong hands beneath the bottom of her shirt and slid it up her spine, fingertips tracing the bumps of each vertebra until his warm palm spread out and pressed into the center of her back.

Rhia stepped backward as they kissed, slowly leading him to the wall. She leaned against it and tugged at the edge of his shirt as he held her body in his arms. She arched her back and felt him slip the fingers of his other hand between the top of her pants and the soft skin of her hip. He held his weight just off her body; she longed to feel the pressure of his chest against her. Her hands clung to his shoulder blades, pulled his mouth deeper into her own, drew his body even closer.

Rhia moved her lips to his cheeks, his neck. William's breath was hot on her shoulder, and she felt him swell. She pressed her hips harder into his and slid her hand down his back to the firm, round muscles of his backside. She squeezed him and tilted her head back, inviting him to kiss her neck. He didn't move.

Her eyes opened, and she realized how tense his body had become. Was he holding his breath?

"William," Rhia whispered.

William exhaled and slowly pushed away from her. His eyes were closed and his jaw was clenched.

"William?"

"I'm sorry. I just . . ."

Rhia watched him for a moment, her confusion giving way to concern. "What's wrong?"

William turned and crossed the small room. "We can't do this here," he said. "Somebody could come in. We would get in a lot of trouble."

Rhia pushed herself away from the wall. "Um, I guess." She tucked a small curl behind her ear and looked at him. Even though she knew it was true, she felt rejected. "Is this because of what Banks did?"

"What? No. I'd better prop open the door," William said. "It's getting hot in here."

"Look, maybe we . . ." Rhia searched for the right words as she straightened her shirt. "Is it something I did? Something you heard?"

"No."

"Do you want me to leave?"

William tugged hard on the latch, and the squeaky door slid open several inches. When he turned around, he didn't look at her. "No. Look, I don't want you to think I don't want to. It's just, we really need to be careful."

"I know." Rhia tried to sound casual. "It's okay. Don't worry about it."

"No, Rhia." William crossed his arms in front of his chest. "I'm sorry. I don't want . . . I don't want you to be angry at me."

"I'm not angry."

"I still want to work with you."

"Got it." Rhia nodded and tried to smile.

"No. You don't understand." William seemed to be struggling for words. He shook his head. "It's not you. It's this place. If we weren't here . . ." He looked at her, finally, and lifted his hands.

"William, it's okay. I understand."

"You don't, but I don't want you to be angry. You and Ruth are the only women I can talk to here, and I don't want you to think . . ."

Suddenly remembering, Rhia said, "Ruth. You haven't seen her."

"No. What's wrong?"

Rhia hesitated. "You saw Banks beat her up at the session last week?"

"Is she okay?"

"She was gone for two days."

"What?"

"She didn't come back until Saturday, and she was really messed up. And now she's talking crazy, like she agrees with the whole thing. She's saying she was wrong and Deacon is right and that she's grateful for Re-ed now."

William cocked his head, confused. "No. No way."

"They had her for days. They must have brainwashed her."

His face looked troubled. "What did she say?"

"She said she was wrong to fight it all this time. She said she needs to make amends for all the things she's done wrong, and that she wants to get better and stop being a burden on society."

William swept his hand across his face, as though thinking hard. "Is she in the Village now?"

"No. She's still recovering, in our cell. She'll probably be up tomorrow."

"Okay." William nodded and, after a moment, turned away. "Okay."

Rhia watched him pace. "What can we do?" she said.

"I don't know. That doesn't make any sense. I just need to talk to her."

"I'll see her after dinner. Do you want me to tell her something?"

William swung about, as if suddenly remembering Rhia was in the room. "No. I have to think about this." He crossed his arms. "I'll talk to her tomorrow in Botany."

"Okay."

William hesitated, as if there was more he wanted to say, but he only shook his head and exhaled. "Look, I'll figure something out. I'll talk to Ruth. Um, for now, we should get some of this wiring done before the guards come check on it."

He headed to the two rolls of wire lying in the corner. "Come here. I'll show you what we need to do."

Rhia watched him for a moment more. She wanted to wrap her arms around his strong back, to feel the warmth and safety of his body again. She wanted him to fill the empty spaces in her heart, born over the past week in this hell, and she silently grieved for the happy moments she could have shared with him if they had met anywhere else. Her hatred for Miss Deacon, the Center, and Captain Banks grew and spread like mold throughout her stomach, black and blossoming as it coated her insides.

~

The sun had moved behind the western treetops, and Rhia and William had completed the wiring in three shipping containers. They began to clean up the tools and ready the site for tomorrow's work. Rhia wrapped a long section of the remaining wire around her arm, spooling it between her elbow and the crook of her thumb and index finger as she walked the length of the last boxcar.

"We got a lot done today."

William sorted the tools into a wooden crate. "Yeah, we work well together." He glanced up at her, an easy smile on his face.

Rhia tugged the spool of wire off her arm and added it to a small pile in the corner. "I guess I'll see you tomorrow in Botany."

Standing up, William brushed the dust off the front of his pants. "Sure."

"Can you try to get there early so we can talk to Ruth together?"

"I think it's better if I talk to her alone." William rubbed his hand over the top of his head.

"Oh. Okay."

"I've known Ruth longer than you have, and I think she might feel like we're ganging up on her. She'll respond better if I talk to her by myself."

"Sure." Again feeling rebuffed, Rhia crossed her arms and looked around the room.

"Nothing personal." When Rhia didn't reply, William crossed the room and touched her lightly on the elbow. "You okay?"

"Of course." Rhia forced a smile and asked the question. "So, are you and Ruth . . . together?"

William's eyebrows crinkled for a moment before realization flashed across his face. He smiled. "Me and Ruth? No. Not at all."

"I just wondered, because you seem to be close, and—"

"No, Rhia. Ruth and I don't have anything like that going on."

"Oh."

"Ruth and I understand each other. Here, in this place, you have to find people who think like you and stay close to them."

"Right. Got it." Rhia nodded and looked away, embarrassed. "Like you said earlier. We have to stick together."

"Right."

"That's why you and I work together—we're just trying to stick together."

William folded his arms across his chest, a wary look in his eyes. "I didn't say that."

Rhia sighed. "But you don't want anything more than friendship. I'm sorry if I was pushing too hard before. If you're not interested in me in that way, it's okay."

"Rhia, it's not that. There are things you don't know. Things about me."

"Then tell me."

William looked into her eyes. "I can't. Some things about this place are just too terrible to talk about."

Rhia didn't understand, but she could see how difficult these words were for him.

"Isn't it enough for us to be here together right now?" William continued. "To just feel safe with each other?"

"William," Rhia touched his hand. "It's okay. I understand." She smiled at him reassuringly and squeezed his fingers.

He took a deep breath. "Let's just take it slow, okay?"

Rhia nodded. "Okay."

William walked to the other side of the box and stooped to pick up the wooden crate. "We'd better get this stuff put away. They double-check all the tools every night to make sure we don't steal anything, and the dinner bell will ring soon."

Rhia tugged the heavy sliding door all the way open and held it as William stepped out into the fading light. She shoved it closed, followed him to the tool rack, and helped him unload the crate in silence. As the last wire cutter was hung up, he turned to her and forced a smile.

"Thanks for all your help today."

"No problem." Rhia squeezed his arm and smiled, leaning just slightly toward him. "Hey, I'll see you tomorrow, okay?"

"Okay. Thanks, Rhia." As William slipped by her, he rested his hand on her shoulder for the briefest moment before walking away.

Rhia bit her lip and turned to watch him make his way between the rusted metal hulks of the shipping containers.

When he disappeared around a corner, she headed in the opposite direction. Finally passing the last boxcar, she looked up at the green grass of the hill she would have to climb to return to her imprisonment. The low sun cast a pink glow over the white stone of the Big House, making it look large and ominous. Rhia's legs felt heavy and tired as she took the first steps.

~

Captain Banks leaned on the rail of her guard tower, high above the dozens of inmates making their way back to their cells and boxes. She'd been there most of the afternoon, keeping watch over the women and men below. She'd seen Rhia seek out William, hours before. She'd watched as they moved from box to box together throughout the afternoon. She'd noticed how close they stood, how they smiled and talked as they worked, the way they touched each other. She'd noticed. And she didn't like it.

~ Twelve ~

"Over here is our titration equipment. This is where Rhia's been working." Laura smiled uncomfortably at Ruth as she led her through the room. "The lab gets cleaned every night, but if you ever see anything where it doesn't belong, just let me or Nadine know." They moved to the far corner of the room. "We store some medicines and drugs here, but they're all in this locked cabinet, so you don't have to worry about coming in contact with anything dangerous. Any biohazards are—"

"Who has the key?" Ruth interrupted.

Laura hesitated. "Um, Nadine and I have keys, but honestly, we don't really ever have a reason to go in there. Ms. Brakille is the one who handles the relay of drugs to the nurses in the Center." She pushed a stray strand of brown hair behind her ear and pointed. "You should note the location of the fire extinguishers and the emergency call boxes, too. Here and over there."

Ruth nodded politely. She could tell Laura was uncomfortable having her here, and she tried to smile.

"This is where you'll be working." Laura brightened as she moved to a lab bench covered with paperwork. "These are the files from the first years of the Center, and we need to sort through them and pull out all the information about varicella vaccination. There's some question about whether or not the chicken pox vaccine alters the efficacy of the TB medicine we're working on now. So we need you to create a spreadsheet listing whether or not each subject had that vaccine."

Ruth stepped to the bench, flipped through a few of the files, and nodded. "What are these big black marks?"

"The names of the subjects have been blacked out so the study's anonymous. Each file has a number code assigned to it, and that code corresponds to the tissue and blood samples. You'll need to use that code in the spreadsheet." Laura leaned over the bench and opened one of the files. "There's a lot of information you don't need in here, but the varicella code is always the same—VC2976. It might be on any page, so you'll have to hunt for it. Here's one, where VC2976 is marked with the nurse's initials and the date it was given. So you know this subject had that shot."

"These are all former inmates?"

"Subjects. Yes."

"But you still have tissue and blood samples?"

Laura looked down at the desk and closed the file she was holding. "They're kept in cryostorage."

"Do these people know you're studying their flesh?" Ruth bristled for a moment before checking herself. In a subdued voice, she added, "I'm just curious about the protocol. Do you need to send out letters to them every time you do a study?"

"No."

"Do you still collect blood and tissue samples from the inmates?"

"Most of the people here now are part of other studies." Laura turned away. "Let me show you where we keep the logbooks. You'll need to start a new one for this project." She hurried toward the opposite side of the lab.

Ruth looked at Rhia, sitting on the other side of the room, and gave her a little wave. She knew Rhia'd been listening as Laura gave the tour. Rhia'd been staring at her for the last two days, and Ruth knew she was just waiting for her to lose her composure, lose her cool, and start ranting and raving against the Center again. But Ruth had gone through too much and worked too hard to stop now. *Miss Deacon wants me to be timid and contrite,* she thought. *And that's what I'm going to be.*

She'd felt a little sorry for William, huddled close to her before botany class started, trying to figure out what was going on, searching her eyes for some indication that this was all a mistake. The more calm and passive she remained, the more frustrated he became. At one point, she'd thought he might actually grab her and shake her, but then Ms. Brakille and the assistants walked through the classroom door and he had to give up.

"Because the logbooks are full of extremely important information," Laura continued, "they're kept locked up." She pulled a small metal ring of keys from her pocket; they were secured to her belt by a long, expandable cord. "When you get here, just ask Nadine or me to open the safe for you." She unlocked the large white safe mounted on the wall. Inside were dozens of logbooks of varying colors, some obviously old and full of years' worth of ink and pencil notations. "Here's a new one. Write your name, my name, and the title of the study on the front. Do you want me to help you set up a spreadsheet on the first page, or do you think you can do it?"

"I'm sure I can handle it." Ruth smiled. "I used to work in a lab of sorts myself. Before I came here, of course. I'm good at taking detailed notes and keeping things in order."

"Really? I didn't know that."

"Oh, it was a long time ago. But it'll come back to me."

"Okay. Well, just ask if you have any questions."

Ruth reached for the file. Halfway there, she turned. "Oh, and I want to thank you for letting me work in here. I think this work is really going to help me reach my goals."

Laura beamed and looked over at Nadine. Rhia just stared.

I can do this, Ruth thought. *This isn't as hard as I thought.*

~

Wednesday afternoon, Rhia made her way down the grassy slope to the Village alone. Ruth and Charlotte had been avoiding her, and part of her was glad. She felt sick every time Ruth talked about her new goals and praised the teachings of the Center. Her head was swimming with the Modern History lecture she'd sat through that morning, and she struggled to shake the phrases they'd been forced to repeat over and over. Each time the teacher said the word *progress*, they were instructed to stand and shout, "Men of the past created war and death! Women of the future create peace and life!" Each time the teacher said *forward*, they stood and shouted, "Down with violence! Up with hope!"

All that standing and shouting had exhausted Rhia and

left her feeling fuzzy and strange. The small box William had told her to make in her mind to hold the teachings and sayings of the Center felt swollen, as if it might burst at the seams and spill out into the rest of her. Her stomach was queasy, and the light lunch of warm beans, cold rice, and foraged greens wasn't sitting well.

The Village was buzzing with activity, with women and men hauling equipment and supplies between boxes. Rhia could hear the sound of hammers, saws, and drills in the heavy afternoon air as she made her way through the aisles. She looked into each box she passed, hoping to find William. As she rounded a corner, she nearly ran into Captain Banks.

Banks was standing with her hands on her hips and her green, sweat-rimmed cap pulled tightly down on her head. She looked like she'd known Rhia would turn this way and had been waiting for her.

"Where do you think you're going?"

"I'm working here today," Rhia mumbled. "This is where I'm supposed to be."

"Looking for anyone in particular?"

Rhia shook her head and kept her eyes locked on the middle of Banks's torso. "No."

Banks raised one thick eyebrow and cocked her head to the side. "Really? There's not a certain man you're trying to find?"

Dread rose in Rhia's throat, and she couldn't stop her eyes from darting up to Banks's face. She knew the woman would be able to see and feel the sudden fear that swept through her, and she tried to cover it. "Do you mean the man I was working with on Tuesday?"

"Uh-huh."

Rhia's words came out fast. "He's teaching me about

electrical wiring. It's a valuable skill. I thought it would be good to learn new skills while I'm here. Things I can use to help society after I leave." Steadying herself, she straightened her spine and looked directly at Banks. "The Center is providing me with many opportunities to improve myself. I hope to be a better citizen when I'm done here."

Captain Banks snorted with suspicion and stared at Rhia for a moment. Finally she said, "There are plenty of women who know about wiring. Find one of them." She slammed her shoulder into Rhia's as she walked past.

Rhia caught herself before falling. She rubbed her shoulder as she straightened up and started forward again. Her heart was still racing as she turned down the next aisle and saw William standing outside a box with two other women. One of them was Briana, the forewoman Rhia had worked with on Monday. She seemed to be giving directions, and William was nodding and gesturing with his hands toward the box behind them. As Rhia approached, she could hear the instructions.

"To wire an outlet so that only the top or bottom receptacle is switched and the other receptacle is hot all the time requires a four-way cable. We're only doing standard switched duplex receptacles, so three-way is enough."

"Even with the addition of rolled solar once the boxes get to towns?" William asked.

"The rolled solar panels have their own relays, to collect power even when the person isn't using it. That won't affect the receptacles."

"Got it." William looked up as Rhia approached. His eyes softened and a small smile curved the corners of his mouth. "Hey."

"Hey."

"I was just double-checking something. We can get to

work if you're ready."

"Okay." Rhia smiled at Briana and the other woman and followed William to the open door of the box. When she passed through the entrance, he rolled the door closed and turned. In one quick motion, he swept to her. He cradled her face gently in his hands and pressed his lips to hers. After a moment of shock, she closed her eyes and wrapped her arms around his waist, pulling him close. She felt the firmness of his chest against hers and the warmth of his hands against her back.

Rhia smiled awkwardly when they parted. "That's a nice way to greet somebody.

"It's good to see you."

"I thought you wanted to take this slow."

"I do."

Rhia sighed.

"How's your day going?" William asked as he moved a few inches away from her.

"I don't know. Modern History this morning was intense. I can still feel the rhythm of those chants in my bones, you know?" Rhia shook her head. "At least I'm still feeling it, I guess. A couple more weeks of this, and they'll probably be so ingrained in my body I won't even notice."

William dipped his chin down to catch her eye. "Hey, you have to keep fighting it, Rhia. You have to turn it off when you leave class. You have to remember, to switch back to normal mode."

"I know."

"Then switch it off."

Rhia pulled him closer and breathed in deeply as she held his gaze. "It's off." She leaned forward and slipped her hands around his back as their lips met again in a long kiss. They stood in the shadowy boxcar, holding each other. She tried to block out the pain and suffering that flowed through the Center like a hot mudslide, wishing the thin metal walls of the boxcar-turned-prison-cell in which they stood could stop it. Rhia thought if they could hold each other long enough, support each other strong enough, maybe, just maybe, she would be able to survive this place.

After a few moments, she leaned back. "Have you been waiting long?"

"No." He spoke quietly, his hands sliding to her hips.

Rhia squeezed the firm muscles in the small of his back. "I'm sorry. I got here as soon as I could." She felt him tense. She noticed the slightest change in the way he moved. His hands held her with urgency and longing even as his feet began to take subtle steps backward. She pretended not to notice, and kissed him again.

William mumbled, "I'm sorry we didn't get to talk yesterday after Botany."

"What did Ruth say?"

"Just what you said. She's turned over a new leaf. She's realized the only way out of the Center is by doing what Deacon says. I don't know. I've never seen her like this. We have to keep an eye on her." William sighed and smiled tentatively. "I'm glad you came to find me today."

"I almost didn't."

"Why?"

"Captain Banks stopped me and told me I shouldn't work with you."

William suddenly stood up straight, a puzzled look on his face. "Banks?"

Rhia saw the lines in his forehead deepen. She wanted to recover the moment that was slipping away. "It's nothing for you to worry about. She just saw us working together Tuesday and said I should find a woman to work with."

William let go of Rhia and stepped back. "She saw us?"

"That's what she said." Rhia reached her hand out and tried to pull him back.

"Why's she watching us? This isn't good, Rhia." He turned to the door. Light streamed in and the metal rollers squealed as he pulled it wide open.

"Wait a minute," Rhia said.

William turned back and with a pinched voice said, "Rhia, if Banks is watching us, we have to be more careful." He exhaled loudly. "I think it's best if we don't work together for a while."

"What?"

"Let's just give it a week and see if she backs off."

"You don't have to worry about it. You're not the one who should be scared of her." Rhia tried to control the tremble in her voice.

Confused, William stared at Rhia for a moment. He seemed to be about to say something, but shook his head dismissively. "No. Banks answers to Deacon. Tomorrow's Thursday. I don't want Banks to think anything's going on between us."

"What does Thursday have to do with it?"

He crossed his arms in front of his chest and looked out into the sunshine. "It's FEmS tomorrow. It's just not a good day to piss her off."

"There are good days and bad days to piss her off?"

"No. Look, I'm just . . ." William stopped. "You don't understand. After this I only have three more Thursdays left in here. Three more, Rhia."

Sunlight haloed his body as he stood in the doorway. That

deep sadness that she had seen in his face so many times before had returned, and it made her heart ache even as a pang of anger flared. "*You* kissed *me.* If you didn't want to start something, why did you do that?"

"Look, Rhia, I'm just saying we need to be careful."

"What are we doing here, William?" Rhia tried to keep her voice down, but saw a man walking by outside glance into the box. "I thought we were in this together. I thought we . . ." Her voice trailed off.

William stared at the plywood floor. "Can we just talk about this on Friday? Can you please just let this go until Friday?"

"What's different about Friday?" Rhia pulled him back into the stillness of the box. "Is it the FEmS tomorrow? Is something happening?"

"I don't know."

"Will they hurt John again? Do you know something?"

"I said I don't know."

Suddenly fearful, Rhia said, "Are you getting an injection? Is it your turn tomorrow?"

"No."

"Then what?"

"Thursdays are bad, Rhia. I just . . ."

"What?"

"It's hard for me to . . ."

"Why won't you talk to me?" Rhia searched his face for answers and was left even more confused.

William said, "Rhia, do you know what Captain Banks would do if she found out about us?" He took hold of Rhia's arm and faced her. "She would tell Deacon, and then I would get punished."

"Punished?"

"And from what you've said about Banks, *she'd* punish *you*. You have to be more careful. Jesus, Rhia, wake up! Banks owns you. She can do whatever she wants to you and nobody will stop her. I'm trying to protect us both here. You don't want to push their buttons. You need to be cautious."

Rhia stepped back. "Why would Deacon punish you? Why is she so interested in you?" She set her hands on her hips.

William stared at Rhia. His mouth opened and closed, as if he was trying to speak but couldn't make the words come out. Finally, he said, "Rhia, I do want to be with you, but it's not that simple. If we weren't in the Center, everything would be different. But we are, and we need to deal with it."

Rhia saw a cloud pass over his eyes and knew he was holding back. "I don't understand. You're the only person I can talk to. Banks is crazy, but I don't want to avoid you just because of her."

William winced and rubbed his right hand across the bottom of his belly. "Look, just give it a few days. Maybe she'll back off."

Her chest felt heavy. She breathed deeply and tried to pull herself together. She thought about her boat, her freedom, and her friends in Miranda, and it only made her feel worse. All the things she loved seemed like a distant memory. One week had felt like forever in this awful place. How could she hope to survive the next two months?

Rhia stretched her spine straight and tried to be brave. "Okay. You're right."

They stared at each other awkwardly for a moment, until Rhia finally spoke again. "I'll go find Briana. I'm sure she'll have a job for me." Her worn shoes clunked as she crossed the floor. With her hand on the edge of the door, she turned to look back at William and tried to smile. "I'll see you."

"Yep."

It took Rhia's eyes a few seconds to adjust to the glare. She lifted her hand to her forehead to shade her eyes and glanced around, looking for Briana. Not seeing her, she walked to the end of the line of boxes and rounded the corner to the next aisle. In the hot, still air, she stopped and set her hands on her hips. Briana wasn't there either.

Rhia noticed movement out of the corner of her eye and turned her head. It had come from the top of the closest guard tower. At first, she saw nothing in the shadowy darkness of the shelter. Then, squinting slightly, she saw what had been camouflaged. In shades of green, standing just inside the doorway, was Captain Banks. She was too far away for Rhia to see her face clearly, and yet Rhia's stomach suddenly felt queasy. She could imagine the smirk pulling at Banks's greasy face, and when she turned and walked away, she thought she could feel Banks's eyes boring into her back.

~ Thirteen ~

When the morning bells sounded on Thursday, the small cell Rhia, Ruth, and Charlotte shared was already stifling hot. Sweat soaked their sheets, and each woman took turns splashing cool water onto their faces from the tiny sink in the corner. By the time the cell door buzzed and clicked open for breakfast, beads of sweat had resurfaced on their foreheads.

The women made their way downstairs to the constant drone of recorded voices blaring out the motivational phrases that had become ingrained in their minds. "Grow More, Use Less! Follow the New Way Forward!"

When Rhia passed through the double doors of the cafeteria, she knew instantly that something was wrong. The rolling metal covers to the food line windows were shut tight, and the usual warm, wet smell of oatmeal and tea was absent.

At the front of the cafeteria, standing on one of the long tables, was Miss Deacon, flanked by Captain Banks and three other female guards. Miss Deacon had her chin tucked to her chest and her arms straight at the sides of her bright white dress. Her hair was perfectly coiffed in bouncy, loose curls that wreathed her face, and the bright sunlight behind her haloed her body, making her look as powerful and terrifying as an angel descending from above.

Rhia's sudden stop caused Ruth and Charlotte to bump into her as they pressed forward.

"What's wrong?" Ruth asked.

"Deacon's here."

Ruth looked over Rhia's shoulder at the spectacle within the cafeteria and snorted. As if checking herself, she cleared her throat and calmly said, "Hmm. I wonder why Miss Deacon's here?" She touched the small of Rhia's back and ushered her to a nearby table. All the women quickly found seats.

A hush fell over the cafeteria. For several seconds, no one moved, their eyes focused on Miss Deacon and the guards. Rhia chanced a glance at Banks and saw a stain of fresh, red blood in the corner of her mouth. Her lip was swollen, and her black eyes burned with anger. Each of the guards showed some sign of abuse—a scrape across the nose or a quickly bruising eye—and Rhia somehow knew from the way they stood at attention that it had been Miss Deacon who had dealt the blows.

At last, Deacon drew in a long breath and raised her head. Slowly taking in the whole room, she met the gaze of each woman seated before her. When her eyes fell upon Rhia, Rhia felt suddenly ashamed, as if Deacon had discovered something terrible about her and was deeply disappointed.

When she'd forced her chagrin on them all, Deacon sighed deeply. "It is with a heavy heart that I am forced to deal with such an unpleasant circumstance as this morning. Like you, I woke happy and refreshed, looking forward only to the opportunities that are held within the rising of a new sun. Like you, I expected this day to be full of nourishment, education, and introspection, and I am aware how much despair the following information will cause among you." She folded her hands gently in front of her skirt.

"You may notice that three of your friends are missing from the group this morning."

Several women glanced around before darting their eyes back to Deacon.

"Two of those women are currently in my custody and will undergo a thorough debriefing today. The other woman is dead."

She waited for the gasps that echoed through the room.

"The woman known as Carol Mueller was found this morning by her roommates with both her arms slashed open from the wrist to the elbow. She was lying in a pool of blood on the bottom bunk of their room. She held a box cutter in her right hand, clutching it even as she passed from this world." Deacon's face was a tight grimace, her eyes darting accusingly around the cafeteria. "And though I am loath to admit it, Carol Mueller must have had help in acquiring the deadly weapon with which she splayed open her own precious body. The usual searches and checks we perform each time you all return from the Village failed us this time, and a woman lies cold on a cement slab in the cellar because of it."

Rhia felt the air rush from her lungs. She had barely known Carol, and yet she felt her death like a punch in the gut. Guilt swelled in her. She should have tried harder to talk to her. Carol and John had saved her life, and she had all but ignored Carol since arriving here. What had she done?

Miss Deacon shook her head and began to pace along the top of the table. "Perhaps our usual searches and checks were not enough to save this poor woman. Perhaps I need to do a better job protecting the women in my care, especially when they are fresh and new here. Believe me, my friends, I carry a large burden of responsibility for this terrible and senseless death. I would give anything to turn back the clock twelve hours and help this poor soul in her darkest hour."

She faced the crowd and held her palms out, pleadingly. "I know it can be a difficult transition for many of you when you first arrive here. I understand the fear and uncertainty that comes when you are brought to the Center. Carol Mueller was overwhelmed when she saw her mate, John, undergoing rebirth last week. Perhaps she was afraid that he would outpace her progress here, that he would change into a new and loving man and find his inner peace before she could complete her own journey. Perhaps she was afraid he would reject her if she did not succeed as quickly as he. Can we ever know what was going on in her head as she made that final terrible decision to end her own life?"

Deacon dropped her arms to her side and continued, "No, my friends. We can never know the thoughts of a dead woman. We will never know the truth behind her decision. But I can tell you this"—she stepped forward to the edge of the table—"we can do everything in our power to find out who helped her. We can do everything in our power to root out the source of the vicious blade that Carol Mueller used to carve open her flesh. And I promise you, my friends, we will find the woman who assisted her, and she will pay."

Deacon relished these words, as if it were her greatest

moment, her grandest achievement to rise to the challenge of this situation. She glowed with purpose and pride even as Captain Banks seethed behind her.

"I know that each of you will do your best to assist us in the search of your rooms," Deacon continued. "I'm sure you are just as horrified as I am by this repugnant crime, and I know you will be willing to do whatever is necessary to ensure the security of our beloved Re-education Center Number Three. Therefore, I am relying on each of you to willingly follow the instructions of the guards as they conduct their searches this morning."

She stretched out her arms and gestured to the four guards behind her. "Captains Banks, Delormay, Juka, and Peen will be leading the searches. I leave you in their capable hands and look forward to resolving this situation as quickly as possible."

Rhia watched as Deacon stepped down from the table and walked, her head held high, to the double doors that led to the long hallway. As the doors swung closed, Rhia turned back to the front. The guards stood waiting, their faces hard and their eyes menacing.

Captain Banks stepped forward, stood at attention, then folded her hands behind her back. Her eyes remained fixed on a spot on the back wall as she addressed the inmates in a loud voice. "You will file quickly and quietly back to your rooms. You will stand by your bunk until two guards arrive at your cell to search it. You will cooperate with every instruction, or you will be punished. There will be no food until the search is completed."

The women sat motionless. After a moment, Banks looked down at them all and bellowed, "Get up! Now! Back to your goddamned cells!" There was a flurry of movement as everyone stood and rushed toward the doors.

Rhia, Ruth, and Charlotte pressed forward with the herd and made their way down the hall to their room. They stepped inside and stood in front of their bunks, facing the open door to the hallway. After a few minutes, the sounds of women bustling outside ceased, and the hall became quiet. Many minutes went by, and Rhia's legs began to feel tired as she stood waiting for the guards to come. She breathed heavily and looked at her roommates. "Has this ever happened before?" she whispered.

"No," Charlotte answered. "Not that I know of."

Rhia looked at Ruth, expecting her to say something, but her jaw was clenched tightly and her brow was furrowed into a hard line.

They waited for nearly a half an hour like that, until Rhia could stand it no longer. "This is crazy. We'll hear them coming, right? I'm going to sit down."

"The guards said to stand," Charlotte said.

Just then, the women heard the loud grinding sound of the main hall door being pushed open, and Rhia leapt back to standing. The hallway filled with the heavy clunking of boots as the guards stomped down the hall. It sounded like at least a dozen guards had been tasked with the search. From the sounds that came to Rhia's ears, she could tell they were starting at the cells closest to the main door. Guards' voices rang out as they entered cells, followed by the sounds of overturning bunks and the thuds of mattresses. After several minutes, the guards left the first cells and began to make their way systematically through the barracks. Bangs and deep voices echoed through the hall, but no one cried out. No shouts or protestations were heard from the inmates.

Maybe it won't be so bad, Rhia thought. Maybe the guards

were simply searching the cells. Then she remembered the vicious look in Captain Banks's eyes as she stood before them in the cafeteria, and she knew she wouldn't escape that anger. The open cell door stood before her like a gaping hole through which a monster would soon appear.

The sounds of the guards came closer. They were only a few rooms away now. Rhia felt a slow drip of sweat trickle down her spine as she stood motionless in front of her bunk. She could hear Ruth's breathing from the other side of the small room, heavy and deep. All three roommates could sense the guards' approach.

"I hope they find the person who helped that poor woman," Charlotte whispered.

"Maybe nobody helped her," Rhia said.

"I just feel so sad for her."

Rhia thought back to the few days she had shared Carol and John's camp. She remembered the way the couple had worked together, moving in harmony in the small home they had made for themselves. Her knees felt weak, and she struggled to push the swelling regret from her mind. "Feel sad for yourself." Rhia's voice cracked as she spoke. "Those guards are pissed off."

Charlotte stood up straight and breathed in deeply. "If it's for the good of the Center, I'm willing to do my part."

Rhia looked at Ruth out of the corner of her eye. Her face was stoic.

"You okay?"

Ruth didn't answer for a moment. Turning to look at Rhia, she finally whispered, "If it's for the good of the Center, I'm willing to do my part."

A chill passed through Rhia at the dead look in Ruth's eyes. She opened her mouth, but no words would come. Ruth turned away.

Four guards passed by the open doorway, heading to the next cells down the hall, and then Captain Banks stepped slowly into view. She stood straight and hard in the doorway, sweat rings darkening her armpits and dark lines streaking down her torso. Her arms hung loose at her sides, and her hat was tucked into her hip pocket, revealing the glistening stubble of her hair. The cut at the corner of her mouth had reopened, and a slow trickle of blood had made its way down her lip. With a sensuous slide of her tongue, she licked the blood away and looked up at Rhia.

"Stand together at the john." Banks's voice was barely a whisper, but all three women quickly obeyed. They huddled close to the toilet, trying to become as small as possible. Banks stepped into the room, followed by another, younger guard Rhia didn't recognize. The name Caldwell was freshly stitched on the front of her uniform, and she hesitated, as if waiting for directions from Banks. When none came, she stepped to Rhia's bunk and got onto her hands and knees to look under it.

Banks moved to the wooden trunk that held the women's single change of clothes, banged open the lid, and began to toss shirts and pants around the room. When it was empty, she swept her arm around the inside, grabbed the back edge of the trunk, and heaved it onto its side. She looked behind it before turning and joining Caldwell, who was working over the bunks.

With efficient movements, they tugged the sheet and pillow from each bed, smashing and pulling at the bedding to check for contraband before throwing it all into the hall. They dragged the mattresses off the sagging metal springs next, slid their hands over the seams and lumps, and unceremoniously heaved them into the hall as well.

Together, the two guards grabbed the side rails of the first bunk bed and pulled it away from the wall. The four metal feet screeched loudly across the cement floor. They looked behind and below it before turning to the second bunk bed and doing the same. The small cell was now a jumble of faded red clothes and flimsy metal and springs, and the guards stomped and climbed their way around the room checking every corner.

When they had completed their search, Banks and Caldwell, sweating heavily from their exertion, turned to Rhia, Ruth, and Charlotte. Banks drew a deep breath before speaking.

"Take off your clothes."

No one moved. Banks dropped her chin to her chest and glared at the three of them, huddled silently at the toilet.

"Take off your clothes." She enunciated each word, her voice a little louder now and her face a scowl.

Charlotte was the first to obey. She stepped away from the toilet, slipped out of her shoes, bent over, and pulled off her socks. She handed each item to Caldwell, who briefly checked them and tossed them into the hall. Ruth stepped forward and began to undress as well, handing her shoes and socks to the young guard as Banks watched. Both women pulled off their shirts, bras, pants, and underwear, passed them to the guard, and stood naked in the middle of the small cell.

As Rhia began to kick off her own shoes, Captain Banks held up one hand and said, "You wait." Banks stepped close to Ruth and Caldwell stepped in front of Charlotte.

"Raise your arms," Banks said.

When the women complied, Banks slid her hands quickly over the length of Ruth's body, and Caldwell did the same to Charlotte.

"Arms down. Bend over."

Ruth bent forward, and Banks rubbed her hands roughly

over her scratched and scabby scalp. She pushed Ruth's head to the side, and Ruth turned around. Banks roughly pulled her buttocks apart, leaned sideways, and looked briefly between her legs.

"Stand up."

Banks nodded to Caldwell, who had completed a similar search of Charlotte. "Take these two out."

The younger guard hesitated. "But, ma'am," she mumbled. "Protocol says we both need to be—"

Banks spun toward Caldwell and spat, "I'm your senior officer. You do what I tell you." She gestured toward the door. "Take them out. Now!"

Caldwell glanced at Rhia. After a moment, she turned and led Ruth and Charlotte into the hall.

Still pressed into the corner by the toilet, Rhia looked to her roommates for help, but they kept their eyes down and filed quickly out the door. The sounds of the searches being conducted down the hall and the banging and slamming of furniture and bedding faded away as the pounding of her own heart filled her ears.

When everyone had left the room, Captain Banks turned to Rhia and put her hands on her hips. "Come here," she said.

Rhia's feet wouldn't move.

Banks crossed the room to Rhia and held out her hand. "Come on out here, gorgeous. You're hiding in that corner like a little mouse." When Rhia still didn't move, Banks reached out and took her wrist, pulling her firmly into the center of the room. "You saw what we did. I just have to check you for weapons."

Rhia felt the bile rise in her throat.

"Do you need me to help you get undressed?"

"No." She kicked off her shoes and bent sideways to pull

off her socks. She handed them both to Banks, who took them and tossed them aside without checking them. Rhia's hands trembled as she gripped the bottom of her shirt and pulled it up over her head. She unhooked the back of her bra and tugged it off, then quickly handed both items to Banks. She rounded her shoulders, trying to curl into herself in an attempt to feel less exposed.

Banks looked down at the faded red shirt in her hands. Slowly, she raised it to her nose and drew in a long breath. "It smells like you." She juggled the shirt in one hand for a second as if considering it. "Maybe I'll keep this as a memento. Then I can smell you whenever I want to." Then, cocking her head to one side, she said, "Take off your pants." She tossed the shirt to the floor and looked into Rhia's eyes. "Take them off."

Though the day was already hot, and the small cell was stifling, Rhia's body shivered. Banks was close, and Rhia had to bend sideways to slide her pants and underwear off without touching her. She handed them to Banks without meeting her eyes.

Banks held the pants for a moment, silently rubbing the folds of fabric between her fingers. "You must feel pretty bad today, don't you? That woman, Carol Mueller, she was a friend of yours, wasn't she? She was probably going to tell Tumwater that you didn't do anything wrong. Maybe help you get out of here. Huh." Banks grunted and tossed the pants to the floor. "It's too bad she's dead."

She looked up at Rhia and grinned. "You want me to tell you a secret? I know nobody helped that idiot off herself last night. This whole search is a waste of time. And, believe it or not, I don't enjoy touching all these naked-ass women all morning. Frankly, most of them are disgusting. But here I am, and here you are, and I have been ordered to search you for any weapons or illegal materials. So,"—she stepped close to Rhia, her face only inches away—"I get to do my duty and search you."

"My roommates are right outside," Rhia whispered. "And that other guard."

"So?"

"They could come in any time."

"You'd rather we had more privacy?"

Rhia hesitated. The rotting smell of Captain Banks's mouth filled Rhia's nostrils. "I'm just saying, this isn't the best place." Rhia's stomach turned and she struggled not to vomit. "Maybe later."

"Maybe both." Banks's voice was cold and hard. "Lift up your arms."

Rhia slowly raised her trembling arms above her head.

Banks reached up abruptly and grabbed Rhia's wrists. She pulled them down behind Rhia's back, holding them together in her left hand as her right hand moved to Rhia's breast. Banks pressed her body close as her fingertips slowly glided down over each of Rhia's ribs to the curve of her waist. Rhia could feel Banks's small, hard breasts pressing against her own, and she tried to curve away. Banks pressed her palm against the top of Rhia's hip and slid it around to the small of her back, drawing her in, pulling her close. She tilted her chin to the side and slowly moved her mouth toward Rhia's. Just before their lips touched, Banks stopped. She held Rhia for several seconds without moving.

Instead of love or passion in Banks's eyes, Rhia saw only cruel laughter and disgust.

"You thought I'd do it, didn't you?" Banks whispered. "You actually thought I'd kiss you. You arrogant bitch." She squeezed Rhia hard, all sensuality gone from her grasp, replaced by rough brutality. "You think you're so beautiful. You think you can do whatever you want. Did you really think I wanted you?" Her voice began to rise. "Did you think you could just fuck your way around this place? Huh? Did you think you'd get special attention from me?"

"No, I—"

Banks pulled away from Rhia, took one step backward, and with all her strength swung forward and slammed her fist into Rhia's stomach. Rhia crumpled to the floor and lay there struggling for breath as pain seared through her body. Banks bent over Rhia and grabbed her by the hair. She pulled Rhia's head backward and, with her other hand, squeezed her jaw hard.

"You're all alike." Banks hissed. "You think I want you? You think I'd want a bitch like you? I fucking hate you." Banks let go, raised her fist, and punched Rhia hard across the cheek.

Blinding light flashed across Rhia's vision, and she fell sideways. She covered her head with her arms as her legs instinctively drew up to protect her belly. Banks jumped on top of her and began to rain more blows down upon her. Rhia tried to get away, tried to get her legs underneath her, but Banks was all over her, clawing and hitting and kneeing into her. Banks wrapped her forearm around Rhia's neck and pulled back hard, cutting off her oxygen. The last things Rhia remembered were the taste of metal in her mouth, the smell of urine, and the full weight of Captain Banks collapsing onto her back.

~

From the hallway, Ruth could hear successive thuds and grunts coming from inside the cell. *She'll be okay*, she thought. *I've had worse.* Out of the corner of her eye, she watched the young guard, Caldwell, bite her nails and pace back and forth. Charlotte hung her head and covered her face with her hands.

"I fucking hate you." Banks hissed, and they heard gasping and choking sounds.

"Shit," Caldwell whispered, and lunged back inside the cell.

Ruth heard a scuffle, then the young guard began to shout. Ruth moved to the doorway and looked inside.

"Shit! Captain Banks? Oh, shit!" Caldwell spun around and shoved Ruth aside as she ran down the hallway. In seconds, a flurry of guards descended upon the room, each as unsure what to do as the first. Finally, one of the captains appeared and shoved her way past the gawking guards and Ruth and Charlotte.

"What happened here?" Captain Juka shouted.

"I don't know," Caldwell answered. "Captain Banks told me to wait in the hall while she searched this woman, and then I heard them fighting and came running in."

"Why is Captain Banks unconscious?"

"She was choking that woman. I didn't know what was going on. I stunned her to stop it."

"You stunned Captain Banks?"

"No!" Caldwell seemed terrified. "I stunned the woman! But the captain was on top of her!"

"Jesus, what wattage did you use?" Captain Juka whispered. She ran her hands through her short brown hair and looked around at the half-dozen guards squeezed into the doorway. "What a fucking mess. Tailen, Meldon, you two stay here. All the rest of you, get back to work! Caldwell, not you!

Christ." As the guards dispersed, she saw Ruth standing naked in the doorway. "You—is this your cell?"

"Yes." Ruth answered.

"Get your clothes on and wait in the hall."

Ruth slowly picked up their scattered clothing, passing some to Charlotte and stealing glances at Rhia and Banks.

"Okay. You three." Captain Juka gestured to the guards awaiting her orders. "Carry Captain Banks to the infirmary, and put this woman in the cellar." She turned to leave the room, then added, "Don't let Banks down there. I want to talk to each of them separately when they wake up."

Ruth watched as two guards lifted Rhia from the floor. Blood trickled from her lips, and there were red welts rising on her back and shoulders. Ruth kept her face stoic as she watched them drag Rhia from the cell.

~ Fourteen ~

William and his three roommates woke to the sound of their boxcar being unlocked and the door grinding open. Four guards burst in. The guards ushered them out into the warm morning air and turned over everything inside, without telling them why. After the men had been stripped and searched, they spent the next hour picking up their belongings and making sense of the trashed boxcar. The breakfast bell never rang.

Later, guards walked through the aisles between boxes and called out orders. William stepped to his open door and listened—FEmS was canceled that morning; stay in your boxes. Hungry and fearful, the men talked quietly among themselves. As grateful as he was to skip FEmS, William worried about Rhia and Ruth, about whatever this trouble was, and he began to fear the repercussions and retaliations he knew would come in the days that followed.

Lunch was not served at noon. Instead, guards walked through the aisles again. They shouted orders for the men to begin their usual work in the Village. William checked out a shovel and a pick from the toolshed and made his way to the hole where a new septic tank pit had been started. As he dug, his eyes often drifted up the hill.

As the afternoon hours passed, women came out in ones and twos and made their way down the grassy slope to work alongside the men. Fresh bruises and scrapes blotted many faces. Whispers began to pass between the boxes about a dead woman in the Big House, and searches happening there. William watched for Rhia, but didn't see her.

~

Ruth squatted on the great green hill as women silently passed her. Her stomach rumbled as she plucked the heat-wilted young dandelion leaves from among the tall blades of grass and wild plantain at her feet. She had a small collection of leaves and flowers tucked into a pouch she had made out of the bottom of her shirt, and when she had nearly three cups' worth, she gathered the fabric together, stood, and walked toward the hangars.

Without the usual bells and gongs to direct the inmates, Ruth had to guess at the time. Judging by the position of the sun, she thought it must be nearly two o'clock. Sitting in the narrow strip of shade cast by Hangar 3 with her foraged lunch, she picked at the mixture of bitter and sweet herbs and plants. As she ate the salad, she paused to look at the sky. Scattered clouds had been gathering in the west since the morning, with wispy mare's tails soaring on a high breeze that hadn't yet made its way down to her. The top portions of the few cumulus clouds were white and puffy, but the bottoms were turning gray.

Ruth smiled and popped the last long dark-green leaf into her mouth. She looked at the ground and touched a few of the rocks that lay in the gravel around her. After a minute, she selected an oblong piece of granite. It was speckled white and black and was big enough to fit nicely into the palm of her hand. She tucked her legs beneath her, brushed her free hand on her pants, and stood up. From across the field, two guards spotted her and began to walk in her direction. Ruth didn't mind. She knew she could talk her way around them. There was a spring in her step as she walked toward the Village.

~

A small electric cart bounced along a dilapidated road fifty miles south of the Center. When the blacktop became too overgrown with weeds and saplings, the cart slowed to a stop, and the quiet hum of the engine was silenced. Agnes Tumwater stepped out of the cart and looked around. She could hear the top layer of leaves in the forest whispering in the faint breeze, but the tall grass growing from the cracks and breaks in the road remained still. She breathed deeply and pursed her lips.

After a minute, she reached into the front seat and pulled out a small paper map. It was dog-eared and dirty, but she traced her finger along a line to the trailhead indicated. Looking up, she surveyed the area until she spotted a break in the trees. *I'm getting too old for this,* she thought. *If the boat's there,*

I'm sending someone else to deal with it. She tucked the map into her back pocket and started walking.

~

When Rhia opened her eyes, she was lying naked on a metal surgical table in a small, dimly lit room. She felt dizzy. Her whole body hurt. Water was dripping somewhere in the distance, and the air stank of mildew. She tried to sit up, but the thick canvas straps positioned across her shoulders, waist, and knees held her down. The strap that dug into her lower belly was also wrapped twice around each wrist, holding them close to her hips.

Don't panic, Rhia thought as she tried to calm her quickening heartbeat. Confused, she swiveled her neck from side to side trying to see the room around her. It was empty except for the table she was on. The unframed doorway was an open, gaping rectangle that looked like it'd been hacked out of the old cement wall itself. She lay her head back down on the cold table and fought to keep the tears from her eyes.

Eventually, Rhia heard the low scraping of a door somewhere down the hall and the soft clunk of boots approaching. The sound stopped just outside of the room before a guard in green camouflage ducked her head to enter. Her hat was pulled low over her forehead, and Rhia felt terror rush through her. When the woman looked up, and wasn't Captain Banks, relief flooded her veins.

"You're awake." The woman looked at an open file folder as she walked to the edge of the table. She stood up straight, the top of her hat nearly touching the low ceiling, and looked into Rhia's eyes. "I'm Captain Juka. I need to ask you some questions."

Rhia's lips opened and closed, trying to speak, but her mouth was so dry. She swallowed hard and said, "Yes, ma'am."

"What happened between you and Captain Banks in your cell earlier today?"

Rhia hesitated. "Nothing."

"What happened?" Captain Juka's voice was clear and direct.

"She was searching our room and told everyone to leave so she could search me. She told me to strip, then became angry and started hitting me."

Captain Juka's gaze was calm but her jaw was tight. After a moment, she sighed and glanced around at the dingy, moist walls. She lifted the file in her hand and said, "Captain Banks has been in charge of all your transfers and checks. Every time you meet with an official or have business to complete, she is the one who tracks you and moves you. Why is that?"

What could Rhia say? This unknown guard could be just as cruel as Banks, just as demented. They were both guards, both captains, and Rhia knew that camaraderie and duty likely meant that they would stick together.

"Are you two in a sexual relationship?" Captain Juka pressed. "Was this all over a breakup?"

"No."

"Then what? Why is Captain Banks so involved in your time here?"

"Ask her."

"I will, when she wakes up."

"What?"

"She's unconscious upstairs. You were shocked by a guard, and she was touching you, so she felt the current, too." Captain Juka shifted her weight and tilted her head. "So, if you have something to tell me, now is the time to do it."

Thoughts of punishment blossomed in Rhia's mind. She was naked and strapped to a surgical table. She was defenseless, and after all she had seen and heard in her short time at the Center, she could imagine the brutality that could rain down upon her if she spoke out against Banks. They could trump up any excuse to keep her here. They could keep her here forever.

And yet, in the same breath that dragged such utter despair into her lungs, there was a fraction of courage. She couldn't abandon hope. There must still be power in truth. She had been in the Center for ten days, and she recognized this as a crucial moment that would decide her fate. Not the fate of how much time she would spend here or what punishment she would be made to endure—those things were as capricious as the wind—but rather the fate of her mind, her soul.

Rhia suddenly knew it didn't matter what Captain Juka would do. She could beat her or torture her, but Rhia had to speak, no matter the consequences. She had to hold on to the power of truth and believe in the tenacity of her spirit.

"Captain Banks has been harassing me since she arrested me." Rhia stared at the damp ceiling, her voice gravelly and quiet. "She's threatened to rape me, and she told me she was able to prove my innocence but wouldn't do it because she wants to keep me here. In my cell, she told me she hated me because I thought I was beautiful, and that I thought I could get out of anything. Then she began punching and kicking me. I didn't touch her."

Captain Juka stood motionless for several seconds, watching Rhia's face. Finally, she nodded sharply and snapped the file down to her thigh. She turned and left the room.

Rhia pressed her quivering lips together, trying to not

make a sound even as her chest and shoulders heaved with sobs. She felt the walls close around her. She could smell the low ceiling. Hell was not a pit of fire; it was a dark, wet hole in which she could be buried alive.

Minutes later, Captain Juka returned, a small bundle tucked under her right arm. She dropped the bundle onto the floor next to the table and began untying the canvas straps that held Rhia down. When the last band was removed, she stepped back, her hands on her hips.

"Get dressed and head back to your cell."

Rhia wiped her arm across her tear-streaked face, slowly rolled to her side, and pushed herself to sitting. The room spun around her, and she gripped the edge of the table for support.

"What about Captain Banks?" Rhia whispered.

"I'll take care of it. Try to stay away from her."

"How do I do that?"

"Do your best."

"Why are you helping me?"

Captain Juka looked at the floor and sighed. "Believe it or not, Ms. Malone, I took this job because I wanted to help people."

She looked up, and Rhia saw tired determination in Juka's eyes, resolution set in her jaw. The captain was in her late twenties. Her light eyes were surrounded by long, thick lashes and her features hinted still at a youth and vigor that simmered just below the surface. Above all, Rhia saw a connection, something shared and kindred with this woman, and her heart twinged. Had they met in a different time in a different place, they could have been friends.

Captain Juka blinked and breathed out the smallest sigh. "You'd better go before Captain Banks wakes up." She turned to leave.

When Juka reached the threshold, Rhia said, “Thank you.”

Without turning, Juka nodded once, and was gone.

~ Fifteen ~

William hit the hard clay layer about an hour into his digging. He stood up straight, stretching his back, and tossed the shovel outside the pit. He leaned forward, reaching for the pickax that lay on the ground nearby, and saw a shadow pass over the area. Resting his elbows on the dry grass, he looked up to the sky. It was the same deep blue as the last two weeks, but clouds were beginning to gather and grow in the west. As he watched, another stray puffy cloud passed over the sun, and its shadow darted across the land around him. Though the sun still beat down hot on his shoulders and back, there was relief in those brief shadows, and the hint of change in the weather. Lifting the pickax, he went back to work in the hole.

"Hey, Bri," William called to the forewoman as she walked past a while later.

"How's the pit going?" Briana stopped and looked into the deepening hole.

"Good. The pickax is getting through the clay layer. Hey, are the guards done searching the women's cells?"

"Yeah. Couple hours ago."

"We're short on staff this afternoon. Were some of the women detained?" William tried to sound casual, leaning on the long handle.

"Some of them haven't come out yet. Sorry, I don't know what's going on any better than you do." Briana gave him a sympathetic look and walked away.

William sighed and lifted the pickax. He swung it high over his shoulder, preparing to bring it down into the dry dirt and rocks below him, but stopped. Two guards were approaching, and he somehow knew they had come for him.

His heart sank. It hurt most to realize he had allowed himself to hope that today would be different from all the other Thursdays. Worrying about Rhia and wondering about the searches had almost distracted him enough to let him believe Deacon had forgotten about him, but as the guards stepped to the edge of the pit, he knew he'd been fooling himself. He wished he could lie down in the pit and hide under the soil, rock, and clay he'd excavated.

"Let's go," one guard ordered.

William drew in a long breath and looked down at the pickax in his hands. He gripped the handle tightly, turning his knuckles white. *Three more weeks,* he thought. *You can do this.* The hint of a cool breeze wafted across the back of his neck, the first inkling of wind he had felt in many hot, still days. The breeze tickled the fine hairs on his nape, and vexed and nettled him as much as pleased him. *Three more weeks.*

He dropped the pickax and climbed out of the hole.

~

The heavy door of the laboratory opened with a squelching sound. The equipment hummed in the cool, dry air. Ruth glanced around the white room. Nadine and Laura were sitting side by side on two stools along the far wall. Their shoulders touched as they leaned toward each other, and Nadine moved her hand to the small of Laura's back. They turned, smiling in welcome as Ruth approached, and Laura's eyebrows crinkled together.

"Hi, Ruth. Where's Rhia?"

"She'll be here shortly."

"You're really late today. Is everything okay?"

"I'm fine, thank you." Ruth made her way to her desk and began to arrange the few papers there. "Laura, could you please use your key to open the cabinet for me? I need to get out the logbook."

"Sure."

Laura crossed to the other side of the room and pulled the ring of keys from her pocket. The long cord that held them to her belt whizzed as she pulled the key up to the lock and opened it. "We heard your rooms were searched today." When Laura turned, she gasped, startled to see Ruth right behind her. "Oh! Sorry. Didn't see you there."

"Here I am." Ruth smiled gently.

"Here's your logbook," Laura said, handing it to Ruth.

"Thank you."

"So, were they?"

Ruth cocked her head to the side, a puzzled look on her face.

"Your rooms. Were they searched?"

"Oh, yes. The guards did a very thorough job, but I'm afraid they found no evidence that would suggest anyone helped poor Carol slit her wrists."

Laura's face pinched slightly at the mention of the suicide, and she looked away. "I'm sorry."

"Sorry the guards didn't find anything?"

"No," Laura mumbled. "Just . . . It's really awful."

Ruth sighed deeply and smiled. "Yes, awful is the right word. I am full of awe. Amazement. To think of what that woman went through . . . Do you know, poor Carol had been here less than two weeks, and she already realized there was no hope of ever getting out alive? She already understood that her time here would be filled with so much pain, and dread, and anguish, that it would either break her mind or break her body. I am in awe of her."

Laura leaned back against the edge of the lab bench and slowly tucked her hair behind her ear. "Um . . ."

"To think that poor Carol figured this all out in less than two weeks!" A small laugh bubbled in Ruth's throat. She reached out and touched the sleeve of Laura's lab coat. "Do you know I've been here for more than two years? Can you believe it?" She heard the quiet squeak of the wheels under Nadine's stool being pushed away from her desk. "That's a long time! Too long, really. If anything, I guess I'm a little embarrassed that it's taken me so long to realize what Carol understood so quickly."

Ruth saw Laura's eyes dart over her shoulder and knew Nadine was walking toward them.

"Let me ask you both something," Ruth said. "Do you think you'll ever leave the Center?"

"Of course." Laura tried to smile. "Nadine and I told you,

we're just doing internships here, Ruth. This is just an internship."

"Right. And then you'll head off to your college, and learn everything about botany, and probably become rich and powerful someday."

"No," Laura laughed mirthlessly. "We just want to help people."

"Which people?"

"Sick people."

Ruth shook her head. "You're too late, my friends. The sickness has already spread. It's not about viruses and germs anymore. It's in our minds." She jerked her index finger up to her temple. "The world has become full of sick people who think it's okay to oppress others to get what they want. The people with all the power think they can beat us and maim us, and do you know the greatest sickness of all? Do you? It's that they can. There are no repercussions. It doesn't matter if a woman or a man is in charge. Being in charge turns you into a different gender altogether. You become a boss, and you lose your gender. You lose your humanity. You're not even human anymore."

"Ruth," Laura said, "I know you're upset about your friend, but the world isn't as bleak as that." Nadine had stepped close to her, and they shot quick looks at each other out of the corners of their eyes.

Ruth laughed. "I don't think it's bleak! I told you, I'm in awe. This is the moment! This is the time!" She stepped closer to Nadine and Laura. "You two have found yourselves at a crossroads, and you need to decide which side you're on. You're young and fresh, and you don't have to follow the herd. You are the ones who will help shape the future." Her voice had become quiet and pleading. "Some day you'll look back on this day and realize that everything started here. You'll understand that this day was the end of the New Way, and the beginning of the True Way." Her eyes grew wide. "This is a day you will never forget."

As Laura and Nadine stared, transfixed, Ruth clenched the rock she'd been hiding in her hand. She swung her arm forward with all the force she could muster. Her fist connected with Laura's jaw, just in front of her ear, sending Laura careening sideways and backward into the lab bench and knocking Nadine off-balance. Before Nadine could correct for it, Ruth drew back and swung again, this time hitting Nadine below the cheekbone.

Stunned, the two women flailed onto the floor, beakers and instruments clattering around them. As they tried to lift themselves onto their hands and knees, Ruth kicked Nadine hard in the ribs and shoved her knee into Laura's back. She pulled a long length of plastic-coated electrical wire from inside her pants and, wrestling Laura's arms behind her back, tied her wrists tightly together.

"I'm sorry to have to do this." Ruth bound Nadine's wrists, as well. "I know you're friends with Rhia, and you've both tried to be nice to me." She grunted as she dragged them one by one to the central lab bench and tied them separately to two metal table legs that were bolted to the floor.

"Ruth, stop," Laura pleaded. She spat out blood that had collected in her mouth.

"Don't worry. I'm not going to hurt you." Ruth undid Laura's belt and pulled off the ring of keys.

"What are you doing?" Nadine growled as her arms struggled against the table leg.

"I saw Ms. Brakille heading up to the Big House." Ruth said. "Was she delivering more of your poison?"

"Ruth, we don't have anything to do with—"

"You work in here." Ruth paused and looked at Laura. "You're just as guilty as them. If Rhia hadn't vouched for you, I'd have to stop you, too. Be grateful."

When Laura and Nadine were secured, Ruth hurried to the large metal cabinet at the back of the room. She fiddled with the keys for a moment until she found the right one, then she swung the cabinet door open. Small bottles and packages crashed to the floor as she rooted through the shelves.

A smile blossomed across Ruth's face as she lifted a small glass vial from the shelf. She let her thumb slide across the smooth label as she read out the name. Psilocox. One by one, she pulled down four vials and set them on the table beside her, along with a large white cardboard box. She began to hum softly, opening the box and pulling out syringe after syringe, inserting the sharp needles into the vials and drawing up large quantities of the hallucinogenic drug.

~

Tumwater could hear the sound of the surf for several minutes before she could see it. The forest was a shadowy tangle of brush and branches, and she picked her way lightly along the rough path, careful not to trip on the exposed roots and mossy ground. When she finally pushed aside the last of the green branches and stood on the edge of the sandy cliff, Thread the Needle dominated her view, the massive sea stack black and towering just past the rocky beach and breaking waves.

As Tumwater's eyes adjusted to the light, she looked out at the dark-gray water. It stretched as far as she could see, connecting in a blur at the horizon, barely differentiated from the thick clouds that had gathered during the last hours. She scanned the sea for the *Elizabeth Maru*. Pulling the map from her pocket, she checked her location again. She heaved a heavy sigh and scanned the horizon one more time. There was no boat in sight.

~

The two guards marched William up the hill and into the main building of the Center. They turned left in the lobby and entered the long, dry wooden hall, their boots clunking on the old floor as they pulled William along. He could feel the weight of his own body and the heaviness of his arms and legs as they drew nearer to Deacon's office. He knew what was coming, and he raced to stow away the feelings and emotions that bubbled up inside him—the rage, the revulsion, and the shame that threatened to consume him.

Too quickly, they were standing outside Deacon's heavy wood door, and the smaller of the two guards was pushing it open and shoving him inside.

Deacon sat at her desk with a pen in her hand, and she looked up as soon as the door closed. A relieved smile graced her face.

"Oh, thank goodness you're all right," Miss Deacon sighed. She stood and quickly stepped around her desk, her arms out wide. As she hugged William, she pressed her body into his and buried her face in the warm spot between his chin and shoulder.

This isn't right, William thought. *I haven't had time to prepare. This isn't fair.*

"I'm sure you're wondering what all the fuss has been

about today." Deacon leaned back, folded her arms behind William, and looked into his face. "Oh, William, something terrible has happened. You may have heard rumors buzzing around, so I'm just going to tell you the truth—a woman was found dead this morning in her cell."

She spoke slowly, while her right hand traveled over his belly and up to his chest, pressing and stroking the strong curves of his muscles. "She killed herself with a box cutter from the Village. That's why we were forced to search the whole Center. We were looking for anyone else who might have stolen a tool or who might be considering such a barbaric act."

"Of course we are questioning her mate, John. I assumed they'd made some sort of suicide pact before they were brought here, but he doesn't seem to know anything. The poor man is simply beside himself. He became so violently upset that we had to sedate him. You know, my heart is simply broken thinking about this poor woman's sorrow and her final, desperate act." She looked up into his face, her eyes glistening. "William, today of all days, I'm so thankful for your company."

William struggled to look away. He'd always had time before. He'd always been in the room for several minutes before she showed up—time he used to prepare himself, steady himself. Time he used to open up that horrid box of putrescence hidden deep within his mind that would allow him to be touched by her, stroked by her, kissed by her. He needed that time!

"For many months now," Deacon continued, her honeyed voice contrasting with her rough grip, "you've been the one bright spot in my otherwise dark and dreary week. Whatever trouble I'm dealing with, when you come to me, it all just fades away." Her eyes lit up with fervor. "Don't worry,

William. The sadness and trouble of this day won't ruin our time together! Here in my office, as the sun sets into the west, you and I will defy the destructive and malicious weakness of one misguided woman by rising above it. You and I, William, will prove to ourselves that she cannot ruin the joyous and holy time we share together!"

Deacon dipped her chin and smiled a coquettish grin. "I've thought of something special for us today, William. Something I know you will enjoy. Something I'm sure you've been hoping to share with me, but have been too shy to ask for." She lifted her chin and leaned in to him.

William felt his heart begin to race as her lips touched his. Did he kiss her back? How did he usually do this? Unable to retreat, he was suddenly horribly aware of her body close to his. He could feel the warmth of her breasts as they pressed into him, and the soft curve of her hips. Her lips were lush and soft, and her breath was hot on his face. He was violently repulsed by her smell and taste and touch. This wasn't right!

Before he could stop himself, he grabbed her upper arms and pulled away from her prying mouth. He looked into her round, white face and pushed her away.

For a second, Miss Deacon stood stunned and confused, but with two quick blinks of her eyes, she recovered. "Ah, I see," she breathed. "You want it so badly you can't even wait. Yes, my love," she said as she backed away from him. "I know what you want." She turned around and leaned her left arm onto her desk. Tossing her bouncy blond curls over her shoulder, she looked back at William with passion in her eyes. Watching him, she began to pull up her white skirt with one hand as she tilted her hips and arched her bottom into the air. "Well, then, come over here and take me."

His mind struggling, William said, "Wait."

Miss Deacon blinked, and smiled. "Wait?"

"I . . . I want to talk to you."

Deacon dropped the hem of her skirt, stood up, and slowly turned to face William. Dryly she said, "You never want to talk. You never say anything."

"I want to ask you a question."

After several seconds, Deacon pushed one of her curls behind her ear and sat on the edge of her desk. "All right." She smiled. "Of course, William. In fact, I welcome this. I would love to deepen our relationship. What do you want to ask?"

"Um," William mumbled. "I've been thinking about my release."

Miss Deacon's cheek faintly twitched. "Your release?"

"I'm scheduled to be released in three weeks, and I've heard there are some steps I have to go through beforehand. Some paperwork. Meetings with Tumwater?" When Deacon didn't answer, William added, "As the director here, I'm sure you could help me navigate that process."

Deacon's smile slowly faded and her face became stony and severe. "Your release."

William couldn't concentrate. The room was buzzing around him, Deacon was a fuzzy white glow in front of him. His words tumbled out. "After all that we've done, all that we've been for each other, I know you'll want to help me. After all we've shared, I thought you'd want to, to . . ."

Miss Deacon breathed in deeply and looked out the window at the grassy field and the darkening forest beyond. Branches were beginning to sway as the wind picked up, and even in this room, the air seemed to crackle with the coming weather. She was silent for nearly a minute before turning back to William and saying, "I must say that I'm more than a little hurt."

"Hurt?"

Deacon shook her head dramatically, stood up, and stepped close to him. "William, William. I knew you would consider leaving me. It's only natural, I suppose. We humans are always searching for something better. Even though you have something beautiful and rewarding right in front of you, you wonder if there is greener grass on the other side of the fence. My husband was that way. I suppose your thoughts about the possibilities have been weighing heavily on your mind as of late." She touched his arm softly, and he suppressed the desire to recoil.

"I want you to know that I have been doing some extra work lately on your behalf." Fear flashed through William's belly, and Miss Deacon continued. "Now, don't worry about me. I'm busy, of course, but I always have time to fit in some extra work for your sake. You see, I've contacted the leaders of your town and have inquired about the status of your former life there."

William felt his jaw clench.

"I'm assured that your position at the warehouse has been filled, and they aren't experiencing any hardship because of your absence." Miss Deacon walked away to her desk, her white skirt swishing. She opened a drawer and pulled out a dog-eared manila file. "In fact," she added as she opened the file, "you don't have to worry about any of the little odds and ends that you left behind when you came here. I've taken the honor of checking on your cousins, Laiken and Harriet, and they are doing quite well without you. Harriet has even decided to take a mate!"

Miss Deacon moved to William's side and showed him the open file in her hands. He saw two grainy black-and-white photographs stapled to the page. In the first, his cousin Harriet squatted in a small garden. Trees lined the edge of the field, their shadows hanging wide over the plants, leaving them small and sickly looking. A young man from the neighborhood stood beside her, and though both looked tired and dirty, there was love in their eyes. He almost smiled at the sight of Harriet, happy to see her safe, but his smile faded as he realized neither of the people in the picture knew they were being photographed. A shiver ran down his spine.

In the second picture, Laiken was hanging laundry in the front yard of a small, rundown house. As in the first photo, this wasn't the house he had shared with his cousins. It wasn't his house, his garden, or his front yard, and he saw the truth.

Two years ago, the neighborhood leaders had decided his house was too big for just William and the girls. They were told to trade with a family of five, to move into the small two-bedroom shack he saw in the picture of Laiken. It was only fair, they had said. It didn't matter how long the house had been in William's family. It didn't matter that he loved it.

He'd protested, and the neighborhood leaders had called a meeting to discuss it. Ten minutes in, he realized there was no hope. They wouldn't let him talk, wouldn't hear him, and he lost his temper. When he knocked over his chair and called them cheating cows, he saw a look of satisfaction in their eyes and knew his mistake wouldn't be forgiven. They'd sent him to the Center to learn how to share and how to behave around women. His house was given to the other family.

He'd fought and argued and thrown his freedom away for nothing. His dreams of going home disappeared like a wisp of smoke.

Deacon snapped the file shut and strutted back to her desk. She dropped the file onto the surface. "So you see, my love, you have nothing to worry about! Everything is fine back in your old neighborhood. Everyone is just fine without you." She leaned her hip on the edge of her desk and smiled with satisfaction. The low sun slipped silently behind a bank of gray clouds and a shadow fell across the room.

"B . . . But," William stammered. He had to focus. Even without his house, he could go back to his cousins. He could learn how to be happy there again. He could make a new home.

"But nothing," Deacon snapped, the slightest hint of venom in her voice. "I told you how important you are to me. I love you, William. I love you with the heat of a thousand suns. And I will always take care of you."

"Then you'll help me."

"I'll do everything I can."

"You'll help me with my release."

Miss Deacon blinked once and smiled, her perfect teeth and beautiful face glowing even as the room around her darkened. "Never."

William felt the low rumble of distant thunder pass through the depths of his chest. His mind was blank.

"What do you mean?"

Miss Deacon slowly shook her head. "William, you know I can't let you leave this place." Her voice was pitched low and condescending, as if she were speaking to a foolish child.

"But I did my time. Tumwater said . . ."

"Ms. Tumwater has no say in this matter, William."

Realization slowly crept into William's brain, forcing itself up from a place in his heart that had somehow always known this truth. "But . . ."

"William, you know you belong here with me." Deacon slowly reached out her hands and began padding closer to him. "We have such a beautiful thing, my love. Why would you ever consider leaving me?"

The first patter of rain began to fall on the wide grass field as Deacon's fingertips brushed the front of William's faded red shirt. He heard the loud swoosh of blood rush to his ears and he closed his eyes. With all his strength, he focused on the sound of his own breathing, the feel of warm air on his skin, and the sound of the stiffening wind in the forest outside. In his mind's eye, he saw the impact of the fat drops as they hit the dry ground in slow motion, bending and splashing among the green blades as each concussion blasted up fragments of dirt and clay from the surrounding earth. He could focus on that space. He could focus and forget everything else that was happening. He could shut off the rest of his brain and retreat to a place of safety and silence where she couldn't touch him. He could lose himself there forever.

"No!" William's voice roared in the dimness of the room. He was *here*, in this office, with this repulsive woman, who had her hands up his shirt and her tongue on his neck. The feel of her skin on his was like a white-hot burning, and the only thing he knew was that he had to get away from it.

William grabbed Deacon and shoved her to the side. Thrown violently off-balance, she tumbled to the floor, hitting her shoulder on the corner of her desk as she fell. Landing, she yelped and rolled, her hair falling across her face. William took two steps backward and stared. She struggled to her knees and held her hand to her shoulder.

"Ouch! Oh," Deacon groaned. Her face contorted into a furious grimace and she groped for her desk. "What have you done?" she hissed.

William instinctively stepped forward, his arm reaching out to help her up. "I'm sorry," he murmured. "Let me help you."

"Get away from me!" Deacon's screech cut through the crescendo of the raindrops that were beginning to beat against the window behind her. She pushed her body away from him. "How dare you!"

"I'm sorry, you—"

Deacon awkwardly lifted herself from the floor. She rushed behind her desk, putting it between herself and William, then puffed out her chest. "How dare you strike me!"

"I didn't strike you, I—"

"You think you can come into my room and assault me? You think that just because you're a man, you can hurt me?"

Deacon glowed with righteous indignation as she raised herself to her full height. "For millions of years, men like you believed themselves superior to women based on their superior strength, and you oppressed us and attacked us, assailing us with blows and the most debased forms of punishment you could come up with. You have—"

"I didn't hit you!" William yelled. "You did this! You did all this!"

Deacon raised her voice above his. "You have badgered and bruised women your whole life, and now you think you can come into *my* room and shove *me* around?"

"I've never hurt a woman! Don't you dare say—"

"Who the fuck do you think you are!" In a furious movement, Deacon swept her arms across the top of her desk, sending her meticulously laid-out papers and pens flying. She slammed her fists onto the top of her desk, her face contorted and ugly. Her eyes closed, and William watched as she drew in two deep breaths, her nostrils flaring, her chest expanding.

When she opened her eyes again, she slowly leaned forward. "I gave you everything," she hissed, her voice menacing. "I gave you everything, and you throw me away like garbage. You will *never* leave me. You will *never* leave this place! You will burn in hell for this."

"You're insane."

"Oh, no, William." Deacon whispered. "I'm in charge."

Her voice was so quiet, William wasn't sure she'd spoken the last words out loud. He stared at Deacon, his body cold and his heart broken. There was no justice in the world. There would always be someone above you who could destroy you on a whim. He looked down, at the faded pattern of flowers on the rug.

A loud thud outside the door to the office startled them both. Deacon looked up, and the door flew open with a bang. Ruth rushed in, her face streaked with sweat and her eyes burning. On the floor behind her, a guard lay slumped and still. In her right fist she gripped four syringes.

Ruth stopped short when she saw William, and for the briefest moment a flash of lucidity crossed her face. "Here you are," she calmly said, as if she had been merely looking for a friend in a crowded place.

"What are you doing here?" Miss Deacon spat. "Get out!" She rushed to the front of her desk, arms raised as if to shoo Ruth away.

Ruth turned to Deacon, and her face hardened again. Without a word, she lunged. Before Deacon could even flinch, Ruth had raised her fist into the air and slammed the four needles into the cool white cloth that covered Miss Deacon's chest. With her left hand, Ruth depressed the four plungers simultaneously.

Miss Deacon's eyes opened wide, and she gasped. She stumbled back from Ruth, the syringes still hanging out of her chest. "What . . . ?" she mumbled.

"How does it feel?" Ruth shouted. "How many times

have you injected this into helpless women and men? Over and over I've had to watch you do this to them, watch as you used this drug to torture their minds and bodies." She grabbed the collar of Deacon's crisp white blouse. Leaning in close to her, Ruth added, "You want to mess with people's heads? Well, now you know how it feels." She shoved Deacon backward into the wall, sending the potted fern crashing to the floor.

Deacon's face flushed deep red and she blinked several times, seeming to struggle with something in her mind. Her left hand swatted in front of her contorting face as her right hand reached behind her, groping at the shelf and knocking down the books and awards that lined it; her feet scraped and slipped beneath her. Suddenly, her body stiffened and convulsed, once, twice, and a third time. Her pupils dilated, turning her bright blue eyes to leaden black, and a thick stream of saliva poured from the corner of her mouth. All color drained from her cherubic face as her jaw went slack. She pulled in one final gurgling breath and slumped to the floor.

The patter of heavy raindrops ticked away several seconds as Ruth and William stood staring at Miss Deacon's body, motionless and pale in the fading light.

"What have you done?" William whispered.

As if just realizing he was in the room, Ruth turned. "William," she said. A wide grin spread across her face, and she looked around at the debris strewn across the room. "You're free! It's all over. Don't you see?" She gestured to the floor without looking down.

William stepped to the wall and squatted beside Deacon. With trembling fingers, he reached out to touch the curve of her neck, checking for a pulse. A fine layer of cold sweat coated her skin, and her lips were beginning to turn blue. He pulled his hand away and wiped his fingers on his pant leg.

“We need to get help.”

“No one can help her.” Ruth was crumpling up the scattered papers and piling them on top of the desk. “Do you want this?” She held William’s file out to him, and when he shook his head, she opened it and began to rip the pages into thin strips. She wadded the final page loosely in her hand and held it above the pile. Then she reached into her underwear and pulled out a skinny orange lighter.

“What are you doing?” William staggered to his feet.

“This is from the acetylene torch rack. Don’t worry, nobody saw me take it. The guards are all too busy searching the buildings.” Ruth spun the small spark wheel, and a tiny yellow flame leapt from the lighter. She touched the flame to the paper, and when she was sure it had caught, lowered it to the waiting pile below. Black smoke curled up from the tinder for a moment before orange flames began to crackle and lick at the whole mass.

“Stop!” William cried.

Ruth circled the desk to where he stood. “Come on, we need to go.”

William pressed against Ruth’s outturned hands, leaning toward the growing fire, but there was little fight left in him. She easily held him back and steered him toward the open door.

As they stepped out of Miss Deacon’s office, William turned one last time to look at the room he had so long dreaded. Through the gray smoke that billowed from the desk and the growing orange glow of the fire, he saw a bright flash of lightning in the sky outside the windows. The still, white-clothed body of Miss Deacon lay illuminated in that momentary flash. Ruth tugged gently on his sleeve, and he turned and fled.

~ Sixteen ~

Rhia sat huddled in the corner of her cell, her knees pulled up to her chin and her arms wrapped tightly around her legs. The places on her face and back where Captain Banks had pummeled her earlier in the day felt swollen and warm. Her jaw was so painful she could hardly open it.

By the time she had dragged herself back to her cell, still dizzy and aching from the stun gun, the other inmates had gone out to their lessons or to the Village. She'd been grateful not to see anyone, to be able to slink back to her room, but now, three hours later, she could tell from the sporadic footsteps and mumbled voices coming from the hallway that the women were making their way back. She heard them quietly complaining about being wet, hungry, and exhausted, and hoping for any sign that food would be served before lights out.

From where she sat, Rhia could see the rain falling against the small, barred window of her cell. Night was coming on quickly. The clouds grew thick and fat, and as the visible sliver of sky darkened, she was overwhelmed by despair. It had been almost two weeks since the storm that had knocked her off Betty, and yet it felt like a lifetime. She couldn't imagine surviving the next two months in the Center.

Rhia lowered her chin to her chest, wrapped her hands around the back of her head, and wept. Lightning flashed outside.

Suddenly, a strange ringing blared from the hallway. It was a bell Rhia hadn't heard before, and it took her several seconds to understand that it was an alarm. Slowly she pulled herself to standing, bracing herself against the wall for support, and made her way to the open door of her cell. Women were peeking into the hallway from their rooms, covering their ears with their hands against the noise. Rhia looked down the hallway and could see an old, gray, metal alarm bell mounted high on the wall. It clanged incessantly.

Several women retreated back into their cells, perhaps hoping to escape the sound or fearful that it indicated another round of searches, but Rhia stepped out cautiously. The fluorescent lights, set on a timer, hadn't turned on yet, and the gloom from the storm outside made the hallway shadowy and dark. Rhia walked down the hall, crouching and covering her ears as she passed under the alarm bell. Two women rushed out of their cell and nearly ran her over.

"What's going on?" Rhia asked.

The women shot past Rhia without answering, ran to the end of the hallway, and pushed through the double doors to the stairs. Rhia followed them tentatively. She grasped the dented metal railing and edged down the steps, her body stiff and sore. The closer she got to the bottom, the louder the voices and shouts became. Several other women thundered down the stairs, and she braced herself as they brushed by.

When Rhia stepped into the hallway on the main floor of the building, the acrid smell of smoke filled her nostrils, and women's shouts mingled with the alarm bell in her ears. A dozen inmates were pressed against the locked metal double doors that led to the entrance hall. They banged their fists and kicked against the doors, their faces pressed up against the small, thick, square peep windows in the center of each. As she drew near, Rhia could see the blurred heads of two guards leaning against the other side of the double doors, reinforcing them to make sure the inmates could not push through. The guards were shouting, but their shouts were muffled and drowned out by the ringing of the bells and the rising panic in the inmates' voices.

Rhia understood that there was a fire somewhere in the building, but she didn't know where. The figures of the guards behind the doors were steeped in a haze, and Rhia could smell smoke, but she couldn't see any in the dim light around her.

Rhia turned in a circle, looking down the long hallway and trying to remember if there were any other exits. The windows that lined every room in this wing were barred, and she couldn't recall seeing any other doors. The only way out was through the double doors that the guards and the locks held shut.

Rhia ran forward and joined the growing throng of women pounding on the thick steel. Quick glimpses through the peep windows showed that the smoke on the other side was getting thicker, and she could see it beginning to billow under the doors and into this wing of the building. Women began to cough and splutter. Rhia's eyes stung. Rhia shouldered her way to the front of the group, shoving several women aside, and looked through the peep window. She could see the top of one guard's head, her short hair pressed up against the glass, her camouflaged hat lost or knocked off.

"Open the door!" Rhia screamed as she pounded on the thick glass. Her body was buffeted and punched by the women behind her. Their fingers scrabbled and scratched at the doors and at the women around them in a vain attempt to get through.

As if suddenly called from somewhere else, both guards lifted their heads and looked to the entrance hall behind them. Without hesitation, one guard stood up straight and ran from her post, disappearing into the growing smoke. The second guard jerked her head around and looked through the peep window. She looked directly at Rhia, at the fate to which she was sentencing the inmates, for only a moment before turning away and disappearing into the darkness.

Panic filled Rhia's chest. By now, more women had rushed to the double doors, and they continued to shove and push, unaware of the futility of their cries. Rhia was desperate to think of another way out of the Center, out of the gray smoke surrounding her. She could barely move; her body was flattened against the metal doors that were beginning to warm. Her cheek was pressed against the glass.

A movement in the smoky entrance hall caught Rhia's eye, and she craned her neck. For a second, it was hidden in the darkness, and then she saw it again. Someone was there. Rhia began to scream for help as her body writhed in the mass of flesh that pressed around her. She saw only a blur as the person approached, and she feared it was the guard, returning to secure the door again. Instead, she felt the subtle shift of the lock and the twisting of the handle that pressed into her belly.

The door flew open. Women tumbled out into the entrance hall, crashing upon each other and trampling one another in their drive to escape the smoke and heat. Rhia fell, felt feet and knees slam down onto her body, and tried to cover her head with her arms and hands. A set of hands seemed to be grabbing at her, trying to get hold of her wrist or arm, even as more women plowed over and around her. Finally, strong hands were able to grab onto her, and she was pulled to her feet.

Choking and coughing, Rhia was dragged through the smoke toward the front doors. They were propped open, and the wind and rain outside was drawing the smoke in billows and curls out into the open air.

Her foot caught on something, and she tripped, sprawling forward. The hands that held her arm wrenched her upward in an attempt to steady her, but her balance was lost, and she tumbled onto a wooden rocking chair lying broken on its side. She landed hard, her knee slamming into the floor and her body twisting sideways as the hands disappeared.

Visibility was down to almost nothing, but on the floor the air was just clear enough to make out the cause of her fall. A woman lay on the ground, her green camouflage shirt bunched up around her torso, her legs bent in unnatural angles. For a moment, Rhia thought it was Captain Banks, and a sickening happiness flitted through her. She bent closer and looked into the woman's open eyes. Then her heart sank, as she recognized the person who had so recently helped her. It was Captain Juka. An empty, clear, glass syringe hung from the center of her chest.

Rhia reached out, in the slim hope that Juka was still alive, but the barrage of legs and feet still flying past her knocked her backward and away from the body. She tried to turn over onto her hands and knees, hoping to crawl to the open doors that led to safety. A knee hit her hard in the shoulder, and she cried out in pain. Once again, hands grabbed her arm, and someone tried to pull her back up.

"Get up!"

Rhia looked up and saw William.

"Come on!" he shouted.

Rhia was half pushed, half dragged the last twenty feet to the front doors, and together with William, she finally lunged out into the darkness and the downpour. She paused at the scene. Inmates and guards were running through the rain in all directions. Near the corner of the building, three guards had corralled six women and were holding them at gunpoint, but even as they shouted orders, other women continued to run past.

"We need to run!" William shouted over the din.

"What's happening?" Rhia hollered back.

"Come on! We have to get out of here!"

Then Ruth was beside William, her face a mask of smoke smudge and dirt. Her eyes gleamed in the orange glow of the fire, and she wore a wide smile.

"Ruth!" Rhia shouted. "What's going on?"

"It's over, Rhia! I've freed us all!"

"Come on!" William begged, and he tugged on Rhia's arm. "Let's go!"

Rhia allowed him to lead her away from the building toward the long driveway that led to the main gate of the Center. Having passed through it only once, in the back of the pickup truck, Rhia didn't really know what security the gate had, but it seemed their best bet in the melee and confusion. The three of them ran with several other women for a minute.

The dirt of the driveway was quickly turning to mud under a hard and heavy rain. Then, as they looked down the long road toward the wide field and the main gate beyond, they saw a row of ten guards standing in the distance.

Rhia, Ruth, and William slid to a stop, William's arm reaching out to steady Rhia beside him. They watched in horror as the guards raised their black guns and fired in unison at the inmates running toward them. Rhia saw women stop short and spin backward into the mud. Even as the guards took aim again, women continued to race toward their doom.

"I know another way," Rhia shouted over the screams of the women below.

"There is no other way!" William cried.

"Yes! By the stream!"

"Where?"

"Follow me. Through the Village. We need a shovel!"

William searched her face for a moment, then nodded. Against all their instincts, the three turned and ran back toward the Big House. Ahead of them, the west wing of the massive stone building glowed orange with fire, and smoke billowed from windows that had cracked and broken in the heat. The dry wood paneling and ancient, desiccated floors had lit up like kindling. Even the east wing, covered in stark cement and metal, was engulfed in smoke.

They ran wide around the Big House, dodging bodies lying on the ground and guards attempting to round up inmates. Suddenly, there was a massive explosion behind them, sending a concussion through their bodies and making them all instinctively duck their heads. They turned and saw a huge fireball blossoming out of the building.

"What the hell!" Rhia shouted.

"Treatment rooms!" Ruth beamed. "Oxygen tanks! This

is the day of reckoning! All the souls that stumbled into this pit and were made low by the demon Deacon are being released back into the universe. The justice of the flames will consume those who dealt out injustice!"

Rhia watched Ruth for a moment, frightened by the rapture she saw in her face.

"I told you she couldn't hold us in here, Rhia! I told you I would destroy her, and now her whole world is burning down around her!" Ruth stared up at the building and opened her arms wide to the spectacle of it—the flames that leapt from the rooftop, the splinters and shards of wood and glass that drifted down from the sky, and the smoke that poured from the barred windows of the east wing.

"Ruth, what have you done?" Rhia gasped.

"I've waited so long for this day! It's just like I'd imagined!" Ruth laughed. "I fooled them all! And to think that—"

Ruth's smile faltered. Following her gaze, Rhia saw movement on the second floor. There was someone in the window, a woman still in her cell. From this distance there was no way to tell who it was, but Ruth's arms dropped to her sides and she said, "Oh, no."

The woman had broken through the small, barred window and was reaching out into the night. They saw her hand open and close, as if she could grasp the fresh air outside. As if it would save her from the choking death of smoke and heat that was overwhelming her.

"It's Charlotte," Ruth whispered.

"What? No, Ruth, you don't know that. That's not even our cell."

"What have I done?"

Rhia saw Ruth begin to move and grabbed her shoulders.

"Ruth, stop! That's not Charlotte! You can't—"

Ruth twisted under Rhia's hands and broke free. Before William could get hold of her, she sprinted toward the fire.

"Ruth, stop!" William shouted after her as she disappeared around the corner of the building.

Rhia started to run after her, but William caught her in his arms. He held Rhia tightly as she struggled against him. "Rhia, no!"

"That's not Charlotte! She can't go back in there!"

"I won't let you go after her! You can't help her."

"You can't let her do this! How can you let her go?"

"Stop! Rhia, she's already gone!"

"No!" Rhia screamed, but she was already leaning back into William's arms, accepting the fate to which Ruth had run. She cried out once more in agony and anguish, her voice lost in the torrent of rain all around her.

"We have to go. Come on." William spoke into Rhia's ear, and his strong arms turned her away from the burning destruction.

The grassy hill that led to the Village was nearly empty, except for a few women and men who frantically scurried around, trying to avoid the guards. As they began their descent, Rhia slipped on the sodden grass. She dug her heels in to stop her fall, her already bruised and swollen muscles screaming out in pain. More carefully, she made her way to the Village toolshed, with William close behind.

"Get a shovel or a pickax!" Rhia shouted to William. She looked at the ground, and seeing a large rock in the mud, fell to her knees and scrabbled her fingers around the sides to loosen it. When it was free, she hefted the rock above her head and slammed it once, twice, a third time down onto the padlock. "There's a hole in the fence where it crosses the stream. We can dig it out." She handed William a pickax and held a shovel firmly in her hands.

"Show me where."

"This way."

Rhia and William ran toward the stream. The guard towers were deserted. The guards had either scattered around the compound or joined forces to keep the inmates from reaching the main gate. Rhia and William passed under a tower and had the stream in sight.

Suddenly, Rhia was slammed hard onto the wet ground, a body landing heavily on her back, the shovel knocked out of her hand. She tasted mud and grass as her lungs were compressed by the weight pressing her down. Above her, Captain Banks began scratching and punching at Rhia's face, interspersing her blows with shrieks and curses. The noise of the rain thundering around her head and Banks's barrage of thumps and slams momentarily deafened Rhia. The next thing she heard was a high-pitched ringing in her ears and muffled shouts as William struggled to pull Banks off of her.

Captain Banks was like a wild animal, frothing and flailing, and William had to use all his strength to drag her even a few feet away. He threw her to the ground and positioned himself between her and Rhia.

Rhia could not get up again. She turned her head and laid her cheek down on the cold wet grass. Her eyes closed. She wanted only to rest, to sleep. The water puddled around her face—she could feel it lapping and splashing with each fat drop that fell from the sky. Her thoughts drifted to the ocean, to Betty's gentle, rhythmic rocking as they sailed throughout the night, working their way back home to Miranda. She could see her boat and her friends again, she could escape the Center, if she could just rest here a while.

Drifting, Rhia inhaled deeply and breathed in the rising water. Her lungs coughed and sputtered, and an instinct deep inside her made her jerk away from the ground. She heard her father's voice in her head, quiet and firm. *Look, girlie, if you didn't drown in the sea two weeks ago, you're sure as hell not going to drown in a fucking puddle.*

Her eyes flew open, and she remembered where she was. Gasping and shaking her head to clear it, she found a hidden reserve of strength, rolled onto her backside, and pushed herself to her elbows.

Lightning flashed through a pitch-black sky, silhouetting William's body above her. His thin shirt clung to his soaking-wet back in the downpour. His arms hung at his sides, the pickax gripped tightly in his right hand. Rivulets of water streamed from his fingers. Captain Banks had pushed herself to her feet and stood facing him. Expecting her charge, William turned sideways and raised the pickax, poised and ready for the attack. Instead of rushing him, however, Banks reached behind her back.

Rhia saw it in slow motion. Banks swept her hand in front of her. She was holding a heavy black pistol. William's shoulders slumped, as if overwhelmed with sadness and realizing that death was about to come. As Banks raised the gun level to William's chest, there was a flash of lightning and the shining, silver reflection of metal as it swept through the air. With a thick clunk, the shovel Rhia had dropped was slammed into the back of Banks's skull, pitching her forward, where she landed face-first in the mud.

It took Rhia several seconds to process what had happened. When she looked up from Banks's body, Laura was standing in the pouring rain, her jaw set, deep resolve shining as she lifted the handle and held the shovel like a baseball bat, ready to swing again.

Banks didn't move, and Laura looked at Rhia. She tossed the shovel to the side and ran, dropping onto her knees to embrace her.

"Rhia!" Laura shouted. "Are you okay?"

"I'm all right." Rhia held Laura even as her eyes darted back to Banks.

William squatted beside the two women and shouted over the sound of the rain. "We need to go! Rhia, you need to get up!"

"Go?" Laura asked.

"Deacon's dead." Rhia said. "It's all gone, Laura. We have to get out of here."

"Where can you go?"

Rhia knew she had to run. Someone would have to be blamed for the fire, and given this morning's fight, she would be one of the first suspects. There would be no justice in this unjust new world. All the inmates who survived tonight would be rounded up. A new Center would be built, and she and William would be locked away for the rest of their lives. They would be punished for crimes against the women who had been the true criminals.

She looked up into the face of her friend. "I don't know," Rhia answered.

"No. Come to the lab! Or you can stay in the hangars! They're not burning. You can stay in one of the boxcars, or . . ."

"Laura, we have to leave. We're prisoners here. They think we're the criminals." Rhia saw the truth wash over Laura's face. Tears stung her eyes as she watched Laura slowly nod her head.

"Where will you go?"

"I don't know."

"Rhia, there's no time. We have to go now," William said as he stood up.

"Come with us," Rhia said.

For a moment, Laura seemed to consider it, but then she closed her eyes and dropped her chin to her chest. "I can't. Ms. Brakille and Nadine and I . . . we want to help. People will be hurt. And somebody has to stay to try to protect the inmates."

"You can't do anything. You said yourself, you don't have the power."

"We have to try."

Rhia looked into Laura's face and felt proud of her courage, but also sad, knowing it would be the last time she saw her. She thought of the years they'd known each other and the life they both might have had in Miranda if Laura had only stayed there, if she herself had only stayed on her boat. One snapped bungee cord had changed it all.

"Laura, tell your mom . . ." Rhia's voice trembled. "Just, tell her."

"I will."

"I'm sorry." Rhia hugged Laura and kissed her cheek before pulling away and standing up. She bent to pick up the shovel on the ground and, without looking back, turned and ran toward the stream with William.

~ Seventeen ~

Rhia and William reached the edge of the bank and looked down at the fence where it crossed the stream. The downpour had turned the bank into a mudslide, and the water raged in swirls and ripples below them.

"It's there," Rhia said pointing to the spot where she had seen the space between the fence and the bank.

"I don't see anything."

Rhia squinted through the rain. She couldn't see the hole. "The water's higher. It must be there!" She grasped the shovel in her left hand and began to make her way down the slippery slope, trying to find her footing on the wide steps the men used when bathing. Her soaked shoes sloshed and squelched in the thick mud. The few rocks embedded in the bank were coated and slimy, and there was nothing to hold on to.

"Grab my hand!" William reached down from the top of the bank and tried to help her.

As Rhia looked up at him, her feet slipped out from under her, and she slid through the mud into the cold, murky water below. Her face was submerged for several seconds until she was able to get her feet under her and push her body up.

Standing in water up to her waist, Rhia dug the shovel into the bottom of the stream and pushed her legs through the swirling whorls toward the fence. The cold and the weight of the water sapped her strength, but, grunting and panting, she forced her way to the place where the hole should be.

In one hand she held the handle of the shovel pressed against the metal links of the fence. With the other, she reached down into the water. She felt around for the edge of the fence. The space was still there and had become even bigger from erosion as the fierce water continued to streak through it, tearing up bits of sand and dirt. Small rocks, sticks, and the detritus of the bottom of the stream were blasting through the space, but it was still less than a foot high and only two feet wide.

"It's here!" Rhia shouted.

William was crouched low, his head turned to scan the field behind him, watching for approaching guards or inmates. Sporadic gunfire echoed across the compound, and screams cut through the pounding rain. His head jerked back toward Rhia and he nodded. Slowly, he began to work his way down the bank, using the pickax for purchase in the mud. Awkwardly, he slipped and slid on his backside until he landed beside her in the stream.

"Where?"

"Reach down here. Under the water."

Rhia grabbed William's hand and pulled it beneath the

surface of the water, guiding him to the spot. His eyes lit up when he felt it, and he looked up into her face.

"We'll have to dig it out," Rhia said.

Without hesitation, William began to poke and prod the area with his pickax, and Rhia followed suit. Together they shoved their tools under the water, rocking them back and forth to loosen the rocks and roots that held the soil in place. The water around them turned the color of chocolate milk, and they were buffeted together against the fence by the flood. After several minutes of digging, Rhia leaned against the fence, panting and exhausted.

William paused and looked up at her. His soaked clothes clung to his body. "Hold me down," he said.

"What?"

"I'm going to dig with my hands. Push me down so I don't float up." He tossed his pickax onto the mud bank above him, stood up, took a deep breath, and plunged his whole body underwater.

Rhia pressed her foot into his back and watched William disappear. She saw bubbles and muddled sediment rise to the surface as his hands clawed and swept at the bottom. The occasional sharp cracks of gunfire seemed closer now, and she could see shadows moving in the field around the guard towers. She felt somewhat hidden by the stream bank above her, but if a guard found them, they would be sitting ducks.

After a minute, William pushed himself up to take a gasping breath before diving back under again. Again and again he went down, until at last he stood up, his chest heaving with ragged inhalations. The water frothed and surged around his wide-set legs. "I don't know," he gasped. "There's a rock in the middle. I can't move it. It might be big enough."

Rhia nodded and slid her hands down the edge of the

fence. The hole was now over two feet high and three feet wide, but she could feel the large rock he'd spoken of. It would be a tight squeeze even without the pummeling of the rushing water. She stood back up and said, "We have to try."

"Go first."

Rhia squared her shoulders and drew two deep breaths, blowing out hard after each. She sucked in the third, held it, and threw her body forward into the water. She grabbed the bottom of the fence and kicked her feet up behind her as she angled her body into the hole.

She kept her eyes closed, knowing the turbidity of the water would obscure her vision anyway. As she pushed her head through the hole, her chest hit the rock, which forced her left shoulder up into the bottom of the fence where it snagged painfully on the sharp wire. For a moment she was stuck and couldn't figure out how to back out of the snag. William's hands were on her torso and legs, trying to push her through. She scrunched her shoulders close to her body and twisted, kicking wildly. The fabric finally ripped free, and she was able to squirm through the hole, using her hands and feet to push and pull herself to the other side of the fence.

With a final kick, she was through, and she flailed around to get her feet under her as the current tried to sweep her downstream. She heaved herself to standing and, as cold water cascaded off her body, grabbed the fence and looked across to William.

"It's tight. It's sharp."

William looked at the blood trickling from the gash in her shoulder, nodded, and sucked in his breath before diving under the surface. Rhia reached down and tried to pull him through. She took hold of his head and tried to guide him forward, but his shoulders wouldn't fit. For all the added strength and force that he could muster, his body was larger than hers, his shoulders more broad, and his muscles more bulky. The qualities and aspects that made him physically superior to Rhia in so many other ways made it more difficult for him to fit through this space.

After nearly a minute, he backed out of the hole and popped up at the surface. Gasping and panting, he leaned against the fence and curled his fingers through the chain link. The tips of his fingers were scraped raw and bleeding. Rhia folded her battered hands over his and leaned close.

"Too tight."

"I'll make it bigger." Rhia moved toward the water.

"No!" William shouted. "It won't work. You have to leave me."

They could hear the shouts of women and men near the guard towers, and knew they were running out of time.

"Bullshit. That's not happening. Get the shovel."

"Rhia, you—"

Rhia didn't wait for the end of his sentence. She plunged back into the water and gouged out more of the loose soil and mud below the fence. She scratched her fingers around the large rock wedged in the center of the hole. When she came back to the surface a minute later, she saw William holding the long wooden handle of the shovel. He was working the blade back and forth in the streambed, trying to pry at the rock from his side. She sucked in another big breath and dove under.

As Rhia excavated more dirt and gravel from the bottom, she felt the rock wiggle. Concentrating her efforts on the front of the rock, she scraped and tore at the streambed—and felt the rock begin to sway. At last, the rock rolled toward her, and with the force of the current and the prying of William's shovel, she heaved it forward and felt it tumble downstream.

Rhia popped back to the surface in time to see William disappear under the water. She grabbed for him in the stream and in seconds had pulled him to her side. He stood up, sputtering and coughing as his chest heaved. Together they splashed to the far side of the stream and crawled up the muddy bank. It was a short run to the forest beyond, and they were lost in the cover of darkness.

~ Eighteen ~

William ran through the forest, following Rhia, keeping the stream on their right. The tree canopy provided some shelter from the slackening rain, but the cool air seeped into his bones like a thousand shards of glass.

"Hold on," Rhia called as she stopped and leaned against a tree. Her breath came in short gasps, her clothes were a mixture of mud, water, and blood, and she was beginning to shiver.

William stopped behind her and reached out his hands to steady her. His chest heaved and he felt the chill of his wet shirt clinging to his body. "We need to keep moving," he panted.

"Give me a minute."

"We should have brought the shovel and pickax." William

wiped his forearm across his muddy face. "We should have hid them in the forest. Once the water goes down, they'll find them and know what happened."

Rhia bent over and rested her hands on her knees. "We can't go back."

"No."

"They'll see the hole in the fence anyway."

"Right." He watched Rhia, worried. She didn't look good. After a minute he gestured in the direction they'd been running and said, "Do you know where the stream goes?"

"The coast. We get there, we can figure it out."

"Do you know where it comes out?"

"No."

"Do you know any place around here?"

"No." Rhia's teeth had begun to chatter. She pushed herself to standing and began to walk. "Let's . . . keep moving."

They stumbled through the woods in silence for almost an hour. William struggled to fight off the cold and the exhaustion, struggled to keep his mind alert and to focus on the ground in front of him. Every muscle ached, and yet he could see that Rhia felt worse. Constant contractions rocked her shivering body. Several times she began to veer too far into the forest, and William gently steered her closer to the stream.

They finally stopped to rest at the edge of a small clearing. William bent over, his hands pressed onto his knees as his chest heaved. Looking up, he saw Rhia standing on a nearby patch of decaying leaves and moss, her eyes nearly closed. Her body began to sway, and as her head nodded to one side and her shoulder slumped, he knew she was going down. William swooped in from behind, wrapped his arms around her and slowly lowered her to the ground.

~

Rhia barely felt William's hands on her body or the soft crunch of the ground below her. Somewhere in the fog of her head she began to hear strange snapping sounds, branches breaking. Minutes later, or maybe hours, she felt him lift her and carry her to the rugged lean-to he had built against a large fallen log. Tenderly, he lifted her damp and clinging shirt and guided it up and over her head. Her eyes fluttered open, and she saw him kneeling beside her in the darkness, his chest bare as he fumbled with the knotted drawstring tie on her pants. With a sigh, she succumbed to the devastation of the day, and slept.

~

Warm sun streamed through the gaps and holes in the top of the small lean-to, sending filtered, dappled light onto the side of Rhia's face. She wanted to sleep, but a faraway nagging in her mind tugged at her until her eyes winked open. For several moments, she didn't know where she was. Suddenly, she noticed the warmth and strength of a body behind her, and for a second, her heart stopped from fear.

Looking down, Rhia saw that she was in her bra and underwear. She could see one filthy, ragged shirt draped over her hip, another flat beneath her torso. Two crumpled pairs of pants, faded red and orange, were tangled around her legs. William's hand curved loosely over her stomach. Slowly, she began to remember the events of the night before, and remembered running.

Taking a deep breath, she rolled toward William, careful for the bruises and swellings that covered her body. Her head brushed against the long branches and ferns that made up the top of the small shelter. His hand pulled away from her belly, and the cool morning air replaced the warmth it had provided.

William lay on his side, naked except for a thin pair of briefs, his shoulder pressed into the twigs and leaves of the ground below. He stared into her face for several seconds, as if trying to process everything that had brought them to this place, and what to do now. Finally, he cleared his throat and spoke.

"How are you?"

"I don't know." Rhia's throat was gravelly and sore. "Warmer."

"You were shivering. Your clothes were wet. I had to take them off. I had to . . ."

"It's okay."

"I heard that somewhere. If you're hypothermic, it's best to get naked together."

"I understand."

"I mean, not naked, but, I took off your wet clothes and . . ."

"William," Rhia smiled. "Thank you. You probably saved my life."

William took her hand and gently squeezed her fingers. "You're welcome." He opened his mouth as if to speak, then closed it again. Finally, he added, "We'd better get up."

Rhia heard his words, but he didn't let go of her hand. She could see hesitation in his eyes, as if he was torn between leaving and lying here with her. Her eyes softened and she edged her body closer to him.

"Um," William said, and he inched away. "I've been wondering. The stream we're following—what happens when we get to the coast?"

"When we get there, I'll have a better idea where we are," Rhia said. "I know the guards drove north from Thread the Needle to get to the Center, so, walking, we might only be only a day or two to Miranda. If we went there, my friends would help us. There are good women there, and they'd hide us . . . but we'd be putting them in jeopardy." Rhia's heart ached, deep and dull within her chest. "I don't think I can do that."

"Once they figure out what happened in the fire, every guard in the region will be looking for us." William said. "We have to go somewhere."

"I know." After a moment, she whispered, "Betty. My boat. If we can get to her, we can go anyplace. We can get away."

Rhia tried to visualize the maps of the coastline she had worked as a runner. "If we're where I think we are, there are a couple small coastal towns between here and Thread the Needle. We might be able to get some food along the way. We'll have to scope it out. I don't know. It might take us a few days on foot, though."

"Do you think your boat will still be there?"

"I don't know."

William sighed. "It sounds like our best bet."

Rhia looked at William apologetically. "It might be best for me to go into the towns alone. It might be easier to find help if it's just me."

"Right."

"You can hide in the woods. I'll bring food out to you."

"Look, Rhia," William said. "Maybe I shouldn't come along."

"What?"

"I mean, I'll understand if you want to split up. I know you don't owe me anything, and you might not want—"

"William," Rhia interrupted. "I want you to come with me." She lifted her hand and pressed her palm into the warm skin of his shoulder. "We're in this together." As she slowly slid her hand down his arm, his eyes darkened, and she felt his muscles tense.

William blinked, his jaw clenched as if he was afraid to speak. His chest rose and fell as Rhia caressed him, her fingertips gliding onto his bare chest. She could feel the heat begin to rise from his body, and she leaned toward him, hungry for his touch.

"Rhia," William whispered.

"I want to be with you."

"We should get moving."

"I don't want to get up yet," Rhia breathed. "I don't want this day to start. Once we leave this place, we'll never stop running." She touched the side of his cheek and he tilted his head into her palm. "Just stay with me a little longer."

William closed his eyes and sighed. "I don't know if I can."

"You can."

"No, you don't understand."

"Then tell me."

William hesitated. "Rhia, I don't know if I can do *this*. It's difficult for me." He sighed. "There were . . . things I did in the Center. Things Deacon made me do."

Rhia lowered her hand to her side, and William closed his eyes. He dropped his chin to his chest and seemed to curl into himself. She wanted to press him for answers, encourage him to trust her, but something in her heart told her to stay quiet. Half of her was afraid to hear the horrors he might have experienced, but the other half wanted to bear witness to whatever he needed to say.

Finally, William opened his eyes and spoke. His voice was little more than a whisper. "I must have done something that made her like me. I never wanted that, I swear. I never tried to make her like me." His gaze was focused on a spot just behind Rhia.

"It started six months ago. At first, she'd have the guards bring me to her office, and she'd just talk. Tell me about things she had to do, her jobs and her responsibilities, people who annoyed her. I never really said anything. I usually just sat there, you know? It was better than being out in the Village in the freezing rain. But every time, she'd find a way to make it clear that she could make things better for me there, easier for me, and that she was the one who could also make it much worse. Then one day she sat beside me. She reached over and touched my leg, then my arm."

Rhia felt like the air had been sucked from the space around her. William's voice sounded muffled and distant in her ears. She could imagine it all—the wooden desk in Deacon's office, the bay windows and the light streaming through. She wanted him to stop talking, to keep his secrets and hide what she knew he was going to say. Part of her didn't want to know.

William's hands began to tremble. "She told me about other men who'd come to her office, how a few of them had been special to her, and how much it meant to her to find those special connections. She told me those men were treated better than the others, but that she had to punish them if they were disloyal to her. I'd seen what she did during sessions. I'd seen how crazy she was. So one day, when she leaned over and kissed me, I let her. What could I do?"

William looked at Rhia. His face was anguished and his eyes glistened. "I didn't want her to touch me, Rhia. I never wanted her to touch me." He hesitated. "But she did. More.

Everywhere. And when it was done, I knew I could never tell anyone. I could never complain, and I could never stop it. She had all the power."

Rhia held her breath. After several moments, she blinked and looked away.

"You have to believe me, Rhia," William pleaded. "I didn't want it. I never wanted it."

"No, of course not."

"You don't believe me."

"I do."

"You're disgusted."

"No."

"But you can't even look at me."

Rhia could hear the pain in William's voice. She squeezed her eyes shut tight and shook her head. When she opened them, she said, "I am disgusted, but not by you or what you did. I'm disgusted by what *she* did. Oh, William, I'm so sorry." She touched his cheek again and held it as tears welled in his eyes. "I didn't know."

They lay together in silence for several minutes. Rhia held William gently and marveled at how her world had changed in only two weeks' time. Once satisfied with her life, her job, and her belief in the people around her, she'd been unwilling to dig into the rumors and stories she was hearing about the Centers. She didn't want to know about government corruption. She wanted to believe it was all working out for the best. She was content in her life, happy with her choices and options. She didn't want to rock the boat.

Through a simple twist of fate, she'd been thrown into a world of terror and fear and saw firsthand the cruelty and injustice of the system. The government she had worked for was mired in the corruption that comes with power, and she knew now that no one was safe from its grasp. Her town leaders couldn't save her, the lawyers couldn't save her, and the word of one woman would never count against that of a person with power. Rhia's eyes had been opened. She could never go back, could never unsee the things she had seen, and she couldn't live in silence anymore. She knew she had to stand up and fight against people like Deacon, and Banks, and every woman or man who would use their power to brutalize the weak and the small.

Rhia had become the reluctant consoler, the reluctant warrior, and now she must become the willing voice of the oppressed. She was a person who knew. She had to become a person who would help others to know.

Rhia took a deep breath. "William, what Deacon did to you—it wasn't your fault. You didn't do anything to deserve it, and in a just world, no one would ever have that kind of power over another person. I'm so sorry. I'm sorry it happened to you and that it happens to other people so often. Too often. I'm glad you told me." She wrapped her fingers around his.

"I want you to be with me. I want to be close to you, but I won't rush you. I didn't know before. I'm sorry. We can go as slow as you need."

William looked into Rhia's eyes, and relief seemed to wash over him.

Rhia smiled. "Let's take it one step at a time. Let's get to Betty and figure out where to go from there."

William squeezed her hand. "Okay."

Together they pushed aside the branches of the lean-to and stood up into the warmth of a sunny morning. The rain had stopped hours ago, but the heavy-laden leaves above them continued to drip fat drops onto their heads and shoulders as they collected their damp clothes and dressed. William scattered the branches and ferns to try to disguise the place where they had slept, while Rhia collected leaves, shoots, needles, and arils for a bitter and unsatisfying breakfast. Within twenty minutes, they were walking through the forest again, keeping the stream on their right, not knowing where it would lead or how long it would take.

~ Nineteen ~

It was midafternoon when they began to drop in elevation, the sound of the stream growing louder as it tumbled over boulders and around thick, exposed tree roots. Rhia and William had to climb over several hummocks and down small, steep slopes to keep close to the water as it quickened and churned. They trudged along, alert and listening for any sign of pursuit, eventually coming upon the remnants of a long-forgotten road that curved along the bank.

They followed it for nearly an hour, finally stopping to rest near a tumbledown trestle bridge. The stream had grown into a small river that cut a deep groove into the land. Rhia sat to rest upon a dark-gray rock outcropping in the fading sun.

"We need food," Rhia said as she took off her worn shoes and dangled her feet into the cool water below. "We can't keep going on pine needles and salmonberries."

William stood beside her and looked around. After a minute he set his hands on his hips. "We can catch fish."

She smiled. "You got a net in your back pocket?"

William looked at her out of the corner of his eye and smirked. "No, but there's got to be fish in this river. It's fast. It's cold."

She watched him and could see his mind working. His eyes sparkled as he paced around the top of the outcrop, peering down into the water below. He looked smart. He looked strong. Rhia smiled.

"Here, in these shadows." William said. "I can see fish!"

"Maybe we could make a fishing pole . . ." Rhia stood and began to look around the riverbank for long sticks.

"Hold on." William peeled off his filthy shirt and began to tug on the drawstring that held up his pants.

"What are you doing?"

Without answering, he pulled the string free of his pants and knelt on the rock with his T-shirt in his hand. Rhia stepped behind him and watched as he experimented with the shirt, folding it in different ways and tying off sections with the string. After several minutes, he had twisted the arms of the shirt together with the neck and tied the string tightly around the top where the fabric gathered. When he turned the shirt upside down and opened the bottom, he'd created a large sack.

"What do you think?" William asked, looking over his shoulder at Rhia.

"Maybe."

William slid off the rock into the cold water and tried to open the shirt-made-net in the river. The fabric folded around his hands, collapsing each time he tried to hold it open. Exasperated, he climbed back onto the rock.

"It won't stay open. A fish couldn't swim into it if he tried."

Rhia looked around. *We need a net,* she thought. *What's missing?* Taking a deep breath, she closed her eyes and imagined her boat, the metal drum that held her fishing nets, the lead weights that dragged the line down in the water and the buoys that held the top up. She pictured her net as a giant red shirt, and thought about what it would look like reeling off the stern deck.

"Something to hold it open," Rhia muttered. She opened her eyes and scurried up the bank to the trees. She returned with an arm-length stick in her hand.

"Try this," Rhia called as she climbed back down to the rock. When she reached him, she picked up the shirt and bent the green stick around the inside of the open end. She poked the ends of the stick through the thin fabric, creating an arc.

"It'll just fall off in the water," William said.

Rhia reached down to her own pants and pulled the drawstring from the waistline. She ripped another hole in the shirt, halfway between the ends of the arc, and used the string to tie the shirt tight to the stick.

"There," Rhia said. "With three points of attachment, the net should stay open." She passed the modified net to William, and he smiled.

~

The third day after their escape, they finally reached Thread the Needle, hungry and exhausted. Rhia squinted into the sun and paced in the sand for nearly half an hour, looking for Betty. Finally, William wrapped his arms around her and held her as she wept.

~

Five days later, Rhia and William were far south of any town she knew. They had stealthily worked their way past the regional trade at Piper Point two days before, stealing or catching food along the way. Now they lay flat on their bellies in a tangle of brush and grasses behind the gravelly berm of a small inlet.

A silent town stood nearby. There were over a dozen houses still somewhat whole, but from the partially collapsed roofs and darkened, shattered windows, Rhia guessed the residents had left this place long ago. The refugees would have taken everything they could carry, everything they would need to survive in one of the neighboring towns, but they wouldn't have taken everything. Rhia and William could find useful supplies there.

They had been hiding and watching for almost an hour, looking for any signs of movement along the beach or among the small collection of broken and tilting boats moored at the three dilapidated docks on the edge of the town. Even from this distance, Rhia could tell most of the boats were useless shells, torn open long ago by a battle that had hailed a storm of bullets and incendiary devices down upon them. There were a few, however, that might still float.

"I think it's clear." William's voice was hushed. His body was close to Rhia's, his hip touching hers and his fingers resting lightly on top of her hand.

"Yeah. We won't find diesel or solar cells. It'll have to be something we can modify to sail."

"Where do you want to try first?"

"That small one up on its edge. The white hull with the

blue stripe. I think it was dry-docked when everything blew. Less damage around it."

"Dry-docked because it was broken?"

"Don't know. Maybe we can fix it." Rhia turned her head and looked at William. His dark eyes sparkled in the sun and a small smile curled the corners of his lips. She stood up and brushed sand off the front of her ragged shirt. She looked at the small, listing boat across the inlet and took a deep breath, pulling fresh air from the nearby ocean deep into her lungs. "Let's find out."

Acknowledgments

Thank you to everyone who helped in the making of this book. Judy Gregoire for invaluable assistance with sailing stories and nautical terms; Heidi Masterson for advice and critique; Kristin Mehus-Roe and Girl Friday Productions for developmental editing; Jessie Chandler for cover design; Kyra Freestar and Bridge Creek Editing for copyediting; Lori Bennett for Ebook conversion and layout.

In addition, I'm grateful to the many friends and fans who supported and encouraged the production of this book. Yes, I'm talking about you!

Thank you, also, to the scientists and foragers who contributed to the details in this book: Cedarsong Nature School, the Washington Park Arboretum, and books by Michael Moore and Doug Benoliel. Although I did my best to accurately describe plants and herbs, please don't trust me, and never eat anything unless you know what it is. Remember, you can eat anything once.

About the Author

Kari Aguila was the recipient of an IndieReader Discovery Award for her first novel, *Women's Work*. She is also an avid gardener, outdoor enthusiast, geologist, and mother of three. Aguila lives in Seattle with her family, and loves to Skype with Book Clubs. Contact her via Facebook, Twitter, or her webpage.

www.kariaguila.com

www.facebook.com/KariAguilaAuthor

https://twitter.com/WomensWorkKA

www.goodreads.com/author/show/7422555.Kari_Aguila

Have an opinion about this story? Leave your feedback as an Amazon rating or review, on Goodreads, at your local bookstore, or on the author's webpage.

CPSIA information can be obtained
at www.ICGtesting.com
Printed in the USA
FSOW01n1524301215
15042FS